AUTUMN'S FEAR

AUTUMN TRENT SERIES: BOOK THREE

MARY STONE

To my husband.
Thank you for taking care of our home and its many inhabitants
while I follow this dream of mine.

DESCRIPTION

Don't fear the dark. It's the light that blinds... and kills.

Forensic and criminal psychologist Dr. Autumn Trent is trying to find her groove in her transition to the FBI Behavioral Analysis Unit. But can her soft heart continue to take a beating? Will her impulsive spirit continue to get her in trouble? Probably.

Using her connections, she begins the search for the sister she hasn't seen since they were both girls. And gets a hit in the Sunshine State.

It's kismet when she's called out on a case with the team— pregnant women are disappearing in Lavender Lake, Florida. The only clue to their fate has come in the form of a single hand...recovered from swamplands heavily populated with hungry gators. The perfect dumping ground for a killer.

A cold-blooded monster is on a holy mission to spread his light into the dark world...but how do you track a criminal who makes sure all evidence is eaten?

Autumn's Fear, the third book in Mary Stone's Autumn Trent Series, is a riveting psychological murder thriller that will leave you scared of the light.

1

Lindsay Welsh forgot absolutely nothing. It was a quality she'd always taken pride in, and even now, as her due date became countdown worthy and the fabled baby brain threatened to take over, she refused to slip up.

Tonight was taco night, which also meant that this was grocery shopping day. It had been that way since before they were married. Josh anticipated the weekly tradition like a child looked forward to Christmas, and Lindsay wasn't about to disappoint her beloved husband. Besides, she was a stickler for keeping a schedule, and if she didn't shop today, she was afraid she'd forget what day of the week it was.

Besides, this might be the only time in her life when she didn't have to worry about her figure or count the calories of each taco to maintain the same number on the bathroom scale. She was clearly incredibly pregnant and had begun to resemble a penguin much more than an hourglass several months ago.

"We'll eat every damn taco in Florida if we want to," she murmured to her rounded belly, stroking the stretched skin.

"All of them." She smiled as her palm received a solid kick in return. An intrauterine high five. She'd take that as a yes.

The checkout lady shot her a glance that implied that Lindsay might be a tiny bit off her rocker. The thought made Lindsay smile. She'd just blame the hormones. That seemed to be the default explanation for anything she did these days. According to the rest of the world, anyway.

Lindsay didn't care. She was nearing the most epic event in her life, one that neither she nor her husband had thought possible. Not ever. As if to remind her that doctors didn't know everything, one of her unborn daughters performed an Olympian-worthy double axel out of nowhere, landing firmly onto Lindsay's bladder. Lindsay gasped and pressed her legs together, sure that either urine or a baby's head would appear at any second.

"Little ballerina almost made Mommy pee herself," she murmured when it was clear that she didn't need to rush to the nearest ladies' room. Taking a deep breath, she almost decided to make a pit stop anyway. She went so much that Josh had offered to build her a cot in their master bathroom.

"The Greengrocer will be closing in five minutes," a voice said from overhead, and that made the decision for her. She'd definitely need more than five minutes to wobble to and fro in her current condition.

Besides, home was only a few miles away, and Lindsay was moderately sure she could make it there before the floodgates opened. Well, assuming the ice-skating competition in her womb was temporarily over.

In spite of the fact that it was January, the Florida air was oppressive with humidity. The winters here were certainly different than what they'd been used to back in Georgia, even though the Peach State was pretty darn warm most of the time too.

Regardless, Georgia seemed a million miles away at this

point. Now, Florida was where they belonged. The peaceful city of Lavender Lake had quickly become home. They were close to Lindsay's family, and having her mom's help with the babies would be a sanity-saving gift from the infant gods. They'd made the move six months ago, and neither Josh nor Lindsay had regretted it even once.

They'd wanted these babies for a long time. Their savings account had all but been emptied to make the IVF treatments possible. Every necessity, along with a ridiculous amount of luxury items, had been bought in preparation for the baby girls' arrival. Countless parenting books had been pored over, but Lindsay was positive that nothing could ever truly prepare them for the change that was soon charging its way into their lives.

It was exciting. It was overwhelming. It was more than she had dared to dream was attainable. Two little girls. They would soon have two precious little girls.

But tonight, they were having tacos.

"Shit. Sriracha sauce." Lindsay gave one last look over her shoulder, but the stern stares from the checkout counters convinced her that Josh would be okay, just this once, without his beloved topping.

I guess I won't be able to avoid a bit of pregnancy brain after all.

She straightened her posture as best she could and held her chin a bit higher. At five-eight, Lindsay knew she was attractive, regardless of the penguin shape she'd taken on as of late. Bright blue eyes, blonde hair, and a pretty face were always in style. So what if she did begin to slip a little? The two bouncing creatures rolling around in her womb were most definitely draining some of her brain power, and whatever was left after that, she'd been putting into training a temp to cover her position as a legal secretary at a local firm.

Even with the depletion of cognizant braincells, she'd

stayed on top of everything like a champ. Aside from the sriracha, Lindsay couldn't think of one other single time she'd blatantly forgotten anything. Josh was a big boy. He'd be fine.

But more so, Josh loved her and was ecstatic about finally becoming a father. She could have made mac 'n' cheese for dinner, and he would still adore her. Lindsay knew this without a doubt, and it brought a soft smile to her lips.

The sweet reverie would have to wait until later, however, because it was taking most of her strength to push the loaded cart toward her minivan, and her phone was going off inside her purse. The ringtone seemed impossibly loud in the silent air of the evening, and she had to stop to take the call.

"Josh, I'm on my way. Just made it out of Greengrocer. Tacos coming at ya, babe." Lindsay's cheery words echoed back to her, and she suddenly couldn't wait to be home with her husband. These long days they'd both been working were making her miss him horribly, even if he did sleep right next to her every single night.

"You were supposed to let *me* pick up the groceries. Is there any power in the freaking universe that can keep you off your feet, Linds?" He sounded upset, but Lindsay knew he was exaggerating. His exasperated laugh confirmed her suspicions.

"It's taco night, but don't worry. Soon, I'll be a worthless zombie lump, fit only for breastfeeding and diaper changing. Let me do what I can *while I can*. I'm seriously fine, okay? Feeling fabulous, actually."

And she was. If she hadn't been so pregnant, this was a moment when Lindsay would have jumped on the cart like a playful child and let it cruise to her vehicle.

"Okay. Just be careful and get your sexy butt home. I'll carry the groceries in." A heavy sigh followed his words. It was full of the exhaustion that he tried—and failed—to keep hidden from her at all times.

"How was the board meeting?"

"Don't change the subject, Linds."

"Don't be a grumpy old man. I'll withhold the tacos." Lindsay smiled at her own threat.

Josh's laughter added to her own. "You would never."

She softened. He knew her so very well. "No. I wouldn't. But...I did forget your sriracha." She cringed, waiting for the adorable little-boy disappointment she knew was coming next.

"How dare you." Mock serious words were followed by more laughter.

"I'll see you soon, okay? Lemme get off the phone so I can push this damn cart." Immediately, she wished she hadn't alluded to the fact that pushing the cart was in any way a struggle for her.

"See? You're doing too much. I'm right. Come home."

"Be there soon. Love you." Lindsay waited for his reply and then tossed the phone back into her purse. Some days she couldn't believe how much she loved that man, and she hoped they would always be this taken with each other.

Lost in happy thought, she almost didn't notice the woman at first. More of a girl than a full-grown adult, the small figure stood beside a banged-up station wagon that had stopped seeing "better days" decades before the girl had even been born. A closer look revealed that the poor thing was crying. She was holding a cell phone, but by the desolate way she jabbed at it, Lindsay could tell that it very clearly wasn't in working order.

Lindsay hesitated as her maternal instincts piqued. "Can I help you? Are you okay, hon?"

A tear-streaked, freckled face looked up at her, eyes wide. The young woman—Lindsay could instantly see that she wasn't quite so young as her tiny stature had suggested—ran a hand through her caramel-blonde corkscrew curls. Giant blue eyes brimming with emotion sought Lindsay's gaze, and almost immediately, a small light of hope seemed to click on beneath the obvious turmoil that had otherwise consumed her pitiful façade.

"I think it needs jumped. My car. It won't start, and my phone isn't working. I don't know what to do!" A fresh tear threatened to spill down her still-damp cheeks.

"I'm pretty sure I've got some jumper cables. Let's give those a try, okay?"

Lindsay couldn't remember the last time she'd actually had to use a set of cables, but she was semi-confident that she'd figure it out. She gave the woman a wide smile, wanting her to know that everything would be okay. The dilapidated station wagon behind them clearly hinted that the distressed creature before her wasn't a stranger to hard times. Lindsay's heart hurt for her.

"I'm Sasha." She wiped her nose on her sleeve. "Thank you. Thank you *so much*. I don't even know what I'd do—"

Lindsay waved a hand to hush her. "It's not a problem. I'm right over there." She pointed toward her shiny new minivan with a small twinge of guilt. "I still can't believe I'm a minivan mom. These babies aren't even out yet, and they're already running the show."

This made Sasha giggle, and the young woman seemed to relax a little. "Everybody loves a soccer mom."

Lindsay grinned, realizing she didn't mind the term as much as she'd always thought she would.

I'm ready for this. I'm ready for the next phase.

It was a serene thought, but when she couldn't seem to find the right button on the vehicle's fancy remote to open the back hatch, Lindsay immediately questioned whether she was ready for any change at all.

"Sorry." She let out an embarrassed chortle and held the tiny device closer to her face, squinting to see the buttons in the dim light. "We just got this. I'm not really used to all of the gadgets yet." That much was obvious, and Lindsay was happy to see that, if nothing else, her struggle had momentarily entertained the stranded young woman.

"It's really pretty. I'm not sure I've ever even *touched* a new car. Does it have that cool OnStar security voice thingy?" Sasha's eyebrows were raised high with interest, and her smile seemed to have overtaken her worries for the time being.

"I think so, or something like that. My husband hasn't set it up yet, and I'll be damned if I know how to use it. But yes, it's in there somewhere." Lindsay laughed at her own lack of tech-savvy skills as the hatch raised slowly.

One of her daughters gave a karate kick somewhere near her rib cage. *Pull it together,* the baby seemed to be saying.

"I'm sure he just wants the best for you and the babies. You did say babies, right?" Sasha was brimming with bright-eyed enthusiasm, her freckled face adorable when it wasn't scrunched tight with worry. "Are you having twins? Triplets?"

"Oh, lord save me from triplets. I think these twins will be just enough to ensure that we never sleep again." Lindsay leaned over the hatch, pulling up the carpet piece that covered the spare tire and—she hoped—the promised jumper cables. Her amiable response didn't touch upon the fact that she and Josh would have happily dealt with ten babies after all the IVF hell they'd endured.

She had just laid a hand on the bright yellow cords when Sasha seemed to lean in questionably close beside her. Before Lindsay's inner alarm had a chance to fully alert her to the possible threat that came with the movement, a sharp sting at the back of her neck pierced through all other thought.

"So sorry about this, Lindsay." Sasha's voice was dark and cold this time. Menacing.

Lindsay's vision blurred for a split-second, and she nearly fell backward, but Sasha's strong grip caught her and pushed her straight down onto the minivan floor. The curly haired woman was small, but she wasn't weak. Lindsay tried to scream, but no sound would come out. She wanted to fight, to do anything other than just lay there, letting what was happening continue. But her muscles were rigid. Her arms, legs, fingers, toes…everything had frozen in an instant paralysis.

She watched as Sasha calmly picked up the remote from the concrete where it had fallen when Lindsay's hands turned to ice. The woman looked down at her, the same large blue eyes having taken on a very different demeanor.

"It's not that hard, Lindsay. The buttons are *clearly* marked. Pathetic." Sasha shook her head, sneering as she hit the proper button and the hatch door slowly lowered to a close. Only a few seconds passed before the van was backing up, and then leaving the parking lot at warp speed.

An animalistic desire to escape had completely overtaken Lindsay's mind by then, but her body refused to allow even the slightest movement. She'd been tricked. She'd been duped like a complete, careless moron. And that woman— Sasha or whoever the hell she actually was—had known her name! She was positive she hadn't shared it.

What now? I can't move I can't move I can't move!

As she strained to make a fist, an unimaginable horror flooded her mind. She concentrated, hoping she was mistaken. Anything but this. She waited for the familiar sensation of her little girls maneuvering around inside of her.

Lindsay Welsh couldn't even cry when she realized her precious babies were no longer moving either.

2

Autumn Trent checked her reflection in the full-length mirror hanging from the back of her bedroom door. She wasn't sure what she was looking for, exactly. Her long, bright auburn hair was neat and tamed to within an inch of its life. Her inquisitive green eyes shone clear. Her black blazer and crisp white blouse conveyed that she was a professional woman who demanded to be taken seriously.

But was she really FBI material?

The transition was unsettling, to say the least. Her current role at Shadley and Latham, where she specialized in threat assessment, had never given her any reason to doubt herself. She was good at that job and more than qualified for it. Her hard-earned Ph.D. in forensic psychology as well as her master's in criminal psychology, not to mention her Juris Doctorate, had spoken volumes to her employers and co-workers about her capabilities.

These capabilities were the same reason that Special Supervisory Agent Aiden Parrish had campaigned so consistently to bring her into the Behavioral Analysis Unit at the FBI's Richmond, Virginia Field Office. The man had a faith in Autumn's abilities and the valuable insight they could add to the BAU that she herself wasn't entirely sure of. Even while the hoops were being jumped through to make her an official FBI employee, Autumn wondered if, at some point in the future, Aiden would change his mind.

Hadn't she already messed up in Oregon? Hadn't she added to that in Pennsylvania? Was there really room for her inexperience in such high-stake cases as the ones she had been and would be involved in?

Autumn sighed and turned away from her reflection. It was time to leave for work, and she refused to be late. Autumn planted a kiss on Peach's head, earning only a disinterested glare from her orange feline. She attempted to likewise kiss her Pomeranian, but that was always a little more challenging. Toad had mastered the art of the sad puppy dog stare, which triggered a deep guilt in Autumn's chest that only a four-legged friend could inspire.

"I'll be back," she promised the dog, but only got a whine in return.

Guilt. Guilt. Guilt.

As she made her way to the Virginia Field Office, Autumn realized there was one thing that she was absolutely sure of, and none of her concerns had changed it. She *wanted* to do this. There was an excitement—a purpose—in being out in the field with the BAU that stirred something inside her. In the FBI, she could make a bigger difference. She could help more people. Her special insight could be utilized in a way that was deeply needed by the seven billion plus human beings surrounding her on this spinning rock.

And it *was* a special insight. Very special.

The brain surgery Autumn had undergone at the tender age of ten had left her with a type of "sixth sense." All it took was the simple touch of another human being to send an instant delivery of intuitive knowledge—knowledge she otherwise had absolutely no way of obtaining—into her psyche.

The particular person's thoughts, emotions, and motives were made clear to Autumn in a mere split-second of connection. Occasionally, she even received short visions of a sort, giving her a glimpse of an individual's past. Though she'd been wary of her newfound ability as a child, in college she had come to see it as a valuable tool.

Now, as an adult, the magnitude of good that could be done by harnessing her gift was not lost on her. She could help the FBI and the plethora of victims they encountered in a way that no one else could. Autumn was a valuable, irreplaceable asset. SSA Aiden Parrish knew this, but more importantly, *Autumn* knew it.

Added to that, there were the signs.

Special Agent Sun Ming had informed her of the pregnant women inexplicably going missing in Florida at the same time that Autumn had received the word that her long lost sister, Sarah, might also be in the Sunshine State. It certainly wasn't the same thing as being offered two free tickets to Disney World, but Autumn took it as an indication that her newfound path with the FBI was inevitably destined.

Others might call it coincidental, but Autumn had long ago learned that the voice of coincidence was booming with design. All doubt aside, these new developments felt significant. Solid.

And it was too late to reconsider, anyway. Just last night, she had spoken with Mike Shadley. Though Autumn was officially still his employee, they were both clearly aware of the transition taking place. She had no problem with Mike, and he had none with her as far as she knew, but Autumn had sensed relief in his voice when they discussed the details surrounding her exit from the firm.

Her other boss, Adam Latham, had plenty of problems

with Autumn. Adam had plenty of problems in general. As Mike's partner, Adam had proven himself to be more of a liability than an asset—a giant, chauvinistic, narcissistic liability.

Autumn thought briefly of the bright red handprint Adam had left on her cheek in the Oregon hotel room. He'd been convinced that she was physically attracted to him, and even more convinced that he was not only her boss but her all-knowing mentor.

Neither of those things had been even remotely true, and when Adam had been faced with this reality, he'd momentarily lost his cool. Autumn had proven herself to be incredibly knowledgeable *and* off-limits. Adam had shown himself to be the absolute douchebag she'd already known he was. And furthermore, now that some time had passed, Autumn had decided she *would* be filing charges against Adam.

The decision wasn't based so much on account of her own well-being as it was on the fact that she wasn't Adam's first victim, and she surely wouldn't be his last. As repulsive as Adam's touch was, it had given Autumn a clear picture of just how many women he'd taken advantage of in the past.

No matter what effect it had on her own career, or even on Mike Shadley's firm, she couldn't let the incident slip quietly by. So many women kept quiet about harassment, indecencies, and abuse. Autumn understood well the reason for the silence, but she also knew that victims had voices that *needed* to be heard.

If Autumn was really going to lead humanity—any part of it—to a better state of existence, she had to start with herself. Leaders weren't silent, even when they were afraid. The more difficult tasks in life were every bit as important as all the rest. Hard or not, Adam Latham wasn't getting away with his indiscretions. Not this time.

As she approached the elevator of the FBI's Richmond

office, Autumn's phone vibrated in her jacket pocket. A couple of swipes opened the text from Victor Goren, the public defender in the case of young Justin Black.

Justin Black has been granted transfer to the Virginia State Hospital.

Autumn sucked in a sharp breath. "That was quick." Her brow furrowed as she stared at the screen. She had just submitted her assessment of his competency to the court the previous day. This was a clear example of a situation that did not feel solid at all.

Justin Black was only nineteen, but that hadn't stopped him from achieving full-on serial killer status. The question was whether or not he was competent to stand trial, and Autumn had more than enough accolades to make her a qualified choice for Justin's particular evaluation.

Upon her return to Virginia, she had been hard-pressed by "the powers that be" to prioritize Justin's competency assessment. The two-day evaluation deadline hadn't allowed Autumn to prove or disprove if Justin was, in fact, faking his mental illness. Although she had tried to make it very clear to the court that she hadn't had sufficient time to prove malingering in Justin's case, no one had seemed to care. Justin was an insane, obnoxious cog in an overworked system. The sooner he was drugged up and mentally vacant inside of a brick-walled institution, the better. For them.

The Virginia State Hospital was the single state-run facility with an Adult Maximum-Security Treatment Program. And although Justin had very much wanted to take the route he'd apparently been granted today, Autumn couldn't help the uneasy feeling that crept up her spine as she thought of him.

Justin wasn't the average serial killer. He'd been raised by none other than Douglas Kilroy, The Preacher, and they later learned was The Preacher's *biological cousin*. Whatever nails "nature" had left loose in Justin's life, "nurture" had fully pounded them in. He was a psychopath whose genetic makeup and life experience had made him a prime apprentice for The Preacher. He'd been dutifully trained to torture and kill and had developed an intense preference for depravity before he'd ever reached adulthood.

Autumn wasn't yet sure of anything other than the fact that Justin was incredibly intelligent and certainly smart enough to fake the symptoms of mental health issues that he exuded during their visits. Either way, she couldn't truly help him without fully and clearly ascertaining his mental state, and when done correctly, that wasn't a short process.

I need more time.

There was another reason that Justin Black's case was so incredibly important to Autumn. He was the younger half-brother of her best friend, Winter Black. Winter was an FBI Special Agent in the Violent Crimes Division of the Richmond Field Office, and she'd become a very important part of Autumn's life. Although Autumn knew Winter was more than capable of handling nearly anything hurled her way, finding out her baby brother was a cold-blooded killer had been a gut punch that her friend struggled with on a daily basis.

Autumn desperately wanted to discover the full truth about Justin because, most of all, Winter deserved and *needed* that closure. Autumn was determined, even now, to give it to her. Eventually.

Autumn's fingers flew across the screen. *Does his sister know?*

Goren responded immediately. *Winter Black has not yet been informed.*

Autumn sighed, her heart heavy. Someone needed to tell Winter, and it was apparently going to be her. She hastily typed one more text, letting Goren know she'd be going out of state for a case in Florida and that she would be in touch when she returned.

Just as Autumn had re-pocketed her phone, a familiar voice called out to her. Special Agent Bree Stafford, one of the most tenured agents in the VCU, approached with a wide smile on her face.

"Guess you're coming aboard again, hm?" Bree seemed delighted by the idea. "You know, if you keep this up, Aiden's gonna get you to stay."

"Ha. I kind of figured that one out for myself already." Autumn returned the smile and would have chatted with Bree longer, but Aiden Parrish appeared as if the sound of his name had summoned the man. She nearly jumped out of her skin at his unexpected presence but managed to maintain her composure...barely.

"Dr. Trent. Might I have a quick word with you?" Aiden's blue eyes stayed fixed on Autumn until she smiled and nodded, though she glanced at her watch, thinking they'd need to be very quick or else they'd be late for their meeting. But it was his meeting, so she could always blame the boss if she was tardy.

Although he normally maintained stony features, he smiled back, causing the corners of his eyes to crinkle. His light brown hair didn't successfully hide the stitches he'd recently incurred.

Autumn tensed at the memory. The man had endured quite the beating at the hands of the last serial killer they'd tracked in Pennsylvania. Several hits to the head had left him in the hospital with a concussion and the now-stitched laceration.

Autumn followed him dutifully to his office but couldn't manage to keep a pressing question to herself. "Are you sure you're okay to be back so soon? It's been less than a week since you were in the hospital."

Aiden turned to face her a little more slowly than he normally would. His expensive suit and tie were just as neat and crisp as ever, and in spite of the recent events in Pennsylvania, he seemed completely relaxed. Or at least, he seemed about as relaxed as SSA Aiden Parrish was capable of being. "When the doctors okay you to leave, you leave."

Autumn didn't quite feel that she'd received an answer to her actual question, but it was as close to an answer as she'd probably get from this very private man. They both sat in uncomfortable silence for a few seconds, and Autumn was aware of the relief that flooded her as she observed Aiden very much alive, and for the most part, well.

"The last time we spoke, Autumn, I'm afraid I was a little hard on you." Aiden cleared his throat and solemnly held her gaze once again. "I'm sorry."

Heat rose to her face, burning her with all the emotion she'd been feeling for days. Guilt. Sorrow. Anger.

"Aiden, *I'm* sorry." She tapped a fist against her chest. "I messed up. I blew my cover, I blew Winter's cover, and I nearly compromised the entire investigation. You had every reason to be upset with me. I'm upset with myself." Autumn earnestly meant every syllable.

Aiden's shake of the head was so small it was barely a movement, making Autumn once again wonder at the extent of his head injury. "It's behind us. We need to move past it and concentrate on the new case." He leaned forward, the corners of his mouth struggling to stay down. "That being said, you should know that you might be the worst speed dater in history."

Autumn threw her head back and laughed, completely unprepared for Aiden's bit of dry humor. When she could speak again, she lifted an eyebrow and said one word. "Vanilla."

The tenured agent went bright red right before he

planted a palm in the middle of his face. "I'm going to kill Dalton." But he was laughing as he said it. "That was the craziest case I think I've ever been a part of."

Autumn hadn't been part of many cases yet, but she had to agree.

A trio of sisters had targeted widowers up and down the east coast, swindling the rich men for every dollar they could. One of the sisters had literally gotten a taste of blood and started taking more than money. She started taking lives.

Clearing her throat, she forced herself to be serious again. "I'll fully focus on this case and give it everything I have. The way this is all happening," Autumn threw up her hands, "I know I'm facing a rather severe learning curve."

Aiden nodded, wincing at the motion. "You're definitely not the average transfer." Autumn wished that she could touch him, just for one moment, and know if the statement carried multiple meanings. She pressed her fingertips together to stop herself from reaching out.

"Overall, I'm just sorry that you got hurt." She fought to keep her gaze from wandering to the stitches as she said the words.

Aiden touched his temple with a soft snort. "I'm sure that wasn't the first woman who ever wanted to beat me over the head." He and Autumn shared a momentary smile before his face went stone serious. "Let's meet with the others."

Business time.

In just a few minutes, Aiden had gathered all the agents together for the briefing. Autumn shot Winter and her boyfriend, Special Agent Noah Dalton, a smile. The smile carried over to Bree, and Autumn attempted to share it with Sun as well. But Sun was, as per usual, less than interested in amiable greetings.

Sun had been much friendlier when she'd been dating another agent, though she would have been mortified to learn that her brief relationship with Bobby Weyrick had been a badly kept secret. The psychiatrist in Autumn wanted to ask Sun about him, especially after the cutting comments Sun made about men during the Black Widow case in Pennsylvania, but she kept quiet. She didn't imagine the surly agent would appreciate either the concern or invasion of privacy.

The only faces Autumn didn't recognize were swiftly introduced to her by Aiden as Special Agents Chris Parker and Mia Logan, both of them BAU agents called in to help work the new case. Autumn forced herself to stand tall, even though she wasn't exactly an established part of the FBI yet. Surrounded by all these great minds, it was imperative for Autumn to remember that *she* was worthy of being here too.

"This is what we have, Agents. Two pregnant women have gone missing in Lavender Lake, a town of about 150,000 residents in Central Florida." As Aiden spoke, Sun tapped at her laptop, and in a moment, the missing women's faces appeared on the smart screen. "The first, Sheila Conlon, went missing two years ago, and the other, Patricia Gorski-Wilson, just this last month."

"Here you go." Sun tossed Aiden the remote for the slides. She grumbled something like, "Lazy ass men. I'm not your slave," but Autumn wasn't sure she heard her correctly.

Aiden nodded his thanks. "Two weeks ago, a fisherman found a hand lodged in a log at one of the local swamps." The images on the screen were replaced by that of the severed hand in question. "Just three days ago, the DNA results came back confirming that the hand belonged to Ms. Gorski-Wilson."

Sun's fingers were flying again, and she didn't look up as she spoke at an equally rapid clip. "CODIS and N-DEx searches indicated an abnormally high number of pregnant women missing in Central Florida alone, and that's just within the last five years."

Aiden tapped the remote again, and the hand mercifully disappeared. "After learning this information, the local sheriff's detective called us for assistance in connecting the cases. That call was only a few days ago, but last night, another pregnant woman, Lindsay Welsh, went missing from Lavender Lake. The case has now been expedited to high priority. We leave for Florida today."

"Are there any leads on Lindsay Welsh's disappearance?" Winter voiced the question Autumn knew they all had.

"Grocery store cameras caught everything. Lindsay appeared to be helping another woman experiencing car trouble. But when Mrs. Welsh raised the back hatch of her van, the cameras lost sight of both women. When the hatch went back down, the van drove away, and all that was left was the shopping cart. Mrs. Welsh's purse was still in it."

"Has the husband been questioned? The primary suspect in any spousal murder is always the victim's partner, especially when pregnancy is involved." Bree's voice was confident, and Autumn knew that the woman's twenty years as an agent had provided her with a plethora of information.

"Exactly. Hasn't anyone considered that this case may have *nothing* to do with the previous two? It seems a bit presumptuous." Chris Parker spoke as though he were trying to out-boom the SSA. He ran a careful hand over his perfectly coiffed blonde hair, and Autumn had the instant premonition that Special Agent Parker was probably not going to be her new best friend.

Aiden exhaled a long breath. There were dark circles under his eyes, and Autumn wondered again if he was really up for this so soon. "I think it goes without saying that the police are following standard protocol for kidnapping, and that includes questioning the partners. All of them. We'll be questioning them as well when we arrive, along with family members, neighbors, and any other possible eyewitnesses."

Chris crossed his arms in mild annoyance. He clearly had more to say but wisely chose to stay silent. His expression said more than words ever could, though.

"No presumptions are being made, but we have to consider the possibility that this isn't the average missing persons case. We wouldn't be expending time and resources if there wasn't the possibility that something much more complicated could be taking place in Lavender Lake. I'm sure you're all bright enough to realize that."

Aiden's words conveyed his obvious annoyance as he tapped the laptop and a pretty woman with blonde hair popped up on the screen. Chris opened his mouth but snapped it closed when Aiden's gaze came his way.

Autumn shifted in her seat, wondering at the clear animosity between the two men. Was it simply a power play or was something more deeply seated creating this thick tension?

Aiden's expression relaxed a bit when he turned back to the others. "It's my understanding that Mrs. Welsh is due within the next few weeks with twins. The working theory is that whoever took her will keep her alive until the babies are born. After that…" He lifted a shoulder, and Autumn didn't need any help filling in the blank.

Aiden flipped to another photo of Lindsay Welsh. It appeared to be one from an expensive maternity shoot. Lindsay looked stunning in a flowing sapphire gown that clung to her swollen shape. Her beauty nearly eclipsed the sunset painting the sky behind her.

There was a murmur around the table, and Autumn's heart squeezed at the serene expression on Lindsay Welsh's face as her hand rested on her belly. "Beautiful," Winter murmured. There were nods of agreement all around.

We need to save her. Save them.

"She could give birth at any moment." Aiden looked as grim as the rest of them clearly felt. "Time is of the essence, so get ready to head south, Agents. We leave in two hours."

Aiden clicked the button, and the screen went dark. Goose bumps raised on Autumn's arms as the missing woman and her twins faded away.

There one moment. Gone the next.

3

There was nothing particularly amazing about Justin Black's new room. It wasn't a prison cell, so that was something, at least. But the walls were a boring shade of beige that irritated him to no end. No imagination, these people. At some point, he hoped to decorate the walls with one of the orderly's blood. Or maybe a doctor's. Or maybe Victor Goren's.

Red was all the rage these days.

If Justin looked at the big picture, things were actually going quite well. Escape was the end goal, and the probability of pulling that off in prison had seemed negligible at best. The authorities had been more than happy to get rid of him. To them, he was the "wrong kind" of inmate for the normal prison setting.

It didn't matter what the hardened criminals around him had done. He still freaked them out just by being in the same building. And while he found their constant state of fear rather enjoyable, he knew it wouldn't do him any good in the long run. He didn't need their fear, as much as he loved it. Some people thought he needed friends.

The word in and of itself was hilarious. Justin had allowed himself very few friends, even when he was much younger. Friends couldn't be trusted. They had their own needs in mind. What he needed was sympathizers. He needed people he could manipulate. Lucky for him, there wasn't a shortage of morons on this planet. In fact, there were so many that the challenge actually became finding the *right* moron for any particular situation.

Justin's lawyer, for instance, was an idiot who served a clear purpose. Victor Goren was really nothing more than a fat bastard with a law degree. But he was Justin's appointed public defender, and Justin would continue to play the pompous man like a fiddle until all of this was over.

And it would be over, one way or the other.

Justin just wanted to make sure his exit was memorable. And it would be.

Right now, ninety-nine percent of Americans knew his name. Goren was a mouthpiece, and that was a hot commodity in Justin's situation. Fame gained followers, and followers became sympathizers, and sympathizers became co-conspirators. And the world turned on and on.

The media, for instance, had blasted so much info about the poor little boy who'd been taken by a serial killer and turned into a monster that the pressure to move him somewhere less severe—somewhere that he could get the help he so desperately needed—had put the heat on the court's heels. Fame had pushed him in the direction he wanted.

He just hoped his mail caught up to him quickly. Justin was enjoying the fan mail he received, including the four marriage proposals from some pretty hot looking women, if the pictures they included were real. Which they probably weren't...lying bitches.

Their letters fueled his hate, keeping him from succumbing to the depression that wanted to sink into his bones at the most inconvenient times. The women's letters were so forward, their pictures so vulgar and raw. Indecent, revolting creatures prancing around the planet like the happy whores they all were...

They were reminders of his mission. Reminders of why he needed out of these walls.

And now that he was here, that day would soon come, he knew.

Justin's competency evaluation had been pushed through so quickly that even he had been a bit surprised to find himself leaving the detention center. But that was what came from feeding the right information to the right people.

One or two morons convincing a large group of morons to raise a public outcry was all that was needed for his transfer. And in this grimy world full of abominations—every single one of them so hungry for information on his case—it hadn't been hard to find a few sympathetic ears.

They had come straight to me.

It was funny, actually, to think of all those idiots putting a hand to their hearts and hoping the very best for his poor, lost soul. Justin would have killed every single one of them without batting an eyelash.

And so many of them *deserved* to die.

He didn't want their pity. It was drenched in the stink of their unforgiveable, unfathomable sins. No, they could keep their pity. What he wanted was for them to see his way as the right way. He wanted justice. He wanted to wipe the world clean.

And if they didn't conform? Well...he was happy to deal out the harshest of punishments.

Which would happen after he was free. He couldn't help cleanse the world of its sins while sitting in a locked room with bars on a window.

And why did they even need the bars? He certainly wasn't

going to risk a jump that could result in a broken arm or leg. Exactly how far would he or anyone else get in that condition? That wouldn't be an escape. That would be a dim-witted move that was far beneath his intellect.

Such measures weren't needed.

In Justin's eyes, they'd basically moved him from a kennel to a playpen. Even babies could get out of playpens.

Grandpa will be so proud of me when I make it out of here. I know he's still with me. I can feel him.

Douglas Kilroy had saved Justin when he took him from the black-hearted sinners all those years ago. He had blessed him. And his blessing, added to the God Almighty's, was all Justin needed. He didn't answer to men.

"Justin? Did you hear me? Justin?" Victor Goren's voice raked across his nerves. The dumb bastard had been blathering on for at least a half hour, and Justin pictured what his face would look like after being bashed into a concrete wall. All the fancy ties in the world wouldn't make him feel better then. His head would be nothing more than a half-mutilated lump sitting on top of a cold body at that point, and he would *finally stop talking*. There weren't many things Justin wanted more in this world than to silence Goren permanently.

Killing him was very near the top of his to-do list.

Tired of it all, Justin shoved a thumb into his mouth and rocked slowly in his chair, honing back in on the piece of shit before him. This act was still necessary, and he was more than willing to play the part. None of it would matter when he was out of here.

"Did you say something?" Justin kept his eyes wide, acting as though he'd momentarily forgotten where he was while drool slid down his thumb.

He never momentarily forgot *anything*.

"I was just saying…you really have to be thankful for this.

It's an incredibly positive development for you. And I'm just so glad that all of the hard work I've put into your case has been worth it." Victor had given this same speech an infinite number of times since they'd been notified of Justin's transfer. Goren was quite proud of himself.

Pride was one of the seven deadly sins.

Justin briefly wondered if Goren even knew that, but quickly decided that it didn't matter. He would teach him all about it. Eventually.

"Th-thank you. Thank you so much." Justin let the tears flow freely, just to add that little extra sentimental touch he knew would make Victor feel even better about *his* victory.

It wasn't his victory. He'd played the exact part Justin had designed for him. He had planned everything. Goren was merely a tool, and Justin couldn't wait until the attorney was one he no longer needed.

Oh, the fun we'll have, Victor.

"Don't thank me, son. I'm just doing my job. What you need to focus on now is bettering yourself. You have an immensely qualified staff here who are going to help you recover."

Justin's insides clenched, and his voice went ice-cold. "I want Autumn."

Victor sighed, irritating him all the more. "Dr. Trent has a lot on her plate, Justin. I'll do my best to convince her to come see you again, but you have to remember that she has no actual obligation to visit you now. She's a very busy woman."

Rage stirred hot in his stomach. "Autumn is *not* too busy for *me*. She'll come. I won't speak to any of the other doctors. Do you hear me? No one but Autumn!" Justin knew his voice had risen to an alarming pitch, but he didn't care. He was mentally unsound, after all. Wasn't he? Now that the competency assessment was over, the insanity evaluation would be next. He sucked his thumb again. He needed the practice.

"Justin, I really think it's best if you refer to her as 'Dr. Trent.' Doctors and patients really shouldn't be on a first name—"

"Shut up! Autumn doesn't mind! I want Autumn! *I want Autumn!*" Justin was screaming now. The whitecoats would be coming soon, and Goren would leave. Blessed silence and rest would follow. It was exactly what Justin wanted...needed.

"Justin, please listen to me. Dr. Trent *has* taken a great interest in your case, and I know she values the insight gained from her time spent with you. I'm not saying she will never come to see you. I'm saying I just can't guarantee it. Calm down. Deep breaths." Victor Goren was about two seconds from pissing his pants. Justin could see it in the man's eyes.

"I. Will. Only. Speak. To. Autumn." Justin knew it would be a good time to start biting himself or simply begin to cry, do something to work Goren's pity button again, but the attorney was just making him too angry.

"I know you prefer Dr. Trent, and she's certainly qualified to see you. But I just spoke with her this morning, and she's currently out of town for a new case." Victor was holding out his hands in a "please calm down" gesture that made him somehow more pathetic than he'd already proven himself to be.

Maybe he *wouldn't* wait to kill the bastard. *He* was keeping Autumn away from Justin, most likely. He wasn't helping Justin at all anymore—just following his own damn agenda. Justin could probably strangle him to death before anyone stopped him. At the very least, he could give Goren the scare of his life.

And Autumn Trent had left? *Again?* Did that bitch not

understand the mistake she was making by shoving him to the back burner time after time?

I was the one who mattered. Justin's case. Autumn was fucking up big time.

Which could work to his advantage.

"How dare she," he muttered, calmer now as he thought everything through.

"How dare she what, Justin?" Victor's fear seemed to have subsided in direct ratio to Justin's drop in volume. He'd really shook him, and Justin knew he was doing his damnedest to return to his haughty lawyer throne that he reigned from in his pathetic mind.

Justin began rocking again, and every molecule inside his body seemed to be expanding and contracting with a variety of emotions. Autumn couldn't just walk away from him. She wouldn't. He knew she wouldn't. Unless Winter had convinced her to.

He stopped rocking. That must be it. It wasn't Victor keeping Autumn away. It was his sister. Winter wouldn't want to share Autumn with him.

"How dare she what, Justin?" Victor repeated, softer this time.

Justin looked at him with all the hate inside him. "You're a worthless dumbfuck, Goren. That's what you are. A. Worth. Less. Dumb. Fuck."

The surprise on his face was comedic. If Justin wasn't ready to murder him with his bare hands, he might have even laughed. The attorney had frozen, no longer knowing what to say for the first time since Justin had met the man.

It was a holy miracle.

But Justin knew he needed to also be careful. Right now, because he'd been such a model prisoner in jail, they weren't keeping him in the most secure part of the hospital. They also weren't cuffing him when visitors came.

Justin needed that freedom. Needed the ability to speak to another person face-to-face, not from the other side of the glass.

To that end, he should focus on finding the balance between insanity and dangerous.

"How dare she abandon me?" Justin cried and began to rock back and forth. "And how could *you let her*? Everyone," he was screaming now, "abandons me! *Everyone*! How dare she! How dare you?" Justin didn't wipe the tears and snot away as he looked up at the attorney. He'd get an Emmy for this performance, he was sure. "You made her leave, didn't you! You wanted to keep the pretty doctor all to yourself! You wanted to make her your own personal whore!"

The whitecoats had arrived, as predicted. Their presence did nothing except add to Justin's rage. He had to tamp it down, though. He couldn't allow any of them to see how much he wanted to kill the fat fuck before him. They couldn't know how Justin would stretch out the torture and make him pay for being such a worthless piece of shit. Make him *suffer* for sending Autumn away.

Wanting to test how far he could push the orderlies, he tried to run from them, but not very hard. He also only half-heartedly fought them when they grabbed his arms and forced him down on his cot. Once there, he shifted from anger to extreme sadness.

A crying patient wasn't a killing patient after all.

He wailed and begged for his mommy. Begged for his grandpa. Begged for Autumn.

But he couldn't bring himself to beg for his sister.

Falling deeper into the insanity hole, he sucked his thumb, mildly aware that there was a slight froth on his lips.

"None of you know who I am—who you're messing with! I am blessed! Do you hear me? Blessed! You will all rot in hell for this! You'll burn in a pit of fire!"

The needle prick he'd known was coming was followed by the sting of the thick meds being pushed into his muscle. The world blurred and his movements began to slow. Try as he might to fight it, his body immediately began to go limp. The orderlies settled him straighter on the bed as Victor stood dumbly in the background. He looked like a cartoon character—one of those useless sidekicks whose only real skill was providing comic relief. Justin began to laugh quietly with what little strength he had left.

Justin knew that even if Victor Goren was shitting his pants right now—literally or figuratively—he'd be back. His case had given ole Vic a glimpse of fame they both knew he'd never see again. He needed Justin. He *owed* him, dammit.

There wasn't much for the orderlies to do after that. They'd succeeded in sedating him, and that was really all they cared about. The brainless gorillas wouldn't even have to strap him down.

Not this time, anyway.

Victor left the room first like the pissant coward he was, and then the whitecoats followed. The door closed on a click, and Justin managed one more weak giggle, just for the hell of it.

It was almost cute that a tiny little lock like that was expected to keep him in this room. When the time was right, he would escape. And God help the people who crossed his path when he did.

The world was fading, and Justin promised himself just before he lost consciousness that he would paint the entire hospital red with the blood of those imbeciles.

Red is all the rage these days...

A small smile, and then nothing.

4

W inter Black closed her eyes and pressed her fingers to her temples. Her head had begun to ache, and she hoped it wasn't one of *those headaches*. The brain surgery she'd had at just thirteen—a result of Douglas Kilroy, The Preacher, attempting to kill her with a brutal blow—had left her with recurring, agonizing headaches that almost always meant a vision was coming on.

The visions had helped her in numerous cases, but Winter had seen enough in the last decade to last a lifetime. Sometimes, the visions offered her an important scene from the past. Other times, she was shown the present. She wished her visions acted more like a crystal ball that forecasted the future. That would have been a handy skill to have tucked in her pocket.

A crammed commercial flight wasn't an ideal place for her "headaches" to act up. Too many people, too much chaos, and absolutely nowhere to hide when she slid back into the current reality surrounding her...dazed, horrified, and nearly always with a nosebleed.

She realized that Autumn was eyeing her closely from the

seat to her right. Concern was written on Autumn's face, and a pang of emotion shot through Winter's body. They'd grown so close to each other and had so much in common that it seemed surreal at times.

"You okay?" Autumn could have simply touched Winter's arm to get a truthful response, and they both knew it.

"I'm fine. A little headache. Not one of *those*, I don't think." Winter pushed back a wayward strand of her dark hair. "I just keep thinking about Justin, whether I want to or not."

Autumn tensed, and Winter immediately knew her friend had something to tell her.

"He's been transferred. I just found out before the briefing. I wanted to wait and tell you when we had a little bit of privacy." Autumn's bright green eyes scanned their surroundings. "But I'm not sure privacy is going to exist for a few days."

As if on cue, a child screamed with intense dissatisfaction, and a man sneezed in the seat directly behind them.

"Transferred to where?" Winter didn't care if they were alone or not. She needed to know everything that Autumn knew…right now.

"Virginia State Hospital. It's the only facility in the entire state that has—"

"An Adult Maximum-Security Treatment Program," Winter finished for her. She rolled the new information over in her mind for a minute, fighting an inner tug-of-war. "Do you think that's the best place for him right now?"

Winter knew her brother had been campaigning hard for a transfer to a "secure" psychiatric facility. Justin didn't want to spend his days inside of a supermax prison, for many obvious reasons.

Autumn twisted a lock of her red hair around her finger, a slight frown furrowing her brow. "I couldn't say for sure.

My time with him was so rushed. I don't think I was anywhere near being done with his competency assessment, and I made sure the judge knew that."

This troubled Winter even more. If Autumn couldn't say it was a good move for certain, then Autumn didn't think it was a good move. Her friend was trying to soften a blow that she knew Winter would find devastating. Worse than that, Winter already felt within herself that the transfer was a mistake.

Justin was dangerous. And clever. He needed bars he couldn't escape. People he couldn't manipulate.

On the other hand…

"I guess the bright side is that he might at least get a little help there. The kind of help he desperately needs." Winter didn't have to add the rest of her thought to the sentence. It was possible that her baby brother was far beyond any type of "help," and Autumn knew it as well as she did.

"We'll see what happens. It's not over yet." Autumn gave her an encouraging smile, but Winter intuitively felt the doubt in her friend's words. It didn't matter who said it or how it was said. No amount of candy-coating could change the truth about Winter's little brother.

All hope that Justin Black could ever return to any semblance of normal had been lost a long, long time ago.

They were silent for a few minutes, and Winter's mind wandered back to the little silky-haired boy she'd kissed goodnight all those years ago. *"Sissy, I love you to the moon and around all the stars in the big, big universe."*

The fact that he'd been taken from her—taken from *himself*—just wasn't fair. Growing up as Douglas Kilroy's protégé, Justin hadn't stood a chance of turning out even remotely normal.

But Winter couldn't stop herself from hoping that, somehow, some way, she'd see her "real" little brother again. She knew it was the same hope that Autumn held on to for her long-lost little sister, Sarah.

As if Autumn could read her mind—which in all actuality she could—her red-haired friend calmly shared a bit of her own sibling update. "I received a message about Sarah from the National Name Check Program. It's very possible that she's in Florida."

Winter's eyes went wide. "Autumn, that's amazing news! I mean, it *is* amazing news, isn't it?" Autumn's trepidation was written all over her face.

"It is. It could be." Autumn twisted another red lock around her index finger. "I just have a very bad feeling about what might have become of her. When I went into foster care and Sarah's dad took her, he promised to come back for me."

Autumn closed her eyes, her entire body seeming to deflate. Winter wiped away a tear of empathy.

"I wanted that to happen so very badly. Ryan Petzke was clean, and it was so obvious that he loved Sarah. He wanted to give her the life she deserved. I just wanted to be lucky enough to be a part of it, even if I wasn't his actual daughter. But he never came back, and now," Autumn turned to stare out the tiny plane window, "I think I was the lucky one. Ryan obviously didn't stay clean, and it kills me to think of how happy Sarah could have been with me and the Trents. She could have had a real family. A real chance."

Winter took her friend's hand, letting her feel the honest compassion flowing through her. "You don't know yet exactly how things went for her. Maybe it won't be as bad as you think." Winter offered Autumn the same sliver of hope that Autumn always gave to her. Autumn's expression once again gave away her thoughts on the possibility.

Maybe it was intuition, or fear, or a mix of both, but Autumn Trent clearly didn't expect to find her sister happy and healthy. Winter knew all too well just how devastating the outcome could be, and she silently willed the universe to spare her friend such pain.

Autumn had been through enough. They both had.

The strange similarities of their situations were a constant source of interest and awe. They'd both suffered traumatic brain injuries as children. They'd both woken up forever changed from comas. They both had lost their half-sibling, albeit for very different reasons. They'd even lost their parents. Winter's were murdered by Douglas Kilroy, and Autumn's were highly abusive, causing the courts to force little Autumn into the foster care system because of it.

But they'd also both somehow managed to find loving homes and real families. Winter's grandparents had raised her, and Autumn had been adopted by the Trents. No matter the suffering that either of them had endured, they'd fared far better than their younger siblings.

And the guilt of that fact nearly crushed them both, every single day.

"It felt like a sign." Autumn's voice had turned light with optimism.

"A sign?"

"Sarah's in Florida. This case is in Florida. Both things happening at a time when I've been so unsure of which path to take next...becoming an FBI agent and finding Sarah seem to be woven together, somehow." Autumn appeared to be firm in that belief, and Winter silently hoped that the theory would prove true.

"Everything happens for a reason, right?" Winter offered, giving Autumn the warmest smile she could manage while wishing she could do more.

Autumn nodded. "I guess right now we should focus on the fact that we have a chance to possibly rescue some other kids from experiencing massively screwed up lives. I'm not sure what humans deserve in general. We're capable of such awful things as a whole, but I'm sure that every kid deserves a happy childhood. We need to find these babies."

"Agreed." Winter blew out a breath full of quiet exasperation. "It's just hard to know where to start. We need to find what connects these women, because there has to be something. But if the unsub is dropping bodies in the swamps…"

She had a vision of the mothers being tossed into the water still alive, their wombs empty as blood flowed from between their legs. The gators would quickly pick up the scent of their terror and slide nearly soundlessly into the murky depths. The victim wouldn't know that death was so close until teeth sank into their flesh. They wouldn't even have time to scream before being pulled under the surface and into a death roll that—

"No bodies, no profile."

Winter was grateful to be pulled from the vision. "Right."

Autumn reached for her iPad. "I overheard Aiden and Noah talking about alligators and decided to look it up myself. Florida has over 1,100 swamps and 1.25 *million* alligators. If the bodies are being eaten by gators and other such predators or scavengers, we're obviously not going to find them. Then again, without bodies, how can we really be sure that the women are even dead to begin with? The hand leads me to believe that whoever is taking the women certainly isn't planning to keep them forever, but that's just one hand. One. They could still be in captivity somewhere, with or without their babies." Autumn clearly understood the obstacles they were facing.

As Winter listened to Autumn's speculation, she forced herself not to smile. She was so proud of her friend. The progress that Autumn had made in such a very short time was impressive. It spoke volumes of what she was capable of in the future, and Winter knew that Aiden had been perusing those volumes since he first met Autumn. He'd known immediately.

Autumn was special. It took five seconds to gather that. Her intelligence was astounding, and her insight was rare. The FBI was lucky that she'd even looked twice in their direction. They needed Autumn Trent, and Winter felt it was safe to finally say that they had her. The loose ends were still being tied into pretty bows, but Autumn was, officially or not, an FBI agent—and an irreplaceable one at that.

"I think what disturbs me most about it is the fact that we don't know what they're doing with the babies either." Winter mentally shuddered as she spoke. "These days there's a pedophile just around every single corner, and some of them *prefer* babies."

Autumn sighed, her face nearly collapsing from worry. "I thought of that too. Infants are nonverbal. Perfect targets. Their abductors can groom them until they reach the pedophile's 'fantasy age.'"

Winter pressed her hand to her stomach. It was impossible to have the discussion without feeling nauseated. "Even worse, some assholes use them for their own perverted pleasures while they're *still babies*. Or sell photographs and videotape of the abuse online to other sick bastards." Winter felt a deep rage at the thought of such monsters existing. But monsters did exist. The Preacher was proof.

So was Justin.

"Do they even get to meet their mothers? Are the women told anything about what's going to happen to them or their baby? Are they even allowed to hold them after labor?" Autumn reached for a tissue in her purse. "I can't think there's anything worse than not knowing the fate of your newborn child."

Autumn's eyes glistened with tears, and Winter squeezed her hand tighter. Due to endometriosis, Autumn would most likely never have a baby of her own. Her diagnosis made the horror of the subject even more personal.

"I think being murdered in that state of fear and helplessness might top it." Winter's rage grew with each word. She knew that both of their hearts were breaking for these women and their children, but her natural tendency was to burn like fire while Autumn's empathy was more like a massive tidal wave of sadness. "The women have to know in the last few seconds that they will never be able to help their babies. They can't even beg for anyone else to help, either. They just die in that horrid agony."

"Maybe the babies are being illegally adopted." Autumn appeared to hope that was the case, as it was far better than any option they'd discussed so far.

"It's possible." Winter let the theory breathe for her soft-hearted friend's sake. "Did you hear about the case also in Florida? An attorney was arrested for running an illegal adoption ring. I know that Aiden has put in a call to the FBI agent in charge of the case, Clay something or other, as well as a Charleston detective named Ellie Kline, I think it was. Aiden is planning to see if our cases might be related."

Autumn turned and looked into Winter's eyes. "You don't think that's probable, though." Autumn called her cards instantly. The intuition between them was amazing, but it also left little room for sugar-coating anything. Ever.

Winter gave Autumn a sad smile. "I *want* it to be probable."

The child who had been crying earlier in the flight was at it again. The crying got worse when a woman yelled, "I told both of you, absolutely *no whining* on this plane! You should be ashamed of yourself!"

"You've got to be kidding me," Winter muttered as both she and Autumn sat in stunned silence while the harried mother stood, holding a little boy who couldn't have been more than two, and yelled at the other child—also a boy and not a day over five.

"Look at the example you're setting for your brother! What is *wrong* with you? You're acting like an idiot!" The younger child was sobbing now too, and it only seemed to make the woman angrier. "Do you want me to take you in that bathroom and spank you? Cuz I'll do it! *I will do it!*"

Winter's skin prickled with anger. Here they were, on their way to help find missing pregnant women who were almost certainly being *forcibly* parted from their newborns, and this screaming hag was taking her two perfectly healthy children for granted.

The universe was not fair. Not at all.

Feeling she was at her breaking point, Winter began to rise. She knew a lot of her fellow passengers were probably wanting to strangle the kids, but Winter was ready to throttle the mother.

Autumn's hand shot up and grabbed her arm before she could fully stand. Autumn was a lot of things, and physically weak was not one of them. Winter's Krav-Maga-practicing friend pulled her gently back down.

Winter's face went hot with guilt and frustration. "I was just going to—"

"I know." Autumn's small smile was adorable and aggravating at the same time. Of course she knew. Winter would have bet money on the fact that Autumn knew the scene that was going to be made even before she grabbed Winter's arm to stop her.

Sometimes a touch wasn't necessary.

Autumn rose and took the few strides needed to reach the horrible woman. Winter watched closely, attempting not to pout, but still feeling like she'd just been put in a time-out by her best friend.

"Ma'am, if you'd like, I could hold one of your little ones

for a while. You look exhausted, and I don't blame you. These tiny guys are a handful! Maybe you could get a few minutes of sleep?" Autumn somehow managed to make the offer without any hint of condescension or judgment. This was good, as Winter knew it was the kids who would pay for any embarrassment or anger caused by a stranger's intervention.

Autumn knew it too.

"Why? Why would you do that?" The woman and her children stared wide-eyed at Autumn. The older one had stopped crying while the little one continued to whimper.

"I just started working a case where newborns are being taken from their mothers. I know you must love your children like crazy, and a little rest would probably go a long way for you and them." Autumn's voice was kind.

The mother sat back down and clutched her little boys tightly. "That's so awful. That's just *so awful.*" She burst into tears, and just like that, the tables turned.

The little one hushed and began patting her cheeks with his tiny hand. "Is okay, Mommy."

The older boy got up on his knees and put his arms around her neck. "I'll be good. I promise."

"I'm just so tired," the mother said after a few moments. "My husband recently passed away after a yearlong battle with cancer, and I'm trying to move back home so the kids and I can be close to my family. Asking for help isn't easy." She looked around, clearly embarrassed by the attention she was receiving. "So many people these days just mommy-shame you and make everything a million times worse."

Autumn nodded sympathetically and smiled as another passenger handed over a small package of tissues. She took one and began to wipe the littlest boy's tears. "Just remember that there are a lot of people who would *understand* your struggles. Not everyone is a mommy-shamer. When you need help, you can't let anything stop you from asking for it. We all need support in this world."

A different passenger handed the woman an iPad with two sets of earbuds. From her vantage point, Winter noticed that *Paw Patrol* was on. Thrilled with the distraction, the children settled down to watch while the mother leaned her head back on the seat. After thanking everyone for their kindness, the mom seemed to fall asleep in seconds.

"I'm an asshole," Winter offered after Autumn was seated beside her once again. "I always want to take a hammer to everything. You get a lot further with your cotton ball approach."

"I wish everything was that easy to fix. My adoptive parents loved me like crazy, but the circumstances that brought me to them were vastly different than what is happening in Florida. Those babies deserve to be with their families. We have to find them before—" Autumn's voice cracked on the last word.

"Before someone like Douglas Kilroy poisons their minds with a deranged, psychopathic sickness that can never be fully undone?" Winter finished her friend's sentence for her.

Autumn met Winter's eyes for a long time before she slowly nodded. Heart heavy, Winter's mind turned to Justin.

If I'd only found you sooner, baby brother.

5

"Excellent!" I couldn't have been more pleased with my newest vessel. Physically, she was, of course, perfect. But even better, it seemed the excitement of her journey to my compound had sped up her incubation process. I would be harvesting my crop much more quickly than I'd expected.

I approached the bed slowly, respecting that the vessel was not yet aware of the privilege that she'd incurred and therefore would perceive me as a threat. Nothing could be further from the truth.

She eyed me and my surgical scrubs warily as I neared her, and I knew that I was correct. She was afraid, and her fear was unnecessary.

"Please." Her voice came out raspy, which was expected. The vessels usually spent quite a bit of energy screaming for help when they were finally able. That was fine. It changed nothing. "Please, let me go. You have to let me go. I won't…"

The vessel struggled to keep her voice calm, and I smiled, knowing I'd chosen wisely.

"I won't tell anyone what happened." Her hands tightened into fists. "I couldn't if I wanted to. I don't know where I am, and I don't know who you are. Please, just let me and my babies go before this goes too far. I'm carrying *twins*."

Her eyes widened, a glimmer of hope causing the pupils to dilate to a point where the blue was a small sliver around the inky black. I waited patiently, wondering what she would say next. It was always interesting to see how the vessels bargained. They always did.

"You've kidnapped *three people*." Her hands fought against the bindings, and I knew she wanted to clasp her belly to protect the seed inside. My seed didn't need her protection, but she wasn't in a position to understand that. "Three. That means you'll be prosecuted three times as hard as a normal kidnapper. You wouldn't want to do something you'll regret. You've taken on too much. It wasn't your fault. You didn't realize. But you have to let me…"

A contraction hit her like a train, made more powerful by the drug I'd injected into her IV line. Pitocin saved me from having to wait so long, and this time it had saved me from listening to her long-winded speech.

A speech that was new. I thought I'd heard every possible plea that a pregnant woman could come up with. The creature was strapped to the bed in such a way that escape was completely impossible, yet she had found it within herself to threaten *me*.

Brave.

It gave me instant, happy hope that my two little girls would come out of this vessel as strong-minded individuals. My children needed to be strong, because together, we were going to change the world.

"Let me go!" The calm bargaining turned into a wail. "Let me go! Let me go!" How quickly the bravery had passed.

I began the vessel's examination without a word. I wasn't a medical doctor, but that was of no consequence here. I was an expert at this. My hands knew exactly where to go and what to look for. This was my *God-given* profession, and I knew *His purpose* trumped any silly degree that a man could ever grant me.

The wailing in the background really wasn't necessary. I would never hurt my children, and right now, they were highly dependent on this womb. That made the womb and the entire vessel surrounding it precious to me. I meant no harm.

Both heads appear to be downward facing. Excellent, excellent, excellent.

I was quite capable of delivering via cesarean when needed and had, on occasion, been forced to use this skill. But the downside of not having all the equipment that modern-day hospitals provided was that I wasn't properly equipped to administer the anesthesia that typically accompanied such procedures.

I did, however, have an ample supply of paralytics on hand. Though I had to be careful not to overuse them. The drugs could hurt my unborn children.

All of that aside, cesareans were messy, and the vessel's screaming was usually of such a horrid volume that my concentration was challenged. Some of the vessels had shown an amazing ability to withstand the shock of the incisions, and therefore the noise carried on for indefinite and completely obnoxious periods of time before they finally went silent.

Yes. Natural delivery was always preferable. It gave my children their best chance at entering this world unscathed and perfect.

All my children must be perfect.

Owning a sperm bank of quite an impressive size had been a heaven-sent blessing from God Himself. It was simply meant to be. All of my amassed wealth gained through my dutiful work as a fertility scientist had arranged my life in such a way that I hadn't even had to change a thing when I set out to put The Dream into play.

The Dream. It was beautiful beyond what I ever could have imagined. The vision had been sent to me years ago as I slumbered, and when I woke, I'd known that my purpose on this planet far exceeded the average man's.

I had been chosen by God to create a pure society of peace amongst all of the world's ugly mayhem. The honor was humbling, and I knew it was my righteous duty to see it through.

I'd purchased a picturesque island off the coast of Florida and named it Eden, just as The Dream had shown me. It was here that my children were sent after they were harvested from my chosen vessels. In Eden, they would grow in perfect peace, and someday they would take their purity back to the mainland. My children would spread my stainless seed throughout the masses, and the immaculate, untainted beauty of The Dream would be woven into an otherwise fallen and sullied mankind.

I knew I'd been chosen because of my own uncommon flawlessness. I was a tall, strong man and my heart was pure. My thick blond hair and clear blue eyes were perfectly representative of the exemplary specimen required to bring The Dream to fruition.

Likewise, I chose my vessels with extreme, meticulous care.

XY Cryolabs, the sperm bank which I solely owned, was located in the happy, quiet metropolis of Lavender Lake. It was there that I pored over the files of fertility-challenged couples to find my vessels. The labor of the search was daunting, but the fruit of the harvest would be worth every minute spent seeking out my worthy vessels.

Blue eyes and natural blonde hair were mandatory. I also made absolutely sure that the medical history was spotless.

Genetic conditions immediately removed a vessel from consideration.

Eden required impeccable vessels to bring about its unblemished society.

The one that lay before me now was everything I could ever hope to find in a solitary female human. These blessed children were going to be exquisite.

"Excellent." It was my first spoken word since having entered the birth room and seemed to shock the howling creature before me into a much-needed moment of silence. "You," I smiled down at her, "have nothing to worry about. The babies are in fine health, and as a God-chosen vessel, your joy should be overflowing."

"I. Am. Not. A. Damn. Vessel. *I am not a vessel!* My name is Lindsay Welsh and you do not have my consent to do anything...*anything*...to me or my babies!"

I didn't take offense, knowing how difficult it was for the masses to understand or accept The Dream. But they would. Eventually.

"I will be right by your side as my children come into this world. Do not worry. You are part of a divine design. You are blessed." I smiled again and proceeded to leave the birth room.

"I'm not part of your design! You're a psychopath! These babies are *mine*! I will kill you...*kill you*...if you so much as *touch* them! Let me out of here! Let me go, you sick son of a bitch! *Let me go!*"

Potty mouth aside, I was again briefly pleased with the vessel's boldness. This one would struggle and fight to the very end, which only proved what a fine instrument I had chosen when selecting her.

My daughters would be exceedingly courageous.

As soon as the door clicked shut, the sweet sound of silence returned. Every cent spent soundproofing the birth rooms had been well-placed. No one would hear the commotion anyway. This building sat in the middle of the ninety-two-acre horse ranch I owned. A bit farther south than Lavender Lake, it was the perfect place for my children to be harvested before they were sent to Eden.

The ranch was beautiful, large, and most importantly, secluded.

No vessel left the ranch alive, but that was a small price to pay for being a chosen one. Their sacrifice was what made The Dream possible. Their sacrifice gave their otherwise meaningless lives purpose, and that purpose would continue on within my children.

We were going to change the world.

"Father." A meek voice pulled me from my sweet reverie.

It was Sasha, my faithful and eager servant. Sasha was of great value to me, although she'd originally been nothing more than the whore-daughter of a prostitute and a pimp. Sasha had spoken of her childhood in great detail, describing through her tears how her father had started selling her out when her mother passed. Sasha had only been ten at the time. She'd spent years as a filthy sex worker, and my heart broke for her.

I'd only met her by chance when she was hired on as a custodian at XY Cryolabs.

Sasha would never be a suitable vessel. Let alone her history of sex slavery, which made her body abhorrent in my eyes, she'd also miscarried an infant while in a jail cell. Former miscarriages meant an immediate disqualification of any possible vessel. While their husbands may have been unable to produce the vibrant seed required for procreation, the vessels themselves must be physically unimpaired in any way.

I knew that Sasha wished more than anything to be a vessel. And indeed, Eden was home to women who had willingly chosen to be a part of my family and serve as vessels. But these women were required to meet the same standards as any vessel I tracked down through my lab's data.

Eventually, Sasha might be allowed to stay at Eden as a caregiver for my children—an Eden Mother. I couldn't blame her for wanting to be there amongst the happy utopia of my family. All the women on the island were there because they'd desperately wanted to be. Not that there was any possible way for them to escape should they change their minds.

For now, Sasha's dedication and enthusiasm served a better purpose on the mainland, helping me acquire the necessary vessels to bring The Dream to full fruition. She was small, but she was strong. And she was young. The vigor that came with being only nineteen was exactly what made Sasha invaluable to me. The resiliency she possessed as a result of the horrors of her childhood was an added bonus.

Sasha had been made for this purpose, and I'd seen the potential in her immediately when she began her work at the lab. She was capable of so much more than custodial work. I'd opened her eyes to this fact, and she'd been unwaveringly devoted to me ever since.

"My child." I placed a hand firmly on each of her shoulders. "Your work securing this vessel was impeccable. You are a priceless asset to The Dream." Her face at once went bright from the praise, and I noted, yet again, how her curls were just a few shades too dark to have ever made her a candidate for being a vessel herself. They were closer to caramel, while I required the lightest shades of blonde possible.

Sasha's freckles were another imperfection that would have eliminated her from consideration, even if she had been a clean woman. And she was not even close to being a clean woman.

"Thank you, Father." The girl humbly lowered her head, but her radiating smile showed me just how pleased my words had made her. "I'm ready to bring in the next."

I smiled at her youthful enthusiasm. "My child, remember that the vessels are chosen through a complex and lengthy process. Plans must be laid ever so delicately before we can proceed with the next vessel. Your devotion to The Dream is appreciated, but I will beckon you when you are needed again."

Sasha's smile faltered slightly, but she nodded in obedience. "Yes, Father. As you wish."

I gave her a lingering kiss to the forehead to reassure her of my appreciation and heard her breathing accelerate with the touch.

She would do anything to be a vessel. But she must let go of that hope.

I walked away, aware that there was a tear building in the corner of Sasha's left eye. Touching as it was, I deeply hoped Sasha's emotions would not interfere with her performance.

It would be a pity to have to eliminate her.

6

Aiden Parrish didn't have the time nor the patience to deal with an FBI agent-hating detective. But as it looked so far, he wasn't going to have to.

His team had landed and made it to the Lavender Lake Sheriff's Department while the afternoon was still young. After a general briefing in the conference room, Aiden had been conferring for at least fifteen minutes with Detective Jacqueline Cohen in the privacy of her office. Detective Cohen was a major crimes detective in the Criminal Investigation Department of the sheriff's office, and she hadn't shown a single sign of resentment concerning the FBI's presence. Jackie, as she had told them all to call her, was legitimately relieved that they were there.

The dark shadows under her eyes told him she hadn't seen sleep in years, and Aiden knew that he didn't look any better. His head was killing him, though he'd admit that over his cold, dead body. Plus, with someone like Winter Black around, it was kind of hard to complain about a headache.

He knew hers were far worse.

After being assigned to the case, Jackie had managed to

link similar disappearances to other parts of Florida. Sheila Conlon and Patricia Gorski-Wilson were both inside of her jurisdiction, and now they had the added possibility that Lindsay Welsh was the third within the county.

"Don't think I can't handle this type of thing. I can, but there may be many connected victims and incidents that cross county lines. The extra help you and your people provide might be what makes or breaks the outcome of all of this." Jackie ran a hand through her cropped brown hair.

Aiden nodded, carefully going through his mental files of what they knew so far. "You seem to strongly believe that Lindsay Welsh's disappearance is a direct part of something much bigger." He was merely observing. Aiden's voice held no judgment.

"Wouldn't you? This isn't the type of thing that normally happens in groups. Lavender Lake isn't exactly a small town, but it's certainly small enough to make three remarkably similar abductions suspicious as hell." Jackie was clearly frustrated.

"The Welshs haven't been in Lavender Lake for long, though, according to my intel." Aiden knew the detective would take his comments as borderline skepticism, but he really was just trying to get a very clear picture of where Detective Cohen's mind was at.

"That's true, but it doesn't change the similarities. Something is up with this." Jackie's hand had moved from her hair to her forehead. "Something *bad*."

Aiden didn't disagree. He knew that Jackie Cohen had fifteen years of work in the force to back up her intuition— seven years as a deputy followed by eight years as a detective. The woman was operating on more than blank guesses.

He had learned, from his own personal career path, that all those years of experience mattered. They sharpened and honed skills and senses you might not have been aware you possessed in the first place.

"I agree with you, Detective. That's why we're here. I assume you're canvassing the area surrounding Lindsay's disappearance?" She visibly relaxed as he spoke the words.

"My officers are going door to door in the neighborhoods surrounding the grocery store where Lindsay was last seen as we speak. So far, I haven't been informed of any leads. If we're lucky, we might get some footage of the vehicle fleeing the scene off a home security cam or two along the way. But even if we get a general direction, finding the destination is going to prove incredibly difficult. They could quite literally have gone anywhere." The frustration was back in Jackie's voice.

"And aside from the hand, we have no bodies. None." Aiden was aware that his expression was grim, but he knew the odds, and so did Detective Cohen.

"Alligators don't much give a damn about official evidence. A free meal is a free meal." Jackie chucked her ball-point pin across the office. "Using the swamps as the dumping grounds for bodies is barbaric, but our killer is smart. All of those clues get chomped up, and no one is the wiser."

"We can't exactly interrogate the alligators, now can we?" The remark was funny, but neither of them laughed. "You don't think these women are being kept captive somewhere, do you? Aside from Mrs. Gorski-Wilson, why even assume they're dead?"

Jackie sighed. "Of course, we would all hope they're still breathing. Alive is better than dead any day of the week. But after we found that hand...I'll shoot straight with you, SSA Parrish. Whoever's behind this is a monster, and they are obviously on some type of mission. I don't think the actual missing women themselves have much to offer this killer after their babies are out, aside from more risk and unnecessary trouble. Serial killers are called 'killers' for a reason."

"What makes you so sure that the babies are still alive, then, Detective?" Aiden was needling again, but that was a major part of his job, when you reduced it to layman's terms. You poked, and you didn't stop poking until you felt there wasn't anything *they* knew that *you* didn't also know.

You didn't lead a witness for a reason.

Yes, the questioning was exhausting for both parties, but that was the point. There was a decent reason as to why the average citizen shuddered at the words "FBI Investigation."

"Why target pregnant women if you don't have a plan for the babies? If the babies were of no consequence, any woman at all could be selected. Those babies are alive, Agent Parrish. I'd bet my career on it." Jackie's face was a tight mask of seriousness. She hadn't been born yesterday, nor the day before that. Detective Cohen was operating on strong gut instinct.

"No need for that, Detective. I'm leaning in your direction of thought myself with this case. I think the infants are alive, and I intend to bring them home." The familiar fire of adrenaline spread throughout his body. Aiden often told himself that he hadn't chosen this profession so much as it had chosen him. He was made for this.

Enough talk. We have an untold number of victims to find.

"Let's do it," Jackie agreed, rising from her desk chair with clear determination. They exited her office and rejoined the team who'd been waiting patiently in the conference room.

"I'm assigning Special Agent Sun Ming with the task of data mining. She's our best and brightest tech, and it frees you up to focus on the investigation." Aiden met Sun's gaze, and she gave a brief nod.

"Thank you, Agent Ming." Jackie's genuine words of gratitude earned her a rare smile from Sun.

"Special Agents Winter Black and Noah Dalton have been

assigned with investigating the spot where Lindsay was taken. They're already on their way. With the info you've gathered, they may be able to uncover some additional leads."

Aiden thought with amusement of the surprised expressions that Winter and Noah had both displayed when they realized they were being paired up. Ever since their relationship was made public knowledge, they had rarely worked closely together. That was normal protocol, but Aiden was bending the rules slightly for this case.

"Special Agent Chris Parker and Dr. Autumn Trent will be interviewing the previous victims' spouses, as well as Josh Welsh. Dr. Trent is a brilliant forensic and criminal psychologist, and she may be able to gather more information on their separate profiles that could point us toward the killer." Aiden hadn't meant to praise Autumn so openly, but there it was. Another slip that centered around Autumn Trent.

There would be a host of opinions about his use of the word "brilliant."

"That sounds good. We need every brain we can find trying to connect these dots as quickly as possible. I can set up the interviews with the spouses. They're familiar with me. And I can also give Dr. Trent and Agent Parker everything I've gathered so far." Jackie was certainly a tough cookie, but she also seemed to exude a happy desire to cooperate.

Aiden couldn't have been more relieved. Autumn smiled widely at Detective Cohen, indicating her gratefulness, and Chris gave a ridiculous thumbs-up.

Why? Why did I bring Parker?

He knew why...because his boss, Associate Deputy Director Cassidy Ramirez would expect him to show equal favor between Autumn and the rest of the BAU team. It had been a long while since Aiden had teamed up with Chris, so tossing him into a few cases would balance those scales.

"Special Agent Bree Stafford will be going through all the

video footage that has been gathered so far from the grocery store where Lindsay was taken, as well as the cameras along all the exit routes." Aiden knew that no one could concentrate for long amounts of time like Bree.

"On it." Bree knew it as well and gave Detective Cohen a nod of affirmation.

"I can't thank you all enough for being here. Now, if you'll excuse me, I have calls to make." Jackie set off to make her calls, and Aiden wrapped things up with his agents before they all dispersed.

There was a palpable electric hum amongst them.

Everyone was ready to catch this bastard—assuming there was only one to catch. The details of this case were complicated. Aiden had a feeling they weren't just looking for a single person.

There was no shortage of psychopaths in this world.

With as much nonchalance as he could muster, he pulled Autumn to the side, aware that they both tensed visibly when he touched her arm, though he wasn't sure why. She stood before him, her bright green eyes as expectant as ever.

Dammit. He'd completely forgotten what he was going to say. He made a desperate lunge for words. "I just wanted to warn you that the spouses you speak to today are bound to be very deeply emotionally scarred. It's typical for that kind of raw pain to be misplaced onto someone who is only trying to help, such as yourself."

Autumn grinned, though he could tell she'd tried not to. "You know, I think I heard something like that back in the day when I was spending years and years in college earning my Ph.D. But thank you for the warning, all the same."

Aiden instantly felt like an idiot. Of course, she knew what to expect in that type of encounter. He *knew* she knew what to expect. But Autumn was still a new hire, and he told himself that he'd have extended the words of wisdom to any newcomer.

Wouldn't he?

The complicated dynamic between the two of them seemed to always somehow muddy up his judgment. Caring more about Autumn's welfare than the rest of his agents would be unprofessional. And yet, he did care more.

Aiden wanted to remind Autumn of the trouble in Pennsylvania, just to make sure she was in her most extreme state of caution when she left his sight today. But his words would have been taken as an insult, and for whatever damn reason, Aiden hated himself every time he offended Autumn.

She was still staring up at him, and he briefly felt like his brain was being probed. "I won't let my emotions make any decisions this time, okay? I know what happened in Pennsylvania. I'll use my best unbiased judgment from here on out, I promise you." She gave him the Girl Scout salute. "Emotions be damned." She flashed him a wide, reassuring smile and turned away to find Parker. Aiden realized that she'd just fully addressed his unspoken comment.

How was Autumn Trent always getting inside his head?

And am I ever going to get her out...

Her red hair swayed as she walked down the fluorescent-lit hallway, and he realized something important. If Autumn were to truly ever stop basing her decisions on her emotions, the world would be losing something. *He* would be losing something.

There had to be a way for her to balance. A way for her to remain safe while still courageously charging toward justice. She was a vitally important member of the team now, but she was also special in a way that Aiden couldn't quite articulate. Or maybe he just refused to articulate it.

Regardless of what he did or didn't feel for Autumn, he was doing his job as a leader. Leaders looked out for their people. "She's a new hire, for god's sake. Of course I'm going to keep an eye out for her." He muttered this to himself, believing the hall to now be empty.

It wasn't.

Sun was a few feet behind him, and he nearly jumped through the ceiling when she said, "What's this about new hires?" He turned to her, taking in her scowl and raised eyebrow. She had a hand to her hip and clearly knew exactly who he was mumbling about.

Sun wasn't a big fan of Autumn. Or Winter. Or humans in general. But especially Autumn and Winter.

Aiden held up a hand. "Just thinking out loud. Brain-storming. Let's get to work, Agent."

Sun was more than willing to be away from him, and after she'd disappeared around the corner, Aiden put a frustrated hand to his forehead. Too many slips today, and they'd only just arrived. He'd blame the recent concussion if the admission wouldn't get him tossed off this case.

He couldn't, so he needed to focus.

Missing persons. Pregnant women. Infants.

Aiden repeated the words to himself silently as he walked. If he was lucky, the mantra would completely drown out the one other word that was rebelliously going off nonstop inside his head.

Autumn.

7

"This is great, isn't it, darlin'?" Noah said from the passenger seat of the sleek black Escalade rental where he'd spread out to enjoy being chauffeured.

Winter shot him a testy side-glance. "Yes, Noah. It's great that pregnant women are disappearing and more than likely becoming alligator snacks as soon as they give birth."

Noah shot her the stink eye in return. "Stop it. You know that's not what I meant at all. I meant it's nice to actually get to work together. Partner up."

"We're always partnered up." Winter smiled slightly, obviously thinking of their home.

Noah let out an exaggerated huff. "You know what I mean."

Winter grinned, and Noah shook his head. How had he fallen in love with such a sassy, beautiful woman? And why in the hell did she actually love him back?

"I'm not sure what Aiden's thinking, exactly. But if he put us together, you can be sure he has a reason." He knew Winter trusted Aiden explicitly. Their history trailed all the way back to The Preacher days.

"Yes, I know. The great and powerful, all-knowing SSA Aiden Parrish always has a grand plan behind his actions." Noah rolled his dark-green eyes dramatically. It didn't matter how much time passed or how much respect he had for the man. He still hated Aiden Parrish.

"Very mature, Dalton." Winter laughed, but Noah knew it would be short lived. They were on assignment. Winter became someone else entirely when she was working a case.

"It's not my fault that the guy is wound tighter than a fishing reel. I frankly don't see why you and I can't partner up more often, no matter our personal relationship." Noah defiantly grabbed Winter's free hand.

"That is exactly why we can't partner up more often, and you know it," Winter retorted, shaking his hand off. "If we weren't a couple, we'd be discussing the case right now. And we *should* be discussing the case right now."

Noah sighed. He knew Winter was right, and he took the case very seriously. At the same time, he was about three inches away from the woman he loved. Pretending he didn't worship the ground she walked on was hard. Regardless, given a choice between the two, he would take Winter's love and partnership *outside* of official FBI business over being just her job partner—any day of any week of any month of any year.

"We'll be there in less than five anyway. Buck up, Dalton." Winter weaved swiftly around vehicles, making the highway her own. She was attempting to be completely professional, but Noah caught the hint of a smile that kept turning up the ends of her mouth.

As it turned out, they arrived in less than three.

The Greengrocer was a small grocery store that boasted of catering to the healthier side of the culinary world. Other than that, Noah saw nothing particularly remarkable or different about it at all. It seemed a very unlikely place for a parking lot abduction.

Then again, that assumption conversely made it the *perfect* place for a parking lot abduction.

The station wagon the mystery woman had seemed to be having troubles with had already been moved to a forensic lab to be dusted for fingerprints. Likewise, Lindsay Welsh's abandoned shopping cart had also been taken in.

As far as they knew, only a few partials had been found and not a single strand of hair. The vehicle had clearly been meticulously wiped down and vacuumed, which was only further evidence that Lindsay Welsh's abduction had been anything but random. Someone had put a great deal of thought and energy into this kidnapping.

When they were seated in the security office at the back of the store, they learned just how careful and precise the unsub had been.

"That wagon was there a good thirty-six hours." The security guard, Fred, was sweating bullets. Noah could see that dealing with two FBI agents wasn't something Fred had probably ever thought he'd have to do. "There was a note on the dashboard claiming there'd been some car trouble, and they'd have it moved by the weekend. Lavender Lake is a nice place full of nice people. No one had the heart to get the vehicle impounded. Kinda wish we would have, in hindsight. You just never know what sick psychopath is gonna show up at your front door, ya know?"

Keeping his tone as pleasant as possible, Noah asked if they could please see the footage from the day when the vehicle first arrived. Fred obliged, and the three of them watched silently as the station wagon in question drove up. A figure swiftly emerged from the driver's side and proceeded to walk away. The mystery person was wearing gloves and a rainsuit, although there had been no rain that particular day.

A hood was pulled up tight around their head, and it was impossible to make out any defining features on the face.

"Clearly, this person knew where the security cameras were." Winter's intense blue gaze took in every detail possible from the footage.

"This was planned out with extreme diligence," Noah added. Their eyes met, and he wondered if Winter was thinking the same thing he was.

Scrupulously conducted crimes such as this were the FBI's worst nightmare. Many killers planned out their crimes, of course, but they often would slip up on a very important detail either before, during, or after they'd carried out their plan. Rushing, panic, interruptions, fascination, and sometimes even horror at their own actions could throw a criminal off-kilter in the blink of an eye.

Nothing had seemingly derailed this criminal. Not a single ruffled feather. The footage of Lindsay's actual abduction was proof.

A solitary woman with a hat pulled low over her face calmly walked to the parked station wagon and waited. Noah noted that the woman never actually *touched* the vehicle. She only stood very close to it. Her demeanor was confident, her actions smooth.

Everything had gone *exactly* the way it was supposed to for this criminal.

Fred informed them that the same girl who had checked out Lindsay Welsh was currently working register five. Noah and Winter wordlessly made their way through the store toward the checkout lanes. The dark-haired girl "working" register five was leaning against her counter, blowing pink bubbles and staring out the front windows as though she wished she were absolutely anywhere but there.

They approached her together, but Winter spoke first. Females often responded much better to other females when any type of questioning was involved. "Carianne? Are you Carianne Simpson?"

The girl's dark eyes lazily traveled toward the sound of Winter's voice and widened slightly as she took in the two FBI jackets before her. "Yes. I'm her. She's me. *I'm me.* I mean," her cheeks turned a deep shade of red, "I'm Carianne Simpson."

Noah thought he would choke on the laughter that had risen up in his throat, but he managed to keep a somber face. Winter continued the questions like a pro while Noah mentally chastised himself for nearly laughing out loud at a possible witness.

"Hi, Carianne. I'm Special Agent Winter Black, and this is my partner, Special Agent Noah Dalton. I'm sure you know by now that a woman, Lindsay Welsh, was taken from the parking lot last night." Winter waited, and Carianne's head bobbed up and down as her cheeks drained of the bright pink color. "We know you were the employee who checked her out, and you might be able to help us find her. Do you remember seeing Mrs. Welsh before?"

Carianne's head continued the up and down movements. "She's shopped here a few times. Maybe more. I'm not sure. But yes, I've seen her."

"Did you observe anything out of the ordinary when Lindsay Welsh went through your checkout lane last night?" Winter waited again.

"No. I mean, she seemed fine. She was laughing and said something about eating all of the tacos." Carianne's eyes glistened and she looked up at the ceiling, blinking rapidly. "She seemed really happy. Maybe a little loopy, but she was mega-huge pregnant, so I just figured hormones, ya know? She was fine."

Noah's stomach churned as he pictured Lindsay, carefree and giggling, patiently watching her groceries get loaded into a cart that would never quite make it to her van. She'd been oblivious. Kidnapping victims almost always were. From the strained look on Winter's face, she'd also found the imagery highly disturbing.

Happy. Pregnant. Gone.

The other clerks echoed Carianne's account, though most of them hadn't even been working the previous evening. Lindsay Welsh was a regular customer. She was nice. She was incredibly pregnant.

Noah held up the screengrab they'd taken from the security footage of the mystery woman. The shot was horrible. Just a partial glimpse of a blurry face. He let each clerk look at the image in turn, ending with Carianne.

Not a single one of them recognized her.

"I mean, that's a pretty bad picture, though. That could almost be anybody. You got any other shots?" Carianne's helpfulness knew no bounds.

Winter and Noah sighed in unison. "Sorry, kid. That's the best one." The defeat in Noah's voice must have been obvious. Every single clerk had gone somber with pity.

"Let's walk." Winter was already moving, and Noah jogged a few steps to catch up with her.

"Whatcha thinkin'?" Sometimes, he wished he could climb inside Winter's mind the same way that Autumn did. But he was one traumatic brain injury and one major brain surgery short to even hope for the sixth sense syndrome.

"I'm just thinking that I want to look at every single aisle. Every single thing. I don't want to overlook the one clue that could save her." Winter's voice was borderline angry, and Noah knew exactly why this time.

They wanted to save Lindsay, but the odds were that if they saved anyone at all—and that was a big if in this case—it would only be the babies. He knew Winter felt like they were fighting blind. They all did.

Noah's eye caught a lanky young man slipping out a side-door exit. He was wearing the same Greengrocer apron the clerks wore, and Noah figured they'd need to question him as well before they left. It struck Noah as strange that there was no alarm at the exit, as it was for emergency purposes only. But alarms could be turned off, especially if the doorway doubled as a smoke-break exit.

He put up a hand, alerting Winter to halt and observe. She focused all her attention on the same skinny boy as he slid behind a large bush directly outside the exit. As if they were one mind working double-time, they both realized something very important at the exact same moment. Winter grabbed Noah's sleeve as he turned to grab hers.

"Someone standing out there behind that bush would have had a straight shot view of the abduction. And the woman wouldn't have had any idea that he was there at all. What are the odds that the kid was working last night too?" Winter's voice was laden with excitement. They were hunting dogs who had caught a scent on a breeze, and it was time to chase.

"Let's go." Noah moved quickly toward the exit as Winter followed directly behind him. He slowed as they stepped out onto the grass, and they each took a different side of the bush to approach the employee.

Noah had a hunch that the young man was smoking something slightly stronger than a Marlboro Light. The hunch was quickly proven true by the telltale smell of smoke that filtered through the bush. Noah didn't want the kid to have a chance at fleeing when he realized that he was facing two federal agents while also smoking a plant that was still deemed highly illegal in the great state of Florida.

Winter stepped into view first, and Noah thought the boy might actually pee himself right then and there. Instead, he twisted around like a pretzel, trying to make his joint disappear in any way possible. The kid ran directly into Noah's chest, bouncing off and nearly falling over backward.

Not missing a beat, Noah and Winter crowded him between them and began their interrogation after introducing themselves per protocol.

"What's your name?" Winter demanded.

"Matt." Matt's voice clearly conveyed his terror.

"Did you work last night?" Noah jumped in, not letting the boy relax for a second.

"Yes."

"How late?" Winter had grown incredibly severe, but it was all a part of their tactic. Back and forth, question after question, overwhelming Matt to the point where he was unable to do anything other than utter the truth.

"Until close."

"Do you always use this exit to smoke illegal drugs, Matt?" Noah dropped the bomb he knew Matt was most scared of.

"No. Of course not."

"You're lying." Winter had transitioned into that other version of herself—the one that was all business.

"I mean, okay, yeah I use this exit for my...breaks. I'm not supposed to, but I turn the alarm off, and no one really cares anyway. Am I in trouble?" Matt's eyes were wide with fear.

Noah held up his phone, showing a clear picture of a very pregnant Lindsay Welsh. "Did you see this woman last night?"

Matt nodded, and Winter shot Noah a triumphant look.

"Did you notice anything about her?" Winter seemed to be using every ounce of self-control she had to not grab the boy and shake him.

"I mean...she was like, really pregnant. Like, *super* huge." Matt's descriptive skills could use a lot of work, but he was a golden ticket to the Wonka Factory as far as Noah was concerned.

"Was she alone?" Noah was tense from the anticipation. A witness. They had actually found an eyewitness.

"Listen, man, am I gonna get in trouble for this? Can you just tell me? Please? Cuz my parents are gonna kill me." Matt put his face into his very bony hands and shook his head in despair.

Winter appeared ready to strangle Matt to death, and Noah took the initiative to allay the boy's fear so that they could get the information needed. "Matt, I'm not worried about your special little cigarette there, okay? We're trying to save a pregnant woman and her unborn children from being killed. You tell us what you saw and leave nothing out. We'll forget about the weed. Deal?"

Matt nodded, the relief flooding his body even as his brow furrowed. "Someone wants to murder that lady? But she's like, pregnant. Dude, what the hell. That's awful."

"Tell us what you saw." Winter's voice was at its scariest yet, and Matt took a small step toward Noah.

"I was just getting done with my, uh, smoke break, and I was gonna head back in. I saw the fat one—"

Winter emitted a low growl, and Matt's face went white.

"I mean, I saw the *pregnant* one pushing her cart out to a minivan. But she stopped and talked to this other lady. That lady was a little sketchy."

"Sketchy how?" Noah's pulse was going insane.

"I dunno, man. She kept lookin' around like, just super *sketchy*. I put my uh, smoke back in my sock and when I looked back, the sketchy one was slamming the hatch. Then she just got in the minivan and took off. The pregnant one was gone too."

"Did it maybe occur to you, Matt, that you should have

told someone about what you saw?" Noah was the one fighting not to strangle the boy now.

Matt scratched at one of the many mountainous pimples gracing his pubescent face. "I mean, it's not illegal to leave a cart of groceries. I didn't actually see anything *bad*."

Winter leaned in close to Matt's face. "That pregnant woman is missing. She's who we're looking for."

Understanding shot across his face, followed by horror. "Oh my god. I didn't know. But I saw her face...the smaller one. I'm really good with faces, even when I'm stoned. I know I could describe her to like, one of those sketch artist guys. I really could."

Noah and Winter locked eyes, and Winter nodded.

"Listen, Matt, you're not in trouble, but you need to come with us immediately." Even as he said the words, Noah wondered if it was all too little, too late.

8

"I think we got the shit end of the stick." Special Agent Chris Parker eloquently shared his feelings with Autumn. She eyed him curiously from the passenger's seat. "A four-year-old Ford Explorer? Jesus. Did you see the wheels that Black and Dalton got? This is unbelievable."

Autumn wanted to roll her eyes completely out of her head. Pregnant women missing. Babies being stolen. Unknown numbers of dead bodies disappearing forever in the massive Florida swamps.

Having the prettiest vehicle didn't quite seem to compete with any of those things.

"I'm sure the rental companies don't have fleets of brand-new SUVs on hand. They don't exactly work for the FBI. Besides, this one is fine. I'm sure Aiden did the best he could." Autumn felt a slight déjà vu, thinking of the time she'd spent on assignment with Adam Latham. Chris didn't seem to be anywhere near the level of "ick" that Adam lived on, but he was still obnoxious as hell.

"Ha!" Chris snorted the word out. "Aiden Parrish is *not*

my biggest fan. I *assure you*, we got this piece of crap for a reason."

Autumn couldn't believe that this was what they were currently discussing. "Aiden wanted you to be a part of this case. That seems like a compliment to me."

"Aiden can't stand Noah Dalton either and yet the dude is always brought along. Trust me, Parrish separates work from personal preference." Chris spoke as if he were relaying top secret information to a small child.

"Well, if that's true, I guess you don't have to worry about him giving special treatment to anyone. Or, should I say, *not* special treatment." Autumn was humored by how quickly Chris had talked himself in a circle.

There wasn't much time to be amused. They were at Brad Conlon's insurance office building in what seemed like a hot minute. The man met them at the door, having been alerted to the visit by Detective Cohen.

He did not look pleased at their arrival.

"Awesome. Now I get to talk to the Feds. Life just keeps getting better and better!" Brad's voice was growing louder with each sentence, and they hadn't said so much as a single word yet.

"Mr. Conlon, I'm Dr. Trent and this is Special Agent Parker. We're here in the hopes that you can help us." Autumn had been expecting something like this, and she thought it best to diffuse the situation as quickly as possible.

"Help you. Yeah, right. I know what you people think." Brad threw a hand up, indicating the business office. "Yes. I had a million-dollar policy on my wife. She had the same exact policy on me. I sell insurance! It's what I do! Of course I'm going to ensure that my own damn family is taken care of. I know how important it is. And you people! You people think that I killed my wife and our unborn babies for some money? We went through absolute hell to have those kids...to have a real family! I would never...*never* hurt my wife! When is the world going to believe that? What do I have to do?"

The man's pain was palpable, and Autumn's heart fractured for him. Chris had managed to listen to the entire tirade without so much as a twitch crossing his face. Autumn credited him for remaining calm, but she knew Chris was nowhere near convinced that Brad had nothing to do with his wife's disappearance.

A part of her wanted to smack him for his lack of emotion. But then she remembered how she had promised Aiden that she would check her own emotions at the door for the foreseeable future.

Aiden didn't believe that for a second. Neither did you.

"Mr. Conlon, could we possibly sit and talk? We're not here to interrogate you, and for what it's worth, I don't personally view you as a suspect concerning your wife's disappearance." Autumn spoke with an empathy that she didn't have to fake.

Brad appeared to calm a little at her words, and he pointed toward the tidy waiting area. They followed his lead and sat, and Autumn wasted no time jumping in. She knew if Chris started talking first that Brad might close off completely.

"I'm sure you've been put through the wringer, Mr. Conlon, and I—"

"You mean being hounded by the media? Having strangers shout obscenities at me on the street? Constantly being asked why I would murder my own pregnant wife? The police have looked through every single thing I own, multiple times. My home, my car, my computer, my phone— I gave them everything. *Everything*." Brad was growing heated again, and Autumn felt how thin the line was between his cooperation and another outburst.

"Your wife's case *is* still an active investigation, Mr. Conlon. There isn't a statute of limitations on murder. That works in your family's favor. If we do find whoever abducted her, we can press charges no matter how much time has passed. But we're here today because we're trying to connect a number of missing women cases." Autumn paused, letting Brad soak in the information.

"Sheila's case could be connected to others? What do you mean?" The small spark of hope in Brad's voice was tragic. Even if Sheila's disappearance was connected to the others, the odds that they would find her alive after two years were so miniscule that they barely existed at all.

"I'm afraid we can't share any information on the current investigation, but we're working on creating a victim profile. Your cooperation could possibly help us narrow down some possibilities and catch the person who abducted your wife. You could help prevent even more women from being harmed." Autumn studied Brad's face as he realized—finally —that he needn't be on the defense. Not today.

"Okay. Well. How can I help?" Brad's voice was hoarse with all the emotion he was swallowing. The man had to know, in his heart of hearts, that finding justice for Sheila was much more realistic than ever actually *seeing* Sheila again.

"Well, maybe you could tell me a few details about you and your wife's life together. You said that you went through 'absolute hell' to have a family. Could you explain that in deeper detail?" There was progress being made here, and Autumn had the fleeting thought that this was what she was made for.

"Sheila and I were happy. We're both incredibly hard workers. Sheila was a marketing executive, highly sought after. The top of her field. And beautiful. Blonde, blue-eyed... she used to run track in college. She liked to stay fit. Healthy.

No one asks about those kinds of things. The things that make her...made her...amazing."

Autumn's heart splintered just a little more as Brad's eyes glistened over. "I'm so sorry." She pressed her palms together so she wouldn't reach for his hand.

He cleared his throat before continuing. "We were successful in every part of life that counted, except for one. We couldn't conceive. And we tried. We tried for a long time, but no dice." He sighed as the memories came back to him. "We eventually turned to IVF. It felt like the only way."

"And did that go well for Sheila?" Autumn shifted in her chair.

"It took three rounds...*three*...for Sheila to get pregnant. We had triplets at first, but one died almost immediately, so we held our breath while the weeks passed. All we could really do was hope that the other two would make it, you know?"

The man was quiet for so long that Autumn didn't think he would continue. "How far along was she when she went missing?" She knew the answer already but hoped the question would put him back on track.

"Sheila was in her third trimester and we were having two babies. Two. It was more than we had allowed ourselves to hope for. Sheila was so happy...she glowed. She absolutely glowed. And then she was just gone. Our babies were gone. I don't even know where they are, what happened, if she was in pain." Brad's voice cracked on the word "pain," and Autumn took his hand in hers, wanting to comfort the man in any way possible.

Despair—black, cold, heart-wrenching despair—flooded her system as she touched the grieving man. It hit like a gut punch, and it took everything inside her to not burst into tears. The man was in pain. Horrible, agonizing pain with no end in sight.

Chris apparently took the moment of silence as his cue to jump right in. It had to have been driving him crazy that Autumn had done all the talking so far. "Brad, if you don't mind, I'll ask you a few questions now." Autumn shot Chris a warning glance, which he ignored. "Let's start with the basics. Describe to me where you were the night your wife went missing."

Autumn wanted to punch Chris in the throat. She watched Brad's face shift back into the angry, exhausted man he had been when they first arrived. "If you want to ask me any more questions, you son of a bitch, you'll have to wait for my lawyer. You can both go to hell."

Chris lifted a scolding finger. "Listen here, I—"

Brad stood and walked away from them but only made it a few steps before he turned back, sweat dripping from his temples. "You *do* think I killed her! I *am* still a suspect! You bastards are wasting your time asking me the same damn questions instead of finding my wife and children! *Go! Find! Them!*" He walked into his private office and slammed the door.

Chris actually looked surprised at the man's reaction. When it appeared that he was going to follow the man to his office, Autumn turned on her heel and headed out the door. A minute or so later, he came skulking out too.

When they were back in the Explorer, on their way to interview Alex Gorski-Wilson, Autumn took the opportunity to share what she felt—what she *knew*—to be true.

"Brad didn't kill his wife. He doesn't deserve to be treated as though he did." Her words filled the tense air between them.

Chris calmly shook his head. "We can't be sure of that. He puts on a good show, and maybe it's the real deal, but we can't know that yet. He's a suspect until he's not. That mindset is harsh, but so are men who kill their pregnant wives and make them disappear like vapor." Chris meant what he said, and though Autumn completely disagreed, she at least had to respect that the man was being up-front and remaining calm.

Chris Parker must be a valuable agent. If he wasn't, Aiden would never have brought him along.

"It's not over 'til it's over," Autumn murmured, knowing that, for now, the best she could do was to peacefully agree to disagree.

Chris relayed that he would like to take the lead on the next interview, and Autumn unwillingly nodded her consent. Parker was doing his job, and she couldn't protest that.

Alex Gorski-Wilson answered her front door after the first knock, and she looked like complete hell. The woman had obviously been crying, and Autumn noticed the way she held her stomach. A small bump protruded from her thin frame, but Alex cradled it in a telltale manner that left little question.

This threw Autumn off a bit. There had been no mention of both wives being pregnant in the case notes.

She recovered before too many seconds ticked by, annoyed that Chris I'll-Take-The-Lead Parker stood there with his mouth agape. Autumn introduced them both, and thanked Alex when she welcomed them inside. Alex seated them all civilly, and Chris proceeded to begin the interview without any of the pleasantries that would give the woman a second to relax in their company.

"Mrs. Gorski-Wilson, could you describe what your life with Patricia was like?"

Alex smiled wanly and twisted a white handkerchief in her hands. "You mean, what was our relationship history? Lesbians, Agent Parker. We were in love, we got married, we were happy." She seemed to be speaking to only Autumn, even as she answered Chris's question. "We wanted a family, just like every other human on the planet. Patricia got pregnant on the very first round of IVF." Alex's eyes brimmed with tears. Autumn couldn't imagine how the woman was coping after learning of the recovery of her wife's hand.

Just one hand. That's what's left of the woman she thought she'd spend the rest of her life with.

"And you, Mrs. Gorski-Wilson, did—"

"Please call me Alex."

Autumn was happy to do so. The woman's full name was a mouthful. "Thank you, Alex. Did you also get pregnant on the first attempt?" Autumn smiled warmly as she made the inquiry, and Chris's eyes nearly shot out of his head. He clearly hadn't noticed a thing.

Alex turned slightly pink and returned Autumn's smile. "It took three more rounds for me. We'd decided we wanted to have...twins, of sorts. We chose the same donor and decided to get pregnant at the same time. It seemed like it might bond the children, to know they had the same father. And both of us wanted to experience childbirth." The tears spilled over this time, and she pressed the handkerchief under her nose. "Patricia was having a boy, and this," she rubbed her stomach with a loving hand, "is our baby girl."

"Two pregnant wives at once?" Chris snorted, slapping his leg with a hand. "What would you have done if you'd both had triplets?"

Autumn was beginning to realize that wanting to punch Chris Parker wasn't a fleeting incident. The urge would be the continual norm. But, in fairness, in spite of the way he had asked the question, Autumn did wonder the same.

"I guess we would have raised six babies together, Agent Parker." Alex's voice had risen with a mixture of sadness and anger. "We had this great life ahead of us, and now it's just *gone*. And you know what the cherry on the top was?" She glared at him. "Smartass cops like you thought I was the primary suspect. *Me.* The person who loved Patricia more than anyone else on this earth!"

Autumn ached for the woman. "I'm sure that's been hard for you, Alex. Please know that it's normal protocol. The spouse is always the first suspect, because statistically, spouses are the most likely to have committed the murders, especially when pregnancy is involved. I'm sorry that you had to deal with that stress on top of the loss of Patricia and your son."

Autumn hoped the words were of some comfort to the grieving woman but was also aware that comfort wasn't truly a possibility for Alex right now. Her grief was fresh. Raw. Brutal in its intensity.

And what if Alex had been farther along? Would the killer have taken her too?

"I will not give up until my son is found. Never." The determination in Alex's voice was striking. She turned to face Autumn more fully, ignoring the man in the room. "Are there any leads at all?"

Autumn tensed, wishing she could share more with the woman. "We've only just arrived today, but my team is committed to working round the clock to bring justice to you and Patricia. I promise."

Alex tilted her head. "Why is the FBI getting involved, anyway? What's happened?"

"The case is ongoing, so I can't divulge much information. But we're working to connect Patricia's disappearance with other missing pregnant women in the state." The tidbit was the most Autumn could share.

Alex's eyes went wide, and she grabbed the newspaper from her coffee table. She held it up, tapping the front-page headline. "This woman? Lindsay Welsh? You think Patricia was taken by the same person?"

Chris held up a hand. "Entirely too soon to tell." Autumn

knew it had to have been driving him insane to simply stand by once again.

"We'll keep you current. I promise." Autumn rose, hoping to remove Chris from the house before he could do any damage.

Alex's face was hard, her eyes aflame. "You better catch that bastard before I do. Because I think we have very different ideas of what justice looks like in this case."

The fury in Alex's eyes left Autumn no doubt that the woman meant her words.

Autumn wanted to hug the woman but held her distance. She didn't think she could deal with the emotional outpouring right then. "Alex, please try to remember that you need to put your baby's welfare above all else right now. Patricia would want you to stay safe and care for the child you both wanted so badly."

Alex's expression made no promises.

On the road once again, Autumn felt the excitement building within her. "I'm going to talk to Aiden. I think there's a connection with the IVF. I think we've connected the first dot."

Chris shook his head. "I can't say that I agree. The IVF is a commonality, yes, but it proves nothing except that we're dealing with cases involving pregnant women. We already knew that."

"It's better than anything else we have right now." Autumn's fingers flew across her phone, texting Aiden at warp speed. He responded immediately, telling her to meet him at the sandwich shop he'd just arrived at. Autumn relayed the directions to Chris and leaned back in her seat.

What troubled her most was the realization that Alex, pregnant and alone, might be in the same exact danger that her wife had been in.

Aiden sensed Autumn's excitement through her text. Whatever breakthrough she may have made, he was eager to know. Of course, that meant having to eat with Chris Parker, which was less than desirable, but Aiden had been the one to bring Agent Parker along in the first place. He would have to deal with the side-effects of that decision.

When Autumn entered the sandwich shop, she was radiant with energy. Aiden thought briefly that the woman never looked so beautiful as she did when she was knee-deep in a case. She locked eyes with Aiden and swiftly made her way to his table.

"Where's Parker?" Aiden was secretly happy that Parker was anywhere except at this table, but he would never say so out loud.

"He told me, and I quote, 'You guys go ahead and take the time to eat. I'm going straight back to the station to work on an alternative profile.' End quote." Autumn grinned, and Aiden realized that Chris's smugness hadn't derailed her in the least.

"So, he obviously doesn't see eye to eye with you on

whatever you're about to tell me. Big whoop. Tell me anyway." Aiden had always pegged Chris as a little suck-up. The man had been gunning for Aiden's job since the first day that he and his ridiculous hairdo had joined the BAU.

This knowledge didn't trouble Aiden. Competition had only ever made him work harder in life, and while he could admit that Parker was a good agent, Aiden didn't feel that his position was even a tiny bit in jeopardy.

Autumn placed her order, stole one of Aiden's potato chips straight off his plate, and then took an incredibly long drink of the iced water the waitress set before her. She pressed the cool glass to her forehead afterward, and Aiden sympathized. Virginia's January temperatures were a long way off from Florida's. And the humidity here was obviously a curse sent straight from the depths of hell.

"IVF," Autumn finally shot out.

"IVF?"

"Sheila and Brad Conlon had fertility issues. She only got pregnant after enduring three rounds of IVF. Alex and Patricia also used IVF. They both wanted to get pregnant at the same time, and they used the same sperm donor. Patricia took faster, but Alex is pregnant right now. Today." Autumn's fingers tapped across the tabletop in quick rolls. "I want to interview Josh Welsh. Immediately. If Lindsay also conceived through IVF, wouldn't that be enough to suggest a pattern? Two victims using IVF could be a coincidence. I get that. But if there's a third? Tell me I'm not onto something here?"

Aiden nodded. "It's definitely worth pursuing. While you're interviewing Josh Welsh, I can try to contact the families of the other missing women in this state. Find out if any of them suffered with fertility issues. But Autumn," Aiden's voice grew sober, "make sure that this lead doesn't close you off to other possibilities."

Autumn's eyes narrowed slightly.

He held up a hand. "I think you're onto something, but you can't get tunnel vision. You have to still consider that the IVF connection may not be the break in the case you think it is or want it to be." Aiden hoped he wasn't being too harsh. He couldn't tell.

Why did everything get so...*blurry* around this woman?

She took a giant bite of the sandwich the waitress served and focused intently on Aiden's face. Her gaze was unnerving—Aiden always felt a bit like Autumn was digging around in his brain with a very soft ice pick. He knew he'd upset her, however slightly, with his admonition.

But he didn't regret it. Aside from her minor in criminal justice, Autumn had never trained in law enforcement. There were certain basic Law Enforcement 101 points that she hadn't had hammered into her head like the rest of them.

"Aiden, do you honestly think I'm cut out for the position you're creating for me?" Autumn's green eyes never left Aiden's face.

"Absolutely. I'm positive. If I had doubts, you wouldn't be here." The statement came out a little colder than he'd meant for it to, but Aiden continued on. "Other BAU team members have transferred to this unit after years of being on the force. You're definitely an exception to the rule, and you will definitely encounter some tough learning experiences. You already have."

Autumn's head hung a little as they both remembered the hard lessons she'd already learned. Aiden knew it nearly killed the woman to accept not only her past mistakes, but the fact that she would make many more.

"You'll learn things along the way—important things. A lot of those things you're going to learn from screwing up. That's just the way it goes. But you have to remember, Dr. Trent, that you bring to this team a combination of skills and knowledge that very few people in this world have."

Autumn eyed her sandwich, her cheeks turning a lovely pink. "I wasn't fishing for compliments."

"I know that. And that's another reason I know you are, without a doubt, the right person for this job. That's why I've made the moves that I have in order to create this position for you. You're valuable. And the rest," Aiden waved a hand in the air, "that will come. We'll get you to Quantico as soon as it's feasible, and that'll bring you up to speed right quick."

Autumn nodded, although he could perceive that she was turning his words over in her mind one by one, picking through them with that mental fine-toothed comb she possessed.

"You know I'll be here every step along the way. I'll guide you as much as I'm able to. Although, it might help if you stop getting so pissed every time I offer you some critique." Aiden couldn't help grinning and was rewarded with her heartfelt laugh.

That's another thing you have that's vital. That laugh.

Aiden was conscious of the fact that he had momentarily been critiquing Autumn in a very non-job-related way and shoved his own sandwich into his mouth. They were two professionals discussing work. He'd die before he admitted anything to the contrary.

Autumn seemed to have grown somber. She was robotically chewing her food and staring past him as she did so. Aiden followed her gaze and found only the blank wall behind him.

"What's wrong?" He'd said the words before considering whether or not he should.

Autumn snapped back to attention and gave him a slight smile, but her eyes were sad. "I'm just thinking about something. It doesn't have anything to do with the job, I promise."

Aiden Parrish suddenly wanted very much to know what was on Autumn's mind.

"We were friends before we were co-workers. You know you can talk to me."

Autumn smiled at him again. Her eyes were still sad, but now they seemed warm as well. "I was just thinking that I have so much empathy for Brad and Alex...and for Josh. I don't know *exactly* what they're experiencing, of course, but I know what it's like to have no idea where someone you love is. To not know if they're okay."

Aiden kept his hands wrapped firmly around his sandwich so he wouldn't reach out and comfort her in a more physical way.

"And worse...to have a pretty deep sense that they're *not* okay at all." Autumn met his attentive gaze. "I really want to find my sister, Aiden. I've wanted to find Sarah for so long, and I think I might actually be close to doing it."

Aiden raised his eyebrows. "You do?"

"I set up notifications through the National Name Check Program. Just in case, you know? I thought that no matter what had happened to Sarah, even if she'd changed her name, there still might be a chance that she'd register in the system somehow. As long as she wasn't, you know. Dead." Her voice wavered on the word, and she swallowed hard.

Aiden bore a dull pain of empathy in his chest as Autumn shared her heartache.

"I was notified that Sarah was in Florida at almost the exact same time...I'm talking minutes...that I learned about the case here. It was odd. Kismet. And now we're here."

"And you want to find her." Aiden let his mind filter the information carefully.

"I don't have much. Just an address, which could be a complete and total dead end." Autumn met his gaze. "I know why I'm here in Florida. First and foremost, I'm here for this investigation. My personal issues will never affect my job performance. I won't let them, Aiden. I promise you."

Aiden sighed internally but kept his face neutral. The inner workings of Autumn Trent's heart and mind couldn't help but affect everything she did. It was her nature, and Aiden was more than aware of it. But he couldn't fault her for wanting to find her sister.

Anything that would bring Autumn peace was important to him.

Just one more thing that he would never say out loud.

"I do need you to focus on the case. Obviously." He considered putting a hand on hers, to assure her of his empathy, but opted not to. "But I also hope that before we leave Florida, you can find the answers you're seeking. I mean that."

Autumn's eyes were dangerously close to spilling tears, and she ran the back of her hand across them. "Thank you, SSA Parrish, for your understanding."

Their eyes locked for a moment, and the humid Florida air outside of the building seemed appealing in comparison to the thick, silent fog that had engulfed them.

Aiden gave a tight smile. "Of course, Dr. Trent. Now, we should probably get going. We wouldn't want Agent Parker to start thinking he's in charge."

Autumn laughed, and the tension dissipated almost instantly. "I'm pretty sure Chris already secretly thinks *exactly* that."

Aiden had to chuckle. If she only knew how right she was. Of course, it was Autumn. She probably did already know. Somehow.

As they walked down the sidewalk to Aiden's Explorer, they passed by a street vendor displaying a wide array of mood rings. Autumn seemed to instantly turn into the teenage version of herself and clapped her hands together.

"We should get these for the team. Then we'll always be

able to know each other's state of mind." Her laugh was the closest to a carefree giggle he'd ever heard come from her.

Aiden shook his head and laughed too. If it had been anyone but Autumn, he would have thought this was the most ridiculous waste of time imaginable. But it *was* Autumn, and somehow that made it...fun.

"Sorry, Doctor, I believe my hands are a bit too big for the likes of this fine jewelry." He held up a large hand to prove the point. Autumn grinned and nodded her concurrence.

Aiden then shocked them both by purchasing one of the rings Autumn had considered and slid it onto her thin finger. She seemed to jolt at his touch but recovered quickly.

Aiden forced a carefree smile back onto his face in spite of the fact that his pulse had started to echo throughout his head like a scream in a cave. "There you go. No more mystery surrounding Autumn Trent."

She tilted her head and grinned up at him. "Oh, don't you ever go thinking that, Aiden Parrish. I promise to remain an enigma until the end of time. *But,*" her green eyes twinkled with playfulness, "I'll be sure to keep this on. At least you'll have no doubt about whether or not you've pissed me off."

Autumn took off down the sidewalk again with an air of lightness that was new to Aiden. He followed behind and couldn't help wondering, in a different world—one where serial killers and missing pregnant women and long-lost sisters didn't exist—how ridiculously happy Autumn could be.

You just put a ring on that woman's finger. Suck it in, and stop being ridiculous.

"Oh, and by the way, Chris knows that you gave him the Explorer on purpose." Autumn blurted the words and followed them with a fresh burst of laughter, climbing into another of the sleek black SUVs that Aiden had seemingly procured for the entire team, minus one Agent Parker.

"Except for the Escalade, we *all* have Explorers. If Agent Parker paid closer attention, he'd have realized that. There's a reason why he's not in charge. However. There were only so many brand-new models available. I did my best." Aiden shrugged, smirking as he turned the key in the ignition. "It was nothing personal."

Autumn rolled her eyes. "You know that I know when you're lying, right?"

Aiden grinned. "Of course I do."

10

A slow trickle of sweat made its way down Lindsay Welsh's temple as pain became a living creature, a predator eating away at her strength and willpower one large bite at a time.

She tried to breathe, using the techniques she and Josh had been taught in her birthing classes...but Josh wasn't by her side, coaching her along. Neither was the scent of jasmine filling the air with its sweetness so that it would be the first thing her babies smelled. The playlist of relaxing music she'd personally chosen was also missing.

She'd been told to plan for the birth and to feel free to personalize the experience the best she could. She was also warned to not be upset if those plans went awry. Although the process of childbirth had a series of steps it usually followed, childbirth wasn't predictable. Her Lamaze teacher had shared that bit of advice to her class of eager faces not that long ago. Water broke unexpectedly. Emergencies that no one could anticipate might veer their checklist down a scary path where nothing but the sound of the babies' cries would matter.

Lindsay didn't think that her current situation was anything the bubbly Lamaze teacher had ever foreseen. No sane person could, surely. A scenario like this couldn't possibly be real.

Had she fallen and bumped her head, or maybe the hormones had gotten the best of her and she'd simply lost her mind somewhere between the grocery store and her home? Another contraction proved the reality of her predicament, and she was brutally reminded that yet another item on her childbirth checklist was missing...pain relief.

She opened her eyes, hoping that the people surrounding her so closely would have disappeared simply because she'd wished it to be so. They were still there. These people were straight out of a sci-fi thriller. Psychopaths. Was she dreaming?

Please be dreaming.

But she wasn't, and she knew it.

The man who had reassured her earlier in the day that he would be right by her side as "his children" came into the world was now between her legs and attempting to deliver them himself. He appeared to be a doctor, and Lindsay desperately hoped, for the sake of her emerging babies, that he was.

Two women were forcefully holding her legs up. The one to her left was a complete stranger. This woman was short and dumpy with a halo of horribly frizzy hair surrounding her round face. She was dressed in nurse's scrubs, which was absurdly comforting in a way that Lindsay couldn't even articulate to herself. She appeared older than the other woman to Lindsay's right.

She knew *that* woman's face entirely too well.

It was Sasha, the small woman with the corkscrew curls she'd attempted to help in The Greengrocer parking lot. There wasn't a hint of sympathy on Sasha's face, nor the other woman's, for that matter. They kept referring to the doctor as "Father," and added to that overwhelmingly creepy fact, *he* called each of *them* "my child."

None of what she was witnessing made any sense at all, and Lindsay wanted to scream at them—to demand that they tell her exactly who they were and what in the hell was going on. How could *anyone* do this to another human being? What in the living hell was *wrong* with these people?

"Aaaah!" The fear for her daughters only increased the intensity of the pain, and the grief that crept in was unbearable.

This wasn't how her little girls were supposed to come into the world. Josh was supposed to be there, holding her hand and whispering words of endearment and encouragement.

Lindsay had envisioned a warm, comforting room, where every ounce of agony her body experienced would soon be replaced by overwhelming joy as their children drew their first breaths. Nurses would be smiling and congratulating them as they wrapped the tiny little humans snugly into...

The scream that left Lindsay was primal as a particularly vicious birth pang gripped her womb. The labor pain was nearly all she could focus on as it grew with ferocious, unrelenting velocity.

Get the babies out safely. Then figure out the rest.

Digging her nails into the mattress, Lindsay roared in absolute anguish as one of her little girls emerged. She was crying—her precious baby was crying—and Lindsay reached her arms out, desperate to hold her firstborn.

Ignoring her, the doctor spoke in a sweet tone to the infant. "You're absolutely perfect, now aren't you? Yes, you are. Yes, you are. The next beautiful piece of the grand puzzle. Proof of The Dream's fruition. Perfection."

The doctor handed the squalling baby to the dumpy nurse, who began cleaning her off. She spoke much as the doctor did, remarking on the child's beauty, cooing and laughing happily at the successful entrance.

Lindsay sobbed, tears mixing with her sweat. She wanted to beg them, kill them, do anything...but the next contraction was arriving full steam ahead, and she knew that her other baby girl was ready to follow her sister's exit.

As each contraction hit, Lindsay could do nothing but push and scream through the anguish. But for the short period of time between the agonizing assaults, the rage spewed out of her like hot lava.

"How can you *do* this? You're a *nurse*! You're supposed to help people! You brainwashed monster! What is wrong with you?" These screams were interrupted by a contraction so strong that the faces around her started to blur.

"Good, good. Push! Yes. Excellent." The doctor spoke kindly to her, as though this were just like any other birth on any other day in any random hospital.

As the contraction subsided, Lindsay's fury turned solely to him. "You're not a doctor! You're a psychopath! You're going to pay for this!" The human claws that held up her right leg sank into her flesh, as though they meant to rip her thigh apart.

Sasha, who refused to even glance at Lindsay, clearly absorbed every shouted word. Her nails alone informed Lindsay of her displeasure.

"And *you*! You're the most pathetic of all. Why are you even a part of this? You're *nothing*! *Do you hear me, you bitch?* You are nothing but a dirty little gopher! I tried to *help you!*" Lindsay instinctively knew that if any of the three were to lose their cool, it would be Sasha.

But even Sasha showed no emotion on her face. They

acted as though Lindsay wasn't saying anything at all. She wasn't screaming obscenities at them. She wasn't howling in pain with each horrendous contraction. She wasn't even there, according to these people. She was already a ghost.

They were soulless. Her words had no effect on them. Anything she said was the equivalent of throwing a champagne glass at a brick wall. Only one of those two things would break, and it wasn't the wall.

It's like they won't acknowledge me. They can't feel. They're pros at this. It's like…

A new terror shot through Lindsay's body, nearly as strong as the contractions taking her breath. These people had done this before. Not just once, but many, many times. They had done it enough times that it was only a matter of going through the motions at this point. Nothing she said mattered. She herself didn't matter. They took newborns from their mothers. This was normal procedure for these bastards.

With a fury she'd never known, Lindsay wrenched her legs together, stretching her hands down to the crowning head of her second baby girl, trying to hold her in. There was hair. It was wet and slimy, but it belonged to her baby. As her fingers stroked the silky, beautiful mess, a desperately forlorn cry escaped her throat.

My baby. You can't have my baby. I will never let you have—

Her mournful thoughts were interrupted by the two women prying her arms back and pinning her to the bed.

"You must push now." The doctor spoke calmly, and the neutrality in his voice scraped against every emotion Lindsay was forced to endure.

"*No!*" She screamed the word, earning her first glances from the threesome.

The doctor simply picked up a large pair of horrid forceps and stared Lindsay directly in the eye. "This is my child. The way she comes out doesn't matter. But she *will* come out."

Lindsay gathered every ounce of moisture possible in her mouth and spit violently into the doctor's face. He only continued to stare at her with his iced-over blue eyes, while Sasha hastened to wipe his face clean.

She wiped him like a servant. A devoted servant. She's every bit as insane as the doctor. So is the nurse. They're completely gone.

Lindsay went limp, her body falling back against the bed as despair took over all other emotions. This was over. It had always been over. It was over the second she'd stopped to help a stranger in the parking lot.

She began to cry, great heaving sobs that racked her body. She didn't know what would happen to her babies, but she knew that she could no longer protect them. These people wouldn't stop. Lindsay was invisible to them. Worse than that, she was aware that they were nearly done with her altogether. She wouldn't be leaving this place alive.

Nature did what Lindsay no longer would, and the second infant rushed out of her with no conscious push from her at all. Her body was simply doing its job...and doing it well.

Lindsay didn't look this time. She couldn't bear to. She'd prayed and hoped and longed for these babies, and now they were being carried away as though she'd never had any right to them at all. Something inside of her had gone silent...had died. Something inside her *welcomed* death.

Her two infants wailed in the background, and Lindsay closed her eyes. All she'd had to do was walk right past that woman. *Don't talk to strangers.* Her mother had been giving her that advice since preschool.

Such a simple thing, really, but now she would soon pay a grave price for her heedless actions.

Lindsay wasn't sure how many minutes had passed when

she felt a strong hand on her shoulder. She studied the compassionate eyes of the doctor. What he had done to her, mixed with his apparent inability to experience any guilt about the actions at all was something worse than a nightmare.

He should have had his own horror movie series. He was far scarier than Freddy Krueger or Michael Myers had ever been.

He smiled warmly, his eyes filled with a compassion his actions didn't match. "Thank you for your sacrifice."

"You're a fucking monster. A demon." Lindsay's voice felt like gravel emerging from her throat.

The doctor sighed, shaking his head. "You must not pass judgement on the things you do not understand."

A minute spark of hope lit in her chest. "Then help me to understand. Please."

Perhaps he would take her on as another servant, and she could worship at his feet until the right moment came, when she could stab him in the neck and flee with her babies.

But the doctor's expression grew sober. "Only the select can comprehend The Dream. You are merely a vessel used to spread my being."

Already confused and overwhelmed, Lindsay shook her head. "Your being? What do you mean?"

"You carried my children, Lindsay." The doctor's smile was back in place, as radiant as ever. "You were such a beautiful vessel, and now your beauty has melded with my essence to sow a new race of *perfect beings*."

He gazed down at her so cheerfully, as though he fully expected clapping and praise. He really believed everything he was saying.

"You've lost your mind. You're crazy." The words were almost whispered as fatigue began to settle deep into Lindsay's body.

"Your words are proof," the doctor's smile was so genuine...so mind-blowingly genuine, "that all is just as I said. My vision is something you could never understand, my dear. But our daughters will, I promise you. They will understand it all *so perfectly*."

Lindsay shot forward with feral mania. Faster than any of them could have foreseen, she grabbed the doctor and dug her fingers into his clothes—*through* his clothes. She wanted blood. She scratched and thrashed, fighting to injure this man who had taken everything away from her.

Everything.

The two women, his faithful servants, were immediately on either side of her again. They grabbed her arms and pinned her back down. Lindsay tried to scream and hurl the foulest words she could think of but discovered she had no voice left.

The doctor picked up a pillow and smoothed the white linen with his hand, clearly unfazed by her attack. She watched him draw closer to her, the smile and warm eyes locked onto her face. He lifted the pillow, and Lindsay froze in terror. When it was merely an inch or so away from her, he paused.

"Would you like the honors this time, my child?"

Sasha reached out and took the pillow from his hands, her eyes glazing over with happy tears. The young woman was excited. Honored.

Sick. You're all so, so sick.

The woman turned toward her, a cold, dark smile on her freckled face. Lindsay briefly remembered how she'd thought Sasha was rather cute when she smiled. Almost girlish.

But Sasha wasn't cute anymore.

Her sadistic grin was thankfully blocked by the white of the pillow that soon grew dark as it pressed onto her face.

11

"That little stoner wasn't lying. He gave a pretty damn thorough description." Noah spoke out loud, but he was really talking to himself. Sun was the only other agent present, and she was busy checking the sketch the grocery store employee provided against the FBI imaging program.

Detective Cohen had lent them an off-duty deputy's office to provide a much-needed private space for their work. Noah was grateful, but the cramped quarters made for an incredibly irritable Sun, which he likened to a nuclear bomb on the verge of going off.

Maybe she just needed to get laid.

Shit.

He was glad he'd kept that thought to himself. First, it was a pretty sexist thing to say, and he was attempting to become more and more "woke" with his knee-jerk thoughts about women. But the second reason he was glad his big mouth didn't give him away was because Sun would absolutely freak if she found out the entire team knew about her down-low relationship with Bobby Weyrick. She'd freak even more if she knew that Bobby had confided in him that he'd tried to get Sun to go with him when he'd been transferred to Chicago several months ago.

Sun cursed a blue streak that was foul enough to make a sailor blush under her breath, and Noah decided that good ole Bobby probably dodged a bullet with the move.

"We're lucky as hell the two partials from the unsub's gas cap contained the necessary points to run them through the system." Sun didn't so much say this as she gruffly tossed the words like darts over her shoulder. She was running the fingerprints at the same time as the sketch, but Noah wasn't fully convinced that what they found would be enough either way.

If there was a match for both the partials and the sketch—and that was a *big* if—it still didn't mean they had enough evidence to convict anyone in an actual court of law. Any attorney worth a dime would be smart enough to argue that an unknown number of people could have touched that gas cap at any time.

And Matt Beckwith's description, however close it was to any image they found in the system, certainly wasn't sending anyone to prison either.

The point of this search wasn't to obtain a clear conviction. The point was to find a lead they desperately needed. That would allow them to at least take a direction and make it possible for them to obtain some solid evidence that *would* be enough for a conviction.

We just need a name.

Sun abruptly leaned back in her chair and turned to Noah. There was a smug twinkle in her dark eyes as she crossed her arms over her chest. "Alexandra Romansky."

Noah glanced from the picture to the sketch and back again. Not bad. The tight, dark blonde curls that Matt had described as peeking out from under her hood hung loose in the computer screen's image. A short nose and high cheekbones gave the woman a girlish demeanor that definitely resembled Matt's portrayal.

Other details that Matt hadn't been close enough to distinguish were obvious in the digital photo. Alexandra Romansky's blue eyes were giant while noticeable freckles decorated her cheeks.

Knowing the partials matched the actual picture of their suspect, which was very similar to the sketched portrait, gave them enough to securely move forward.

"Good work, Sun." The printer whirred to life as Noah printed out the pages. "Maybe do a little more digging, but this is good."

"Bite my ass, Dalton. I know what to do." Sun's snark knew no end, even when she was pleased with herself.

Voices in the hallway alerted Noah to the fact that the team was returning to the station just before Aiden and Autumn walked past the office door.

Noah stood, thankful for the chance to stretch his legs. "I think it's briefing time." Sun gave him no acknowledgement whatsoever.

In a few short minutes, Aiden, Noah, Autumn, Winter, Chris, Bree, Sun, and Jackie had all convened in the conference room. It was time for an end of the day recap, and SSA Parrish appeared eager to get the meeting started.

"Agents, I know each of you have been working your asses off all day, and your efforts are greatly appreciated, as always. Who would like to share what they've gathered first?"

Noah wasted no time in stepping forward.

"Winter and I went to scope out the grocery store Lindsay Welsh was abducted from. The security footage didn't show much more than we already knew. An unknown woman entered into conversation with Lindsay in the parking lot, but unfortunately, there were no clear shots of the unsub's face." The information was less than thrilling, and Noah knew it. It would get better, though. He glanced at Winter, and she took the tag team.

"The clerk who checked Lindsay out didn't provide any helpful information except to say that Lindsay appeared to be in high spirits. But we *did* luck out with one break-taking, weed-smoking employee." Ears perked at this bit of news. "He'd *also* been on break the previous night at the same time Lindsay was abducted and had good line of sight to the section of the parking lot in which Lindsay's van was parked. He saw Lindsay and the unsub talking outside Lindsay's van before she disappeared."

"And why, exactly, did the boy not share this information with local law enforcement immediately?" Jackie Cohen was incredulous with disbelief.

"He didn't realize he was witnessing a crime. He turned away for a moment, and that was when the actual kidnapping part happened. He wasn't even aware that Lindsay Welsh was missing." Exasperation was evident in Winter's voice.

Nearly everyone groaned. So many hours lost due to the only eyewitness *just missing* the act of villainy at the crime scene. The fact was a tough pill to swallow.

Noah hoped to raise their spirits back up with the next bit of information. "The kid, Matt Beckwith, was able to give us a pretty detailed description of the unsub. Sun just cross-ran the sketch with the fingerprint partials, and we think we might have found our mystery woman."

Sun hit a few buttons on her laptop, and every cell phone in the room simultaneously began dinging.

"This could be our unsub?" Aiden turned when the larger image flashed on the screen. "Do we have a name?"

"Alexandra Romansky." Noah nodded to Sun. "It was Agent Ming's find. She's the computer genius."

Sun rolled her eyes at him, but Noah knew she appreciated the recognition. More importantly, she deserved it.

Aiden nodded at Sun too. "Well done."

Any hint of pleasure slid from her expression, and her face settled back into a blank stare that was ten times worse than a scowl. Yep...both Aiden Parrish, one of Sun's past lovers, and Bobby dodged a treasure trove of ammunition with that one.

Autumn raised a finger, gaining Aiden's immediate attention with the simple gesture. "Agent Parker and I spoke with Brad Conlon as well as Alex Gorski-Wilson. We found a possible connection involving IVF treatments. Apparently, both couples experienced fertility trouble and had gotten pregnant *only* through utilizing IVF." Autumn's exuberance steadily grew while Chris's expression darkened.

Detective Cohen flipped through her folders. "Here it is. The case notes include that Josh and Lindsay Welsh also turned to IVF treatments, and they were incredibly open about their fertility issues. Lindsay even had a blog set up for the sole purpose of detailing their struggles, and ultimately, their success."

Autumn's head was bobbing up and down, and Noah wasn't quite sure he'd ever witnessed her that charged up about anything. She was beaming with excitement at this additional intel. "I'm interviewing Josh in the morning. That information is especially helpful, Detective Cohen."

Noah grabbed his iPad and pulled up Lindsay's blog. He clicked on the oldest blog post he could find, which was written over five years ago. Scrolling past the blog itself, Noah found the comments section and read through them. He was struck by a somewhat familiar name attached to one of the comments. *Sheila C.* Could that possibly be Sheila Conlon, the pregnant woman who had disappeared two years ago?

While he continued to scroll, Agent Parker cleared his throat. "I tend to differ with Dr. Trent on this point. I'm working on a profile that includes a much wider range of fetal abductions. My take is that these kidnappings are far more random than Dr. Trent believes." Chris paused and glanced around the room, letting his words sink in as deeply as he thought they should.

Noah glanced at Winter and knew by her expression that she wanted to punch the man in the face for discrediting Autumn so openly. The two women were so protective of each other that it was nearly suicidal to put either on the spot in any sort of negative light when they were both present.

"If you take into consideration the fact that nearly a third of American couples seek fertility treatment of some sort, then even three instances of IVF treatment don't seem as abnormal as one might think. Coincidence is more probable. I certainly don't think we have enough of a lead with this IVF theory to push our investigation in that direction." The smugness on Chris's face was maddening.

"I assume you have your own direction you'd like for us to consider instead?" Aiden's question was fair, but Noah knew the SSA well enough to detect the faint hint of annoyance.

Chris didn't miss a beat. "I'd say that, initially, we are searching for multiple unsubs. A fetal abduction requires careful planning, clear thinking, and organization. It would take a long time to pull off and would be nearly impossible to accomplish alone. The odds are very unlikely that one woman could have stolen two babies only a month apart from each other."

"What you're saying makes sense, Agent Parker." Jackie gave the validation Chris had been waiting for. "Who would take care of the first baby? How could she possibly have time to befriend and groom a second mother?"

"Exactly." No one could miss the triumph on Chris's face.

Noah noted that disliking Agent Parker might be the only thing he and Aiden could thoroughly agree on.

"I assume you're leaning toward a particular motive?" Aiden stared intently at Chris, and Noah found it hard to decide whose blue eyes were icier.

Chris was prepared for the question. "The motives behind abductions like these are pretty wide-ranging, but the most common are that the abductor has delusions of fulfilling a partner relationship or experiencing childbirth vicariously. Often, the abductor befriends the pregnant victim, sometimes pretending to be pregnant themselves. There have even been instances when the abductor purposely gained weight or used prosthetics to appear pregnant."

Winter stopped taking notes and peered up at him. "If your theory is true, and we're tracking down multiple unsubs, then it's possible the perpetrator isn't trying to fulfill a mother fantasy at all. Maybe the babies are being sold on the black market. An infant a month would be very profitable."

Noah loved the fact that his girlfriend was in no way worried about stepping on anyone's toes.

When Parker had no response for that, Bree stepped into the conversation. "I've gone through the majority of the video related to the kidnapping with the assistance of the sheriff department's techs. When we combined all the footage from homeowner's cameras with what we gathered from the traffic light cameras, we were able to ascertain that Lindsay Welsh's van left The Greengrocer and turned south."

Noah was relieved to know the van hadn't disappeared as abruptly as Lindsay Welsh had. "Any direction is better than no direction."

"Precisely. I've called for help from the neighboring counties to provide assistance in getting additional video footage.

I'll be going through those first thing tomorrow." Bree was upbeat as ever, and the team as a whole appeared rejuvenated by the bits of positive news.

"I've tried to narrow down missing persons in the U.S. who resemble the physical profile of our three Lavender Lake victims." Sun tapped a few keys and a graph appeared on the screen. "There were over 609,000 missing person victims last year across the country, and 235,367 of them were females over twenty-one."

Noah let out a low whistle of surprise.

"Florida alone has approximately six people missing out of every one hundred thousand." Sun shot the data out as expeditiously as the high-tech computers she worked with.

"*Pregnant* missing persons?" Autumn's voice was edged in disbelief.

Sun shook her head. "That part's harder to nail down. There isn't a field on missing persons reports that specifically addresses pregnancy, so the unborn aren't always mentioned on the forms. Officers will sometimes note pregnancy on the form, but not always. It'd be impossible to know exactly how many pregnant missing women there are, let alone how many of them are related to our case."

"It has to help that our three victims are all visually similar. Blonde hair, blue eyes—"

Sun held up a hand before Autumn could continue. "Physical similarities do help, but they aren't everything. I'll keep working on narrowing it down as much as possible."

Aiden clapped his hands together and all eyes turned to focus on him. "Great work, Agents. For only being here one day, you've uncovered a lot."

"And I think I just uncovered something else." Noah swung his iPad around. "Lindsay Welsh's blog contains comments from a 'Sheila C.' *and* a 'Patricia W.' It's another possible connection."

Aiden moved closer to the screen as another ripple of excitement moved around the room. "That's definitely worth researching. I want you and Winter to follow that thread and find where it leads." He turned to address all of them. "We have a chance here, Agents. Don't let up. We reconvene in the morning."

The meeting adjourned, but Noah couldn't take his attention away from Lindsay's blog. She'd named it *My Baby Miracle*, which he knew was meant to be uplifting and filled with good cheer.

In hindsight, though, it seemed as though Lindsay's miracle might also be the direct source of her doom.

12

———

Autumn should have been resting. The team had disassembled for the night and this was her one chance to get real sleep in the surprisingly comfortable hotel bed.

On top of the exhaustion, she was starving. The pissant sandwich she'd eaten at the shop had barely filled a quarter of her stomach, and the recurring, rumbling growls emanating from deep inside her would not let her forget her hunger for a moment.

Talk less. Eat more.

Autumn could have smacked herself, but there wasn't any point in focusing on the "should haves" right now. What she was in the actual process of doing would require every ounce of concentration she had left.

Driving through the dark Florida night alone, Autumn couldn't believe that Sarah might only be an hour away. It didn't seem possible.

How long had she wanted to find her sister? And now, with a simple address typed into her phone, the GPS was leading her along as though her quest had never been that difficult to begin with.

The thought nearly angered Autumn, because the arduous task of finding Sarah had been anything but easy.

And you still haven't actually found her.

Autumn shook the thought off. She would find Sarah because she had to. Sleep wasn't even remotely possible with the knowledge of her sister being so nearby. The time to act had arrived.

Visions of Sarah's sweet babyface sleeping peacefully in the bed next to her own flooded Autumn's mind. Sarah was only two years younger, but Autumn had felt it was her duty to protect her even when they were both barely more than toddlers.

As a child, Autumn had thought of her life like something of a macabre fairy tale. Her father was the most obvious villain, but there had been many. His evil schemes hadn't mattered, because she'd known that someday Sarah's father was going to come back for her—save her—and she would live happily ever after with her sister.

That never happened.

Autumn had spent many tough years learning that *no one* was going to save her. She had to save herself. And even after the Trents adopted her into their loving home, Autumn had retained the belief that she would be her own caregiver in life.

The way she viewed family, nothing was guaranteed. The Trents could have dropped dead at any given moment for a multitude of unfair, unexpected reasons. And she would be on her own once again. All the love in the world couldn't have wiped out what Autumn knew to be true far before she became an adult.

She was alone, and she always would be.

But Sarah doesn't have to be. Not anymore.

"In a quarter mile, turn right, and you'll reach your destination."

Autumn's hands tightened on the steering wheel. In her best robotic GPS voice, she absently murmured, "You may or may not find what you are seeking upon your arrival. Thank you. Have a nice life."

She snorted, amused and disgusted with herself.

Just a quarter mile stood between her and the answers she so desperately needed. Then again, she could just be driving straight into another dead end.

After the final briefing, Autumn had approached Noah and asked to borrow his vehicle. This had set off a series of questions from both Noah and Winter. Of course they were curious as to what she was up to. Autumn had fully expected as much.

Her only explanation, which she'd delivered as more of a plea, was that she had something she wanted to do, and she needed to do it alone. She could fill them in later. Tomorrow. Next year.

Winter instinctively understood, and Noah had been quelled by Winter's compliance. Autumn doubted that Winter was as clueless about the little mission as she'd acted.

Autumn slowed the Escalade as she neared her destination. Chris would have been insanely envious that she was driving the sleek black SUV. Since his tirade about Aiden and favoritism, Autumn had paid closer attention to the group of vehicles the BAU was using.

Except for this one, they *were* all Explorers. And aside from the fact that Agent Parker had been assigned a slightly less sparkling gray model, there was barely a difference amongst them. Chris's Explorer couldn't have been more than a year or two older.

The difference was infinitesimal, but Chris hadn't missed

it. And Autumn was quite certain that Aiden had known he wouldn't.

Idiots. They might be FBI agents, but they're still men.

Autumn was convinced that pissing matches must have dated back to the caveman days and beyond. The human race would probably be extinct before evolution was able to stop the male species puffed-out chest contest.

Smiling, she pushed the thoughts aside. She'd arrived.

Autumn parked the Escalade and surveyed the scene. The "destination" was actually a trailer park, which was largely concealed by the darkness of the night.

Four rows of ramshackle mobile homes sat in all their decrepit glory on sand heavily littered with trash and cigarette butts. Just how far the rows stretched was a question whose answer lay hidden in the shadow of the night. Autumn was convinced that the establishment had experienced its best days at least forty years ago.

Maybe longer.

Autumn wished the address was a mistake, but she highly doubted that the National Name Check Program made errors. *She* had made the blunder herself by ever holding on to the smallest hope that her sister was living a happy, accomplished life.

As she drove, Autumn had promised herself that she would only locate where Sarah lived, do a little reconnoitering to get the feel of the place. The day was ending, and Autumn knew that dropping in on a long-lost sibling in the middle of the night wouldn't exactly be the prime way to start this reunion off.

Besides, she needed sleep. She was utterly drained, and there was so much work yet to be done if they were going to solve the case and save Lindsay Welsh and her babies. Hadn't she promised Aiden that Sarah's whereabouts would in no way affect her job performance?

You can come back. In the daylight. Like a normal person.

But Autumn wasn't a normal person.

There was a row of dilapidated mailboxes standing at the border of the property, and Autumn couldn't help herself. She had to know more, and those boxes were less than five feet away.

"I'll check her box, and then I'll leave."

Leaping down from the oversized vehicle, she shut the door quietly and approached the row. According to the report, Sarah's number was 1126. Autumn spotted the corresponding mailbox immediately, and after a few quick glances around, went to it.

Getting caught going through someone else's mail was not an attractive proposition. Opening the mail was a federal offense, but a quick peek carried a risk Autumn deemed as acceptable.

Autumn wasn't just anyone, after all. She—sort of—had FBI credentials. And she was a doctor. She knew that neither of those things meant she could randomly break the law, but this was involving *Sarah.*

She had to know.

There weren't any actual names on the boxes, only the numbers, but when she stooped to peer into the box marked 1126, she found it stuffed to the very top with mail—mostly junk and flyers—bearing Sarah's name.

Why was it so full? What could that mean? Did Sarah rarely check her mail?

Maybe she's already gone.

Frustration had Autumn gritting her teeth. The scene before her was depressing, at best. Bent siding, chipped paint, rotting makeshift porches, cracked windows. Autumn couldn't believe this was where Sarah had ended up. One of the trailers was missing a front door.

A Rottweiler from a trailer two doors down barked

raucously at Autumn and another dog across the street. This set multiple babies wailing, the cries angry through open windows.

"Now you listen to me, Darrel," a rageful female voice trumpeted through the park. "Don't you dare tell me I ain't no good at cookin' when you can't barely use a damn fork right! Do you even know where the kitchen *is*?"

"D'you know where *the bedroom* is, Lucy Mae?" Darrel clearly didn't appreciate Lucy Mae's attack and shot back with one of his own. "Cuz *you* damn sure can't barely find your way 'round nothin' in *there!*"

Living in such an environment wasn't any better than what Sarah had experienced as a small child. Autumn only hoped that her current situation wasn't even worse.

She could come back tomorrow when sunlight was on her side.

Or she could take a quick walk through and try to locate Sarah's trailer.

And then I will leave. I will.

Autumn crept slowly down the sandy lane that connected all the homes. She scanned each of them for the correct numbers, but most of the trailers didn't have them at all. The ones that did were so worn they'd become illegible.

There were very few people out and about, but Autumn was still exceedingly grateful that she'd changed out of her business suit into a simple pair of jeans and a t-shirt. Two unruly school-aged girls passed by her, giggling and then running away. Some old folks sitting in folding chairs on their porches gazed at her with curiosity. Random adolescents sitting on the hoods of beat-down cars eyed her warily.

And of course, Lucy Mae and Darrel were still going at it.

"There's gotta be something to find 'fore you can find it, you limp dick dumbass!"

Autumn studied every face. There was no doubt in her

mind that she would recognize Sarah at first glance. But she spotted her sister nowhere. And with no numbers on the trailers, her quiet search seemed to be in vain.

Just as she had decided to give up, a male figure emerged from the blackness shrouding the small neighborhood. He walked unsteadily toward Autumn until he was close enough that she could smell the liquor on his breath.

"Hey, Sugar Tits. When you gonna bring that fine ass back over to my place so we can get it *on*?"

Autumn froze in confusion but quickly understood. She and Sarah, in spite of having different fathers, could have passed for twins. This man knew her sister.

He laid a heavy hand on her shoulder, and the touch instantly informed Autumn of just *how well* he knew Sarah. The slew of depraved thoughts that assailed Autumn with the touch was revolting. She shook the man's hand off in disgust, careful to keep her face friendly.

"Hey there, big guy." Autumn's voice had transformed into seductive and smooth. "How 'bout you remind me when the last time was that the lord blessed me with screwin' you?"

The man was unshaven. His two front teeth were missing on the top. His t-shirt barely covered a classic beer belly, and little tufts of chest hair popped out around the collar. A faded pair of boxers revealed skinny legs that were comically small in comparison to the rest of his body. No socks. No shoes. No pants. She inhaled…and no deodorant.

This is what Sarah goes for? This repulsive ogre?

"Honey, if you ain't remembering that I fucked you silly just last night, I must not be doin' it right." Loud, drunken laughter followed his words, and Autumn took it as a good sign. He was drunk, but he was a happy drunk.

For now.

Aiden would lose his shit completely when—*if*—he ever discovered her response. She batted her eyelashes and gave him her sexiest little grin. "Oh, I'm just playin'. You know me. Why don't you take me back to my place and maybe we can pick up where we left off?"

"Well, of course, little lady." He stuck his arm out gallantly and Autumn took it, reconnecting the endless wire of pervert radio shooting out of the man nonstop.

He weaved a bit as he led her deeper into the park. Autumn fought to keep her nose from wrinkling while she let him guide her. "Guide" certainly wasn't the right word. Autumn was practically carrying the man by the time he stopped in front of a tiny trailer near the very back of the lots.

Autumn saw her chance and immediately embraced it. Whirling around, she pressed a hand to her stomach and emitted a low groan. "Oh man. I must have eaten somethin' bad. I think I'm gonna throw up. I'm sorry. We'll hook up later, okay?"

Autumn rushed toward the trailer, bounding up the three cement block steps, and banged fervently on her sister's door. There wasn't any response.

Drunk Romeo was quickly closing the ground between them, staggering like a *Walking Dead* extra on set. Autumn tried the doorknob. When it turned agreeably, she pushed her way in and whipped the door shut. Once the latch was secure, Autumn breathed slowly, surveying her surroundings and attempting to block out the drunk rambling outside.

"Sarah?" Calling for her sister was ridiculous. Anyone would have been alerted by the commotion she just made by busting in. But maybe not. "Sarah?" This time reality had settled in before she even finished saying the name.

Sarah wasn't here. No one was here. At least, no one was here right now. The trailer was empty.

And messy. Perhaps even a little smelly, though that could have been the lingering aroma from her unwashed Romeo. A mattress lay on the floor, covered in rumpled blankets and sheets. The kitchen, which was adjoined to the main room— the only room—was littered with stacks of dirty dishes. The remnants of several meals remained on the majority of the plates, and some had started to mold.

With a heavy heart, Autumn turned toward a folding table that sat in the center of it all. She pieced through a large stack of mail, noting her sister's name but finding no clue as to where she was employed, or any other place Sarah could possibly be.

Sighing, Autumn allowed herself to fully consider the position she was now in. She'd gone from promising herself she wouldn't even get out of the Escalade to locking herself in her sister's tiny, shitty trailer with a piss-drunk idiot hell-bent on screwing her directly outside.

Once again, she'd impulsively thrown herself into the middle of a dangerous situation. It wasn't just Aiden who would kill her. Winter, Noah, Bree—they would all wring her neck.

When would she ever learn her lesson? Maybe Quantico *was* necessary. Some marine training, perhaps. A permanent bulletproof vest. And when had she become too busy for her Krav Maga?

I'm slipping.

Maybe she should abandon the pursuit of an exciting FBI career altogether. The possibility was high that she belonged back at her safe little desk, cocooned in Corporate Land until retirement.

The thought made her sick. She might throw up in here after all.

A Disney World magnet caught her eye from the fridge. Autumn walked to it, sucking in a sharp breath at the picture it held. The image was one of Autumn's only happy memories of her family. Apparently, Sarah had the same sentiment.

Her parents had taken them hiking that day. Autumn's father had very few "good days" as far as his addiction was concerned, but that had been one of them. The two little girls were grinning, each of them proudly holding out a bouquet of dandelions.

Sarah had rubbed hers on her cheeks until they were yellow, making them all laugh. Together.

Autumn's heart clenched in her chest. As much as the bad memories hurt, the good memories were far worse.

The good memories were torture.

The door to Sarah's trailer burst open violently, and Drunk Romeo stepped inside. Autumn nearly screamed in alarm at the intrusion, and she scanned the surrounding area for a weapon. She needed to get out of here.

"C'mon now, Sweet Tits. Why you playin' hard to get? My money ain't good no more?"

The words struck Autumn like a slap, and any last lingering hope she had for Sarah's welfare crumbled inside her chest. Her sister was selling herself for money. The little girl with dandelion-smudged cheeks peering out of that picture on the fridge had turned to prostitution.

Fighting the tears in her eyes, Autumn forced a smile onto her face. "You know of any good places hiring 'round here?"

The man's laughter bounced off the walls of Sarah's tiny home. "Did The Booby Trap fire you already, girl? I told ya, yer just too damn mouthy for your own good. But," he leaned in close to Autumn, "I got some cash in my pocket right now and it's as green as your stripper money ever was. How 'bout we go a round?"

Drunk Romeo proceeded to grab his crotch with one hand and make a "v" on his mouth with two fingers of the other. His tongue slithered out, insinuating some rather vulgar activities.

Autumn thought of her sister and the fury was overpowering. She kicked the man square in the balls, enjoying the startled look on his face as he fell to his knees. She nearly kicked him again for good measure before running out the door and back through the trailer park.

As she sped away in the Escalade, hot tears threatened to blind her.

"No. I will not cry. *No*."

She was wrong.

Dr. Autumn Trent sobbed the entire drive back to Lavender Lake. What if Sarah was damaged beyond repair? Maybe her sister wouldn't even *want* to rekindle a relationship.

Then again, at least Sarah was alive.

Autumn hadn't received a message informing her that her long lost sister's hand had been found in a swamp. For that, she was grateful.

Damaged was better than dead.

13

The sun was just beginning to rise, and I let the light's glory fall on me as I stared out the large picture window. Eden was coming to pass exactly as The Dream had shown me.

A quiet knock at my door roused me, and I opened it with a peaceful smile. My servant—just one of many faithful and devoted individuals—was waiting with my morning coffee. Her joyous face struck my heart with pure love.

"Thank you, my child." I graced her with a kiss on the forehead, and radiant happiness flooded her face as she backed into the hallway, shutting the door behind her.

I knew that many would not be able to understand The Dream, and for a long while, this limitation had saddened a part of me. Eventually, I came to understand that comprehending The Dream was a rare and wonderful gift. There was no place for sadness in Eden.

Only bliss and purity lived here.

I took a sip and proceeded to admire the grandeur of the sky once again.

Someday, Eden would be everywhere. *Eden would be*

everything.

Another knock at the door, but this time it was my loyal assistant, Timothy.

"Your helicopter will be ready for the return trip to the mainland in just over one hour."

"Thank you, Timothy. You are a dear and faithful servant."

Timothy beamed with pleasure before respectfully bowing and returning to his tasks.

Flying my sweet little ACH135 was one of my greatest pleasures in life. Soaring through the sky allowed me the bird's-eye view necessary to observe the world my seed would purify.

I had thought that perhaps I'd acquire some much-needed rest on my yacht before returning, but there simply wasn't time for that. The Dream moved forward with clarity and perfection regardless of all else.

I needed to be back in my office. There was much work to be done.

Abandoning my cup, I left my private quarters and strolled down the long hallway of my home. Everything in my house was meticulously white—the walls, the floors, the furniture. The color represented the unsoiled essence of The Dream.

I exited through the back, inhaling the balmy morning air with a grateful heart. I often liked to visit the nurseries before leaving the island. My children provided me with a fresh breath of inspiration I could then carry with me to the mainland.

The sprawling building was comprised of separate rooms that divided the children by age. I walked slowly down the gleaming white hallway, breathing in the blessed ambience.

Each expansive room of the nursery was made visible through a wide pane of exquisitely clean glass. I stopped first at the room which contained my eleven-year-old crop. Three flawless blonde heads slept peacefully on their pure white pillows.

These were the first—the brightest stars of Eden. Here, there was no knowledge of good nor evil...only the faultless peace of God. My elevens had been the beginning of a new world. Their births had set into motion the wonderland of unrivaled magnificence my seed would spread throughout the masses.

How intensely I wished The Dream had come to me sooner.

I'd simply woken one morning with a divine clarity regarding my life's mission. The brilliant, vivid vision I'd been gifted with as I slept had shown me a beautiful, utopian society of harmony. I was to create this new world—a garden of heaven on Earth. As Eden grew, my children would one day leave and take my message to the far corners of this aching planet.

My seed would stretch across the land until *all* was Eden.

The night nurse stirred, rising from her chair as she became aware of my presence at the window. I sensed her exuberant eagerness at the mere thought of having a moment of my time and gave her a gentle nod.

She was at the door in mere seconds, opening it softly and beaming with the joy that all my followers displayed at my arrival. The exhilarating scent of fresh lilacs enveloped me as she came close, and I opted to bless the woman with a kiss to her forehead.

"Well done, my child." She trembled at my touch, and I understood how very earnestly she wished to be a chosen one. Her nose, however, was far too large for her to bear one of my fruits. She served Eden much better by caring for my seed.

"Thank you, Father." Diligently, she returned to her

duties, and I continued my tour.

Harvesting my fruit through the vessels involved a tedious selection process, and I couldn't allow any imperfection to sully my seed. But God was good, and I'd been blessed with five lovely beauties who lived permanently on the island, incubating my unborn children.

These faithful women enabled Eden to grow at a much more rapid pace than the selected vessels alone could have allowed. I hoped one day to bring more flawless angels to the island to receive my essence and carry my children into this world.

Of course, all of the women were artificially inseminated, just as the mainland vessels were. I desired no intercourse in the process of creating Eden. The animalistic human act would have tainted my seed and The Dream's vision.

I moved on to the ten-year-olds, all four of them resting in the arms of holiness. Next came the nines. There were six of them. Eden had been in the early stages of its creation then, and the harvest that year had filled me with elation.

The next window was humbling. Only one eight-year-old slept in the large room. This fruit had been born the same year I'd decided to purchase the island and also moved my offices from Chicago to New York.

The move had been wholly successful, and the eight seven-year-olds slumbering in the next room were proof.

More expansions to Eden's mission had provided a record-breaking year for the sixes. Ten holy fruits had been harvested that year, only to be followed by twelve the next. These twelve who dwelled in the five-year-olds' room had inspired me to build another wing for the nursery. My blessings were of such great number that Eden must grow to accommodate the increasing influx of the harvest.

The expansion had been wise, as the next year brought fourteen precious little ones to join my family. However, the year of the threes had been greatly disappointing. Not even one child was present in the three-year-old room, and I always did my best to avoid thoughts of that year's failure.

I would not allow myself to be brought low by obsessing over times of tribulation. Hardship only made The Dream's reality more beautiful.

Eden had experienced an unexpected difficulty that year. Selfishness had slithered its way into the heart of one of my most faithful followers. She'd become sullen and discontent, which had grown into outright resentment and subversion.

I was convinced that given a day or two more, this servant would have turned on her family fully. Eden, my children, and The Dream itself had been threatened.

Of course, I'd quickly ordered her elimination, but the ruckus she had caused was considerable. I'd been forced to abandon all my plans for that year, and every single day I mourned the loss of the children who could have filled this room.

The tragedy of the threes had inspired my move to Florida. I needed to be much closer to my family. The Dream would suffer greatly were another insubordination allowed to fester and grow.

My offices were now less than an hour-long helicopter flight from Eden. I was apprised of every single event that took place on my island. Threats were immediately eliminated.

No evil would ever be allowed to weave its way into Eden.

I had desperately needed to discover the rainbow after the storm of that year, and it came to me upon my move. Florida had provided beauteous relief with its bright sun and promising light.

I knew I was finally where I belonged, and Eden could only flourish after the move. I could visit my family every day if I wanted to. I could also continue my professional work, which allowed me access to thousands of potential vessels. The Dream was set to thrive as never before.

The blessed land of Florida even offered a beautiful solution for disposing of used vessels. The gorgeous yet brutal territory of the swamplands allowed me to recycle the vessels dutifully back into nature, which could only work to further purify humanity.

The following year of the twos had gently blanketed the heartbreaking loss of the threes, producing nineteen unblemished fruits. My joy had never been greater.

I viewed them now through the window, chuckling softly at how many of them were already awake and toddling around with their Eden mothers. Such a beautiful year. Three sets of triplets and four sets of twins. The harvest had been bountiful.

In spite of my work on the mainland, I knew I must return soon to spend more time with these youngest blessings. The success of The Dream was highly dependent upon the necessary time spent bonding with the babes. They needed me to imprint my limitless love upon them.

The same went for the one-year-olds. My most successful garden to date, twenty-five of them had been harvested— three sets of triplets, five sets of twins, and six singles. These tiny little lights would someday illuminate the world.

A wave of emotion came over me as I viewed the ones. To be given this vision, this family, was marvelous.

The last of my children awaited in the newborns' room. January wasn't even over, yet I had already harvested six unblemished fruits. I was sure that this would be a record-breaking year for Eden. A new wing was already under construction for the nursery, and I'd made plans to build a new compound on the other side of the island.

The older children would move to this new site, and there

they would receive the best education and most extensive training that money could buy. The purpose of the new compound was to bring out their full potential and transform them into beams of exquisite, sparkling light.

A smile of deep gratitude stretched across my face as I entered the room where my six infant children slept. All six of the Eden mothers immediately rose, their faces returning my warmth and unconditional love.

Approaching the cradle that held my two newest arrivals, awe overcame me at their precious, beautiful faces. My daughters were perfection.

One of them began to whimper, and I nodded toward her Eden mother. She swiftly had the baby in her arms, and I observed as the hungry little mouth latched onto the offered breast. My daughter nursed vigorously, and soon her sister began to fuss as well.

Her appointed Eden mother immediately was at the cradle, lifting the dear babe to her own breast and allowing my daughter to suckle the milky nourishment.

I licked my lips, momentarily wishing that I could stay and feed myself as well, but I simply did not have the luxury of time. Soon, though. I never allowed myself to let too many days pass without partaking of the sweet, pure elixir that only an Eden mother could provide.

There was a great responsibility on my shoulders. The Dream required my watchful dedication, and so much work was yet to be done.

As you sow, so shall you reap.

And I intended to reap abundantly.

As a child, Lindsay would wake from a nightmare and immediately take off running to her parents' bedroom. Her mother would rouse from even the deepest of sleeps and cuddle Lindsay's tiny body close. Eventually, the fear subsided while she lay at her mother's side.

The ease with which Lindsay's world settled back into its proper place then was magical.

But waking up to this day's reality and having to accept that the nightmare lay on the *conscious* side of the fence was an entirely different sensation. Her mother couldn't help her now.

She'd immediately known that she wasn't supposed to wake up *at all*. They had killed her...or so they thought.

They had failed.

A car door slammed, and Lindsay went completely limp. A firm grip encased each leg, and she was dragged from the car trunk where she'd awoke.

Dead. You're dead. Be dead. Stay dead.

The arms that had pulled her roughly into the early morning air dropped her promptly to the cold, wet ground. The impact of the fall was agonizing on her spent and swollen body, but she remained silent.

"Jesus Christ, you're a heavy bitch."

Lindsay knew the voice. It was Sasha.

Sasha was dumping her body.

A tough kick to her hip sent Lindsay rolling down a sharp, grassy incline, and the splash that stopped the roll instantly informed her that the danger was far from over. The dank, musty scent was unmistakable. She was floating face-first in a swamp.

A *Florida* swamp. The kind teeming with hungry, ruthless, man-eating alligators. Childbirth had left her bleeding and weak, reducing her body to nothing more than easy, tempting prey.

Lindsay held her breath, waiting for the headlights of Sasha's car to fade away. If Sasha didn't leave soon, Lindsay would either drown or be forced to give up her ruse altogether. In her current state, Sasha could easily finish the job.

But soon, the lights were fading away entirely. Not waiting until they were fully gone, she began half wading, half crawling through the shallows of the murky, slime-ridden water until she reached the bank.

The second she was sure that her feet were out of the swamp, Lindsay collapsed to the damp ground, her body sinking into the muddy bank. All her strength was gone. Her lungs burned mercilessly, and her entire body ached with a pain she'd never known before.

The cold was unbearable. In spite of moving to the Sunshine State, Lindsay was aware that even in Florida, January nights could drop to as low as forty degrees. Her teeth chattered violently while she tried to piece together the events that had led her here.

The grocery store. The parking lot. Sasha. The sudden paralysis. Shock. Confusion. Blackness. And then...that bed. The blindingly white walls. The horrible, smiling man. Was he really a doctor?

The women had called him "Father." He had called them both "my child." They had *all* forced her to give birth to two perfect baby girls while barely acknowledging her existence.

What had he called her? A vessel?

Lindsay's heart twisted at the foreign sensation of emptiness in her body. They had taken her babies. What would become of them in the care of such a deranged psychopath?

Hot tears stung her eyes.

Your beauty has melded with my essence.

Lindsay knew what the words implied, but she refused to think they could be true. That man was delusional. *All three of them were.*

Sasha had *grinned* at her before attempting to smother her to death.

Didn't quite get it done, you bitch. You failed.

Lindsay's instincts told her that failure was probably not something the good doctor took lightly. Father or not, Sasha was more than likely going to be in a great deal of trouble if Lindsay managed to make it out of this hellhole alive.

A nearby splash was like an explosion in the quiet, bringing Lindsay back to the very near and present danger. The only other sounds were of birds and insects, and the darkened sky made even the musical tweeting seem ominous.

Another splash...*much* closer this time. Adrenaline shot through Lindsay's spent body, and she began to claw her fingers into the muddy ground, managing to move barely an inch with each surge of determination.

She had to survive. She had a family. And no matter where that crazy piece of shit was keeping her children, *she would find them*. She would save them.

The water began to churn as an unknown number of gators started to splash in a frenzy. Lindsay was afraid to look back. She didn't want to know which of the beasts would win the prize.

Although she continued to claw her way through the mud, Lindsay braced herself for the sharp teeth that were sure to sink into her flesh at any given moment. After that would be the death roll, and regardless of how hard she had fought to stay alive, she'd end up just another snack in a giant reptile's belly.

Josh would never know what had happened to her or the girls.

Though she couldn't see the danger coming at her like missiles, Lindsay knew they were coming. Felt them coming. She hadn't moved fast enough, and what movement she *had* managed was clumsy and loud.

I've announced myself as breakfast, and now I'm going to die.

The commotion behind her grew thunderous, and she closed her eyes in acceptance of the end. A horrendous keening ripped through the air, and the water exploded in a frenzy as the alligators attacked...something else.

In the dim light of the early morning, Lindsay made out a small gathering of deer to her right. Tails waving, they bounded back into the trees. The beautiful creatures were probably coming for a cool drink of water before bedding down for the hot day, though not all of them survived long enough to get that chance.

Lindsay shuddered as she watched two massive alligators continue to roll and thrash with their catch. The cycle of life was painful to witness, though the deers' suffering had given her yet another chance to live. For some silly reason, she wished she could show them her gratitude.

She crawled with renewed strength, simultaneously petrified and hopeful. A last glance back at the bloody mess caused her a pang of pity, which shifted into horror. It could have easily been her trapped in the relentless jaws...her blank eyes stuck in an eternal stare before she was dragged down to be stored for a later feast.

"Thank you for your sacrifice," she whispered, thinking of the mad doctor's words. If the deer hadn't distracted the alligators...Lindsay shuddered.

Stop it. Focus on getting help.

Turning away from the carnage, she began the ruthless climb once again. The sun was growing hot by the time she made it to the road Sasha had parked on. Blood loss and trauma threatened to knock her out, but Lindsay kept crawling. Inch by inch, she was leaving the swamp behind.

She wasn't dead. Against all odds she had survived.

"Mommy's coming, girls."

With their sweet cries firmly in her mind, Lindsay Welsh continued to crawl.

14

L avender Lake Hotel provided a respectable spread for their complimentary breakfast, which had made Winter's beloved special agent partner a very happy man. Winter grabbed a single bagel and coffee, while Noah piled a plate high with a little bit of everything, snacking on bacon while he made his rounds.

Damn...she loved that man. Even this early in the morning and even with bacon grease on his chin, she was so glad she'd let down her walls enough to let him into her life. In Winter's world, love equated to worry, and worry distracted her from her goals. But Noah Dalton was a big boy, literally and figuratively, so while she still worried, he offered her such a warm, safe space that the benefits far outweighed the risks.

Autumn appeared just as they were sitting down to eat and headed straight to their table. Noah's keys flew his way, and he snatched them out of the air while popping yet another piece of bacon into his mouth.

Autumn looked impressed with Noah's fine motor skills and reaction time while the keys reminded Winter, once again, of Autumn's evening getaway. She was burning with questions.

"Thanks for letting me use your wheels." Autumn gave them both a bright smile before turning to the buffet tables.

Winter studied her friend. Nothing appeared out of the ordinary, but she knew *something* must have happened last night. Autumn certainly hadn't been going out to catch a late movie.

It had been long after midnight before Winter had fallen asleep last night. She'd been worried about her friend, unable to stand not knowing if Autumn was okay. Things often didn't go as planned in this world, and Autumn Trent's life was no exception. Winter had witnessed the woman make more than one dangerous decision.

But Noah had eventually calmed her down. He reversed the situation, asking Winter what she would want her friends to do if she'd set out alone the way Autumn had.

"I would want my friends to trust me. And leave me alone." Winter's answer had dutifully proven Noah's exact point.

After that, she slept.

Autumn settled down at their table with a plate stacked nearly as high as Noah's. "A girl's gotta eat." She stabbed a piece of sausage, nearly inhaling it in one bite.

As minutes dragged on, filled only with chewing noises, Winter thought she might explode from curiosity. "Your night went okay?"

"Yep. Sure did." Autumn spoke through a mouthful of pancakes.

Noah flopped a piece of bacon back and forth, studying Autumn nearly as closely as Winter. "We thought you might let us know when you got back in."

Winter shot him the stink eye. He'd said the words innocently enough, but Autumn's bright green eyes had gone on alert.

"Oh…it was late, and I figured you'd be sleeping. We all needed sleep so badly. It seemed mean to wake you." Autumn's voice was stiff, and Winter didn't think her friend had gotten much sleep at all.

There were the telltale dark circles under Autumn's eyes, but more than that, they appeared slightly swollen. Had Autumn been crying?

"Slept like babies." Winter cringed, unable to believe she'd just allowed that out of her mouth. "Sorry. Poor choice of words."

Noah swatted a speck of bagel from her jacket. "It's okay. It's not like the word itself is offensive."

"But speaking of, we should probably all head to the sheriff's office. I'm sure Aiden's already there and waiting for us." Autumn jabbed her fork into a chunk of scrambled eggs. "Mind if I ride with you guys? I'd like to avoid Parker for as long as possible."

Noah snort-laughed, and Winter smiled. What was it with Chris? He immediately gave off a vibe of extreme obnoxiousness. She knew Aiden didn't care for him, although, to be fair, Aiden Parrish didn't care for a lot of people.

But Autumn didn't like Chris either, and Winter knew that the caring psychologist gave everybody a chance.

He must have blown it.

They all stood, and Winter glimpsed that Autumn's plate was cleaner than Noah's. The girl could eat. Autumn had proven that the very first night the two of them met with a rather impressive chimichanga eating contest.

"What are you smiling about?" Autumn's voice was near her ear, as though they were about to share something conspiratorially.

"I didn't know I was." Winter threw a friendly arm around Autumn's shoulders and wished the physical connection could tell her as much as it told the woman at her side.

The move had been a mistake because Autumn read *her* immediately.

Autumn stopped and held Winter's arms, waiting until their gazes connected before giving her a warm smile. "I'm fine. Promise. We'll talk about it...eventually. Right now, we've got babies to save." Autumn pulled away with a smile and took off for the parking lot alone.

"What'd you do to her?" Noah had grabbed another coffee for the road and caught up to Winter just as Autumn sped ahead.

"Me? You're the one who got her guard up with your whole 'why didn't you let us know you were back' crap." Winter gave him a playful elbow to the ribs. "You came off like the father of a teenager."

Noah elbowed her right back, nearly knocking her over with his strength. "I was just trying to make conversation. You know. That thing people do when other people are around."

Winter rolled her eyes to the heavens. "Next time, talk about the weather, Agent Dalton."

The drive to the station was short, and none of them were capable of small talk. Winter thought it was mostly due to the elephant in the room. Or vehicle. They had no idea where Autumn had gone last night, and she didn't seem like herself this morning.

At least not to Winter.

Once parked, the three agents exited the SUV and dutifully made their way down the sidewalk to the station's front door.

"Okay, girls. Let's brief it up." When they both just stared at him, Noah held up his briefcase with one hand. "Get it?

Brief? Cause we're going into a *briefing*. Tell me you guys caught that."

Winter loved the man, but his humor was somewhere between dad jokes and *Sesame Street*. "You know, people say silence is golden for a *reason*."

Noah let out a "har de har har" while Autumn cracked up completely. Good ole Noah, always great at breaking tension with a laugh.

Maybe today was going to be a good day after all.

Aiden, Sun, and Jackie were already waiting in the conference room. Chris and Bree arrived just a few minutes later.

"Okay, Agents." Aiden already had a marker in his hand. "Let's not waste any time this morning. Agent Ming, I believe you said you'd like to start off the briefing?"

"What we now know," Sun pulled up the mug shot of Alexandra Romansky to the screen, "is that Alexandra, or 'Sasha' as she goes by, was and may possibly still be a sex worker. She has several arrests on her record. The last arrest notes that she was pregnant and suffered a miscarriage while in custody."

"I knew it," Chris muttered.

Aiden shot him a stern glower.

"She was released sixteen months ago and hasn't been seen since. Until the kidnapping video, of course. That's assuming it was indeed her, and we don't know that for a hundred percent certain yet." Sun clicked across her keyboard, pulling up some official forms.

"There's more?" Bree's tone was alert and ready.

"Sasha skipped out on her parole meetings, violating the terms of her release. Naturally, there's already an active warrant out for her arrest." Sun closed her laptop. "That's it."

"I want an APB out on her immediately." As soon as the

words left Aiden's mouth, Jackie was up and headed out of the room to do just that.

Winter's eyes met Autumn's. Both women were troubled by the addition of "sex worker" to Sasha's profile, but Autumn's face had a particular upset on it that Winter couldn't quite read. Her friend had turned ghostly pale and raised a hand to her mouth as though she might actually throw up.

"This clearly fits the profile I've been working on. A lone woman targets a pregnant woman. That's what this case is about. And I don't know why we should assume at this point that any of the other cases are related." Chris spoke smugly. Perhaps his smugness was what irked everyone he came into contact with. The man nearly defined the word.

"We don't have enough yet to assume they're not, either." Noah almost barked the words, and a rare flash of approval crossed Aiden's face.

Holy mother of crap. Miracles do happen.

"I'm profiling Alexandra Romansky as self-centered, narcissistic, and anti-social. She lacks empathy. That's how she's able to sacrifice a human life to get what she wants. It's not that Sasha didn't know what she was doing was wrong… *she didn't care.*" Chris finished his oration and glanced combatively at each of them in turn. He was clearly hoping someone would challenge his theory.

Winter wasn't sure. She was far from thinking that the cases weren't related at all. There were too many coincidences. But Chris's profile of Sasha did appear to be somewhat accurate. Maybe the mistake was in thinking that this was an "either-or" situation. Perhaps it was a combination.

"Noah and I read through Lindsay Welsh's entire blog last night at the hotel. I'd like to interview Brad Conlon and Alex Gorski-Wilson and find out if their wives ever spoke about the blog. There could be an even deeper connection there."

Winter immediately received Aiden's nod of affirmation. He wasn't ready to call the cases unrelated yet, either.

"Good luck with that. Brad Conlon will *not* be glad to see you. I doubt he'll tell you anything without a warrant *and* his lawyer present." Chris laughed as though Winter's pursuit was amusing.

"That man has been through a lot." Autumn spit the words at Chris like venom. She had transformed into Dr. Autumn Trent before everyone's eyes, morphing from good-natured and caring to professional and dominant in a second. "He lost his wife and children. Then he was blamed for their disappearances. He spoke with us just fine until you opened your damn mouth."

Everyone was stunned.

Although she completely agreed with Autumn, the outburst was alarming. That wasn't how Autumn normally operated, regardless of her opinion.

Winter spotted Aiden eyeing Autumn with deep concern. He also knew that something was clearly wrong with her.

Surprisingly, Chris had nothing to say in response. Winter was positive that he'd been deeply offended, but the shock had rendered him silent. She was beginning to think that none of them would ever speak again when Detective Cohen re-entered the room.

"APB is out, and if it helps, I still have the cloned versions of both Sheila and Patricia's computers."

The world whirled back into motion.

"Agent Ming, I'd like you to connect with our tech team in Virginia and go through those clones with a fine-toothed comb. There could be other clues in there that were missed." Sun nodded at Aiden and turned back to her work without so much as a word.

"I should be receiving loads of video footage today. I'll

scan through them all. Won't let anything get past me," Bree vowed.

"Excellent, Agent Stafford. Dr. Trent, I assume you still plan to interview Josh Welsh today?" Aiden's voice softened ever so slightly when he spoke to Autumn. It was a small enough change that most people wouldn't have picked up.

But Winter heard the difference.

"Of course." Autumn had pasted her normal, agreeable expression back onto her face and was gathering her things.

Aiden turned to address Winter and Noah but was interrupted by a firm knock on the conference room door. A deputy stepped inside, his countenance grim.

"Sorry to interrupt you, folks, but we've got another pregnant woman missing."

Winter met Aiden's gaze before it went from her to Noah to Autumn.

The agents were on their feet immediately.

WENDY ARNOLD WAS a twenty-three-year-old stripper struggling to make ends meet. She'd unexpectedly become pregnant with her boyfriend's baby and had taken a break from her flashy career to wait tables on the night shift at a run-down twenty-four-hour diner.

Her boyfriend had kicked her out when she was seven months along, and since then, Wendy had been crashing with some friends. These friends were the ones who had reported her missing that morning.

The deputy shared that he hadn't thought much of it at first. After all, adults escaped from reality every day, and strippers were no exception. He'd taken the report and given the typical speech. They'd look into it. Nothing to go crazy about just yet.

Then the friends had told him that Wendy was only a week or so away from giving birth. That had gotten his attention, and he'd taken off to find Detective Cohen.

They had an address for the apartment Wendy had been staying at and not much more. Noah and Autumn tried to find anything they could on Wendy Arnold while Winter drove like a maniac to the given address.

As Noah knocked on the door, Autumn considered kicking it in but took a calming breath. Her emotions were getting away from her again. But hell...another pregnant woman was missing. The case was spiraling out of control.

Two rather shocked twenty-somethings answered. After being informed that their visitors were FBI agents, they shakily introduced themselves as Kyle Petrie and Laura Hopkins.

"We didn't even think the police were gonna do anything about it. The dude we talked to literally ran away mid-conversation." Kyle's face was a mixture of frustration and fear.

"I was just gonna start calling all of Wendy's friends. She didn't have a lot of them but...still." Laura pushed messy brown hair away from her face. She'd obviously been crying.

"Can we come in? Your friend might be part of a bigger investigation, and we can't waste any time. Understand?" The formidable tone of Winter's voice left Kyle and Laura wide-eyed and silent. Their heads bobbed up and down before they led them inside.

Noah went over to a wall of photos. "Wendy was staying here, correct?"

"Yeah. We let her crash on the couch for a hundred bucks a month." Sweat dripped down Kyle's temple as he spoke.

"She was better off here anyway. Her boyfriend was a dick. Obviously. Who breaks up with their pregnant girl-friend?" Laura was clearly closer to Wendy than Kyle, and her face was a conglomeration of emotions she was trying to hold back.

"Do you have a picture of her?" Autumn spoke directly to Laura. Social media had given them nothing. Wendy apparently wasn't a Facebook type of girl.

"Yeah, like, on my phone. Hold on." The girl grabbed her cell and swiped a few times. "Here." She held it up for the agents, and an attractive blue-eyed blonde stared back at them.

Physically, Wendy was a clone of the other three victims.

Autumn exchanged glances with Noah and Winter.

"Can we take a quick peek around?" Noah asked, but it wasn't really a question.

"Go for it." Kyle took a step back as Noah and Winter began exploring the apartment.

"You told the deputy that Wendy worked at a diner. Could you give me that name and address?" Autumn still focused on Laura and gaining any information possible.

The girl quickly acquiesced, providing the information and fighting back the tears that had been building in her eyes since the agents arrived.

"I know you guys know she's a stripper, but she's not a bad person." Laura's lips trembled. "Wendy's really sweet. Do you think something bad has happened to her?"

"We're going to find out." Autumn was just about to promise that they'd find her but managed to hold her tongue in time. She'd learned firsthand that not every case had the outcome she wanted. "Was Wendy ever involved in any type of prostitution that you know of?"

Laura's tears finally spilled over and ran down her cheeks. "I don't know. I think so, but she needed the money. I'm telling you, she's not a bad person." The crying turned to sobs.

Autumn laid a gentle hand on Laura's shoulder. The girl's

misery was bracing, and it flowed through Autumn in violent waves. "Laura, I absolutely believe you. Good people get into some tough situations sometimes. We're going to find your friend."

Winter came back into the living room with Noah at her heels. Her eyes met with Autumn's, and Winter gave a discreet shake of her head. They'd found nothing useful, the gesture stated.

"I've got the diner address." Autumn was halfway to the door but turned to offer Laura the only assurance she could. "We won't give up."

The diner was closer than they'd thought. If she hadn't been in her last trimester, Wendy could have walked to work. Winter brought the Escalade to a screeching halt, and the trio dispersed.

"According to the deputy, this is the last place Wendy was seen." Noah scanned the area, going down on his haunches to peek under a car parked on the street. "She left her shift early this morning, and then boom. Gone."

"You guys go in. I'll check around back for her car." Autumn didn't wait for a response before walking toward the back lot where she assumed the employees parked.

Kyle and Laura had provided a brief description of Wendy's vehicle, but they weren't sure where it actually was. Autumn knew she was searching for a late nineties four-door Toyota Camry and nothing more.

The door jingled as Noah and Winter entered the diner. Autumn quickly rounded the corner of the building, scanning the unimpressive collection of vehicles. The back lot was nearly as empty as the front, and Wendy's vehicle was nowhere to be seen.

Autumn growled with frustration.

Physically, Wendy matched the other women. But professionally, she was much more like Sasha Romansky. Stripping. Prostitution.

Sarah.

Refusing to think of her sister, Autumn surveyed the cracked concrete surrounding her. There was nothing. The clues were as absent as Wendy.

Turning back to join Winter and Noah, the sunlight reflected off something that had fallen into a crack in the concrete. Autumn stooped, focusing on the object but not touching it. It was a vial. A full vial. And the label read oxytocin.

Oxytocin was a drug used to induce labor.

Autumn called Winter. "Out here. Now. We need an evidence bag."

Within moments, the vial was collected, and the three of them studied the ramifications of their find.

Noah finished marking the date and location on the bag. "Maybe Wendy struggled, and the abductor dropped the vial? It's full. Unused."

"Wendy was a stripper and a prostitute, according to Laura. Remind you of anyone?" Autumn's eyes darted from Noah to Winter.

"Alexandra Romansky." Winter was nodding, and her brow furrowed as she turned the information over in her mind.

"If Sasha is selling the babies, maybe she needed one fast? It's possible that Lindsay's twins didn't make it. Sasha may have had a contract to fulfill." Autumn was deeply disturbed by the theory.

Noah followed the train of thought. "Or she had to fulfill her motherhood fantasy. Either way, this abduction wasn't meticulously planned like the others. Too fast. Sloppy."

"Or this snatch is a completely different profile, the physical similarities are a coincidence, and Chris Parker was right all along." Winter's nose wrinkled, and Autumn knew why.

If Parker was right, they would never hear the end of it.

But that wasn't important.

They couldn't possibly know where Wendy was now, but Autumn knew one thing for certain. Wendy and her baby were in a great deal of danger.

15

Sasha's excitement grew in intensity with each step she took toward the building.

She had done it. She'd kidnapped a beautiful pregnant woman by herself and brought her directly to the horse ranch compound.

The Father would be so pleased. And if she kept pleasing him so greatly, possibly he would let her go to Eden for good. Sasha would leave this world in a heartbeat to be a part of the paradise they were all helping to create.

She could be pure again. Happy. She could finally have a family that loved her.

The expression on Tamara's face as Sasha entered the building with a half-cognizant Wendy Arnold leaning heavily on her shoulder was the exact opposite of Sasha's expectations.

"Why? Why would you bring that pregnant woman here?" Tamara's voice was severe, and Sasha feared a slap might be coming her way. It had happened before.

"For the Father, of course. I found her all by myself on the drive back from the swamps. She's a little drugged, but I made sure she was awake enough to push. The oxytocin is already kicking in." Sasha was still brimming with excitement in spite of Tamara's cold reception.

Tamara, fully garbed in her nurse's scrubs, appeared ready to murder Sasha, let alone slap her. "The Father has taken his newest children to Eden. He'll be back shortly, I expect. But he has a *very busy day* ahead of him." The nurse's face was crimson with anger. "This was *not* a part of the plan. Why would you *ever* secure a vessel without specific instructions? You know how particular the selection process is."

Sasha stood her ground, feeling secure in her actions. Tamara was obviously jealous. Sasha knew that Tamara secretly pined for the Father—that she wanted to be a vessel herself. Tamara was just too freaking ugly to ever pull it off. "She's *beautiful*! And her baby is coming *now*. She must be a gift from God, sent to help the Father's mission."

Tamara's countenance was cold as she considered the pregnant woman before her.

Sasha was sure if Tamara would just take a second to think—to *understand*—that she would grasp what a miracle this was.

But maybe she would be jealous of that as well. The Father wasn't presented with such an unexpected gift every day. And Sasha was the one who had brought it to him.

Tamara hadn't had a single thing to do with this surprise.

Wendy began to struggle within Sasha's tight grip. The woman was breathing heavily and clearly in a great deal of pain. "This isn't the hospital. You told me we were going to the hospital."

The panic was weak, but it was there.

"Hush." Tamara snapped at Wendy, shooting Sasha a frigid glare. "Follow me. We have to get her to a birthing room before the baby drops out on the damn floor. I cannot believe you've done this. You've messed up."

Sasha followed after her, mostly dragging Wendy's full weight. "It's okay," she whispered to the woman. "It's all part of his plan."

Instead of comforting Wendy, Sasha's words increased her fear. The woman became alarmed at being informed she was a part of *anything* and tried to pull away.

She lacked the strength to do so.

Tamara assisted in pulling Wendy's laboring body onto a clean, white bed, ignoring her attempt to struggle altogether. "You have no idea what you've done." She shot the words at Sasha like a bullet, and for the first time, Sasha experienced a terrifying doubt about securing the vessel.

As if he'd been summoned, the Father appeared at the doorway of the birthing room. His crystal blue eyes absorbed the scene before him, and his face became a tight, expressionless mask.

"I've brought you a gift. Another family member who is about to enter this world *right now*." Sasha's smile faded when the Father showed no sign of joy or gratitude whatsoever. "Did I do something wrong, Father?"

He ignored her and walked swiftly to the birthing bed. He quickly examined the situation to confirm that the woman was giving birth this instant.

She most definitely was.

Sasha perceived the Father's jaw flex and fought the instinct to run as he focused a severe stare directly on her. She had never witnessed the Father's anger. Part of her had believed that he wasn't capable of the emotion. He was too good…too pure.

"You didn't follow the rules. You must always follow the rules. I gave you no order to do this. Worse than that, Sasha, can you not recognize that this woman is not the right stock for my family?" The Father wasn't yelling or even raising his voice, which somehow made him even more frightening.

"But...she's...beautiful, isn't she? That's what the right stock requires, isn't it? Her eyes are blue, her hair is blonde, and she's gorgeous. She's even prettier than the last vessel." Sasha's entire body tensed when the Father's expression didn't soften even a tiny bit. Maybe he was upset because they had no idea who the baby's father was. "I only wanted to give you what you want, Father. I believe in you and your vision and your family. *I believe in Eden.* I thought...I thought—"

"You were wrong, Sasha. Wrong."

Sasha's heart ached with the full realization that the Father was not only displeased with the vessel. He was angry *with her.*

Wendy let out a horrifying scream, and the trio instantly went into birth mode. The mistake would be dealt with later.

But still, Sasha had faith in her actions. She hadn't made a mistake at all.

He'll see. Once the baby is out, he'll love it so much that he won't care how it got here. He'll change his mind. He'll be grateful.

But that wasn't what happened at all. Wendy gave birth only a few minutes later, and even as the baby screamed its first breath, a waterfall of blood soaked the end of the bed and floor.

Tamara wrapped the newborn and surveyed the vessel's condition. "She's going to die without proper medical attention." There wasn't a hint of concern in her voice. Tamara was merely stating a fact.

The entire scene reminded Sasha of a middle school science experiment gone wrong, and she nearly giggled but managed to cover the sound with a cough just in time.

Father's face brightened, and her terror subsided a little. He turned to her and smiled for the first time since entering the room. "I think there's a way you can salvage this, Sasha. I want you to take this woman and her baby back to her car.

Tamara will follow you. You will leave the car deep in the forest on a backroad, but close enough to town to clearly differentiate the woman's circumstances."

Sasha nodded eagerly, willing to leave a thousand women and babies anywhere if it meant the Father would forgive her for her mistake. She noted Tamara's intensified displeasure, and a part of her was very entertained.

"If this is done correctly, it will appear as though the woman simply took off on her own, went into labor, and died soon after. Maybe someone will find the baby before it perishes, maybe not. But the fact that the baby is with the mother will disconnect her entirely from our other work. This woman is not one of my vessels, nor is that my child. Go."

Tamara wasted no time wrapping the woman's bleeding lower half with thick layers of pads and gauze. Sasha grabbed Wendy's upper half, and Tamara took her feet. The baby lay squalling in a nearby medical bassinet.

By the time they'd shoved Wendy into the back seat, the woman was unconscious. Blood leaked through her bandages and coated the cracked vinyl in thick, reddish-black swirls.

Sasha ran back to retrieve the infant, placing it on the floor behind the passenger's seat. The damn thing would not stop crying.

The drive wasn't long—a half hour at most. The great thing about Florida was that you didn't have to drive very far in any direction to reach a patch of little-traveled swamp-land. Sasha had the backroads memorized.

Piece of cake.

As she drove, she mentally went over the events that had just taken place.

Surely, the Father would forgive her. His love was limitless, and Sasha was a faithful follower. A valuable servant. All she needed to do now was not screw up again.

He'd be reminded of her great devotion to him, and this would all be put behind them. Perhaps she would have to wait longer to get to Eden, but she deserved that. Sasha wasn't afraid of some hard work if it earned her a place in the Father's family. And it would, eventually. It had to.

Tamara would hate her forever, but that bitch had never liked her. She hadn't even pretended to. Sasha couldn't think of a single kind word Tamera had spoken to her in the entirety of her service to the Father.

Tamara didn't matter. At some point, there would be an opportunity to take her out. Of course, Sasha would have to be very careful about eliminating someone so close to the Father. Much more careful than she'd been today. He could never know why or how Tamara had disappeared.

Sasha could figure out those details later. For now, she'd just have to put up with the bitch. And after this drive, with a newborn baby screaming its face off nonstop, Tamara wouldn't seem so bad anyway.

When she felt she'd gone deep enough into the middle of nowhere yet close enough to be discoverable, Sasha pulled Wendy's car to a stop. The damn baby was *still* wailing, and she briefly wondered how long it would take the thing to just shut up and die.

As she was exiting Wendy's car, Tamara came charging toward it.

"What are you doing?"

Tamara ignored her and opened the back door. She pulled a pair of surgical scissors and a plastic grocery bag from her pocket and deftly cut the bandaging off in one quick movement. She then stuffed the bloodied material into the plastic bag and hung it from her wrist while she lifted the screaming newborn up, placing him on Wendy's stomach.

Sasha hadn't even registered if it was a boy or girl before now, but that was definitely a baby boy. She had been much more concerned with the Father's disapproval before. Tamara backed away from the vehicle as Sasha peered at her in confusion.

"She wouldn't have bandaged herself, you idiot. And I highly doubt she would have left the baby on the floor." The words stung, but Sasha reminded herself that Tamara wouldn't be around forever.

And as much as she hated to acknowledge it, even to herself, the nurse was right.

The older woman flung a package of disinfectant wipes at Sasha, and they both set to work wiping down the entire car as speedily as possible.

When they finished, the women took a final survey of the bloody mess in the back seat. There was certainly no wiping *that* up. Blood was *still* leaking out of Wendy's lower half, but at least the baby had finally stopped crying. Sasha wasn't sure if this meant he was dead or just exhausted. She didn't really care either way, as long as he stayed silent.

"God, that's disgusting. You've got blood all over your hands. You need to wipe them *good*." Her eyes were still locked on Wendy and the baby and the gore, but just one glance at Tamara's gloved hands had made her nauseated.

"Yes. It is disgusting. And that blood you're disgusted by..." Tamara pointed a bloody finger at Sasha's chest, "is on *your* hands. Literally and figuratively. You killed both of them for *no reason at all*. This is not the work of Eden. This is not the Father's plan." The hate in Tamara's voice was clear, but again, the woman's opinion of her was not at the top of Sasha's worry list.

She wasn't even sure what "figuratively" meant anyway.

Tamara and her big words were going to look amazing rotting away at the bottom of a swamp, and that Oompa

Loompa body of hers would sink like a rock. Or maybe Sasha would make a special trip and feed Tamara to the sharks instead. Alive.

Nothing but the best for you, you hag.

The two women returned to Tamara's car and drove in silence back to the compound. The farther they were from the chaotic scene behind them, the easier it became for Sasha to breathe deeply...calmly.

Problem solved. The Father would be so pleased.

16

R oger waited impatiently behind the steering wheel. He'd followed them to this desolate area and parked ever so carefully behind a thick stand of trees that ran perpendicular to the backroad Tamara and Sasha turned onto. Waiting, he gave the women a few minutes before exiting his vehicle.

He had witnessed the entire scene like a ghost hovering in the shadows. Everything but the birth, of course. For that, he'd listened through a crack in the birthing room door. He'd heard it all. Had been appalled by it all.

But even through his anger, a plan had formed.

Stealthily maneuvering through the trees, he ventured as close as he dared before kneeling and peering through the dense foliage.

The two women were wiping down the mother's car. He couldn't make out exactly what they were saying, but the tones of their voices alone told him they were not pleased with each other. Not that he hadn't already known that.

"The Father" was his brother, and Roger had been a faithful servant to The Dream since the beginning. His brother's zeal had been too overwhelmingly real for the vision to be anything but a gift from God.

But he was past believing that now.

He was past believing in anything, especially miracles.

The wailing of the babe in the car tugged at Roger's heart. He and his wife had wanted their own family since the moment they'd said their vows. Either he or Amanda were apparently incapable of making that happen, though, and after years of trying, he'd begged his brother for assistance.

Hadn't Roger assisted him all these years? Hadn't the family grown so large in part because of Roger's faithful service?

His brother owned a sperm bank, for Christ's sake. He had the tools, knew the people, and could make it happen for Roger and Amanda.

Only he *wouldn't*.

"The Father" interpreted their inability to conceive as just another sign of confirmation that he was meant to repopulate the earth himself. Alone. No other man was pure enough. No other man was worthy.

And certainly, Amanda was not equal to the holy vessel standards. Not according to Roger's brother.

He had stared Roger straight in the face and told him that fatherhood simply was not in the cards for him. They were infertile for a reason. "It's all part of the plan," the Father had told him. "It is another confirmation of The Dream's truths."

Roger's teeth ground together. "Part of the plan my ass." How could his own flesh and blood say such things about their struggle? Their pain?

Roger's brother had added that he and Amanda were already a part of a family, and Roger needn't forget that. There was no need to want for more.

Then the bastard had hugged him. *Hugged him.*

That conversation had been the beginning of the end as far as Roger's allegiance was concerned.

Amanda needed a baby. Every year that passed found her more withdrawn and consumed by the sorrows of her barren body. She wasn't the same woman he had married—she couldn't be. Her only desire had been motherhood.

She'd asked him just days ago, "What is left to live for?"

Roger had harbored a terrifying, mounting fear that her words had been an omen. A warning. If something didn't change—and soon—Amanda would find a way to kill herself.

Meanwhile, Roger had witnessed his brother deliver baby after baby, creating a veritable army of perfect, towheaded children.

"The Father" was certainly bringing The Dream to life. Roger and Amanda had a front row seat to that truth. But Roger had, at some point, ascertained that The Dream was merely *a dream*. And *that* dream didn't even remotely provide the happiness Roger knew he and his wife deserved.

Worst of all, his brother didn't even care. All that mattered to him was the creation of Eden.

Roger and Amanda's concerns were of little consequence to The Dream.

The Dream was bullshit.

The poor infant's screaming blasted through the forest. They were just going to leave it there to die. His brother had so many children that this "unworthy" babe was disposable in his eyes.

What a wonderful father his brother was.

While Roger had grown numb to the idea of the vessels being eliminated, he had never before witnessed his brother order the same for a newborn child.

Roger's job as an apostle at the compound kept him in very close quarters with the birthing rooms each and every day. When a new vessel was delivered, Roger knew. When the crop was harvested, Roger knew.

And today, he'd caught every word spoken as Sasha's "gift" to his brother labored away in one of those rooms. He had eavesdropped through the baby's first cries and Tamara's comment about the condition the vessel was in. His brother had calmly ordered the two women to abandon the vessel *and the infant.*

Roger's first instinct had been to offer his assistance. Despising his brother hadn't changed the fact that he'd spent years being a brainwashed peon. Roger was a servant to The Dream. Anything that helped The Dream move forward naturally was something he would volunteer for.

But this time he had stopped himself.

This was *his* chance. This was *his* gift. That baby was meant to be with Amanda and him.

Screw the Father.

Without a glance back at the compound, he'd followed them. Of course, he stayed far enough back to not be detectable. But he never allowed himself to lose sight of the two cars.

Roger was just as familiar with these backroads as Sasha could ever be. The second they turned off, he knew which road he would take and where he would park.

Now, all he had to do was wait.

The child's wails had stopped, and Roger was overcome by a mixture of sadness and rage. If that baby died before he could rescue it, there would be consequences.

There was a time when he'd worshipped his brother— long before The Dream. They were two normal brothers doing normal things. Playing with G.I. Joes and Ninja Turtles. Watching Saturday morning cartoons. Betting on who could do the best "underdog" on the swing set.

They had laughed and fought and cried and daydreamed.

They'd loved each other dearly. Or at least, he'd assumed they had.

Try as he might, the images inspired not a single ounce of affection within his heart now. He hated his brother. His brother had ruined his life. His brother was insane.

Roger also knew that he was teetering on the edge of absolute madness himself.

But he didn't care. He couldn't deny that he wished the Father would die. His brother was a selfish, egotistical asshole. He'd killed enough. If this baby died too, simply because it wasn't deemed "pure" by his dick of a brother, Roger might lose his mind completely.

Years ago, Roger never would have thought he was capable of even thinking about hurting his brother.

Those years were over.

If this baby died, Roger would kill "the Father," and he would enjoy watching him suffer through to the very end.

The sound of an engine pulled Roger back to the present. Tamara's car pulled away. He waited an agonizingly long three minutes before he was certain the women were gone.

Roger ran. The shrieks had started up again, and they pierced through to his very soul. This was fate. This was the baby Amanda had been waiting for.

The hot Florida sun assailed him, and he was covered in sweat by the time he reached the car. The back door of the passenger's side had been left open, and Roger slowed to a walk.

There lay the woman—absolutely covered in blood— holding the yowling infant.

She's still alive.

Roger hesitated for a moment. Doing this, taking this child…would be crossing a line he could never slide back over. He would be betraying his brother, his "family," and the entirety of Eden. He was directly defying The Dream.

"Screw the dream," he muttered, stretching out his arms. As he took hold of the baby boy, the mother's eyes fluttered open.

She was dying, and there was nothing he could do to help her.

"Please. Save him." The whisper was so weak that Roger barely understood her words.

"I will." A deep sense of certainty settled into his bones. He was doing the right thing.

The woman's eyelids closed again. She was either dead or would be very soon. Roger stepped back from the car, the tiny babe secure in his arms, and surveyed the scene before him.

Such a waste. Such a horrible, meaningless waste.

That girl shouldn't be dead. She never should have been at the compound to begin with. Roger's brother had developed such an enormous god complex that he couldn't even keep his followers in line anymore.

Sasha was a problem, and Roger had sensed it immediately. He knew Tamara had also. Yet the Father let her run around like a little psychopathic sidekick, putting them all in danger.

He knew his brother well enough to be expecting Sasha's immediate elimination.

But the damage had already been done.

Roger did not for one second believe that there wouldn't be a trace of Sasha or Tamara's DNA on or in that car. They had been careful, but they weren't forensic experts, either. They would be discovered.

Whether or not Sasha lived long enough to be arrested was certainly up for debate, but Tamara would be around. Tamara was a faithful, heartless troll.

The police or the Feds or *someone* would get ahold of her, and eventually, through whatever means necessary, they *would* get her to talk. Roger was sure of it.

This was the perfect time for his family—his *actual* family —to get the hell away from here. He and Amanda had their own private little house on the horse ranch, and it was far enough away from the main compound to mask a baby's cries. Ninety-two acres was a lot of land. But there would be visitors. Fellow servants dropping by just to say hello and spread the love of Eden.

His stomach turned.

"Screw Eden."

As he drove, the baby boy in his lap now staring up at him curiously, Roger knew it was time to leave. He would take the baby to Amanda, and then he would make a store run. They would load up with baby supplies, and Amanda could pack some clothes and other personals while he was out.

Roger drove through the ranch as though nothing was wrong. He turned on the drive that led to his home with Amanda.

No one paid attention, nor would they bother to. He was *the Father's brother.*

That fact didn't stop fear from pumping through his veins.

He pulled to a stop and carried the baby into the house after being certain no one was around.

Amanda was bent over, pulling a fresh pan of cookies from the oven. His beautiful Amanda, whose skin had grown sallow and wan from the depression that kept her indoors. When she caught sight of her husband and the bundle in his arms, two dozen snickerdoodles flew to the floor along with the clanging pan.

She walked carefully toward Roger, her eyes filling with tears. "Is that? Is it ours? Do we get to keep it?"

"Him," Roger corrected, placing the infant in Amanda's arms.

She was crying and laughing simultaneously. The joy on her face was the final sign Roger had needed.

This was meant to be.

This was *his* family.

"Amanda, we have to leave. We have to leave *fast*." His somber tone left no room for the possibility that he could be joking.

Amanda didn't hesitate for an instant. "I'll pack some things."

"I'll make a run to the grocer."

She smiled at him, the baby in her arms creating a light in her eyes, something he hadn't witnessed in years. "We'll be ready."

The locks clicked into place after he shut the front door. Amanda was wise, and he was confident that nothing on this planet could take that baby away from her now.

The drive gave him time to consider some details. He had plenty of money, so that was of no concern. He also had loads of experience, thanks to his big brother, in navigating the legal system. A name change would be necessary, which wasn't an issue. He'd had new papers created for them both years ago. Now, he just needed some for his son.

Son.

The word pleased him greatly.

He had a son now, and both he and Amanda needed to stay hidden from Eden and from anyone who might be searching for their child.

But everything was doable. The things he had learned over the years while assisting with the Father's plan would make this new life possible.

Screw the plan.

Roger knew exactly what he was doing.

He had his own plan now.

17

"Autumn, will you be my therapist when this is all over?" Noah's voice was flat and dull.

"You're a seasoned pro, Dalton. This should be nothing for a guy like you." Autumn returned the banter, but the words were just as empty as Noah's.

"Maybe Sasha knew Wendy? They both stripped. It's possible." Winter seemed to be thinking out loud as she drove.

Autumn considered the possibility. She wouldn't put it past Sasha to take out a co-worker. One of the only things she agreed with Chris Parker about was that Sasha had extremely narcissistic traits. She behaved as if she had no conscience, no soul.

But the girl hadn't exactly had a fair shot at life, either. What would become of any female whose father whored her out for money at just ten years of age? And right on the heels of the loss of her mother. Sasha never stood a chance.

That was the side of things that Autumn wished the world could comprehend. Criminals were humans. They had a history. And except for rare and extreme cases, these humans could have ended up in a very different place if just one thing in their lives had gone differently.

Had gone *better*.

Even Justin Black had stood a chance when he was born.

So had Sarah.

Autumn, Winter, and Noah were on their way back to the station, and the mood had gone dark. Wendy's disappearance already gave the impression of being just as mysterious as the others, and even the vial of oxytocin didn't tell them anything they didn't already know.

Someone was taking babies. Every last one of the agents were well aware.

Winter's phone went off, and she put the cell to her ear with lackluster enthusiasm.

"Phone calls and driving are heavily frowned upon in Florida." Noah was attempting to be light, Autumn knew, but the humor fell flat.

"Special Agent Black," Winter barked into the phone.

In the rearview mirror, Autumn watched Winter's blazing blue eyes grow wider with each passing second as she concentrated on the call. Why her phone wasn't connected to Bluetooth was something Autumn would deal with later.

Something had happened.

Winter threw her phone in Noah's lap and pulled a death-defying U-turn that put the most intricate of roller coasters to shame.

"Okay, *that* is *definitely* straight-up illegal." Autumn smiled. Even now, Noah couldn't help but attempt to provide a bit of levity to any situation.

"Shut up, Dalton." Contrary to her harsh words, Winter's tone was gentle. Her foot wasn't. It smashed onto the pedal, pressing Autumn into her seat from the force. "They found Wendy Arnold. She's nearly dead from massive blood loss. Found all alone in her car on a side road. She gave birth within the last few hours, but there was no sign of a baby. The deputies are scouring the area for the newborn right now, and we're going to the hospital. We *have* to talk to Wendy."

Noah's face went grim. "Do you think she'll *make* it to the hospital?"

Winter said nothing, and Autumn closed her eyes.

Please don't die. Please, please, please don't die.

There was so much information they still needed if they were ever going to make this madness stop. Wendy *had* to live. She just had to.

Winter pulled into the Lavender Lake Medical Center's emergency room receiving area and was immediately followed by the ambulance, sirens blazing. All three of them raced to the back of the vehicle, anxiously waiting for Wendy to appear.

But when the doors flew open, the paramedics' faces were bleak.

Winter shook her head, despair and frustration furrowing her brow. "She's either dead or close to it."

When the gurney was lowered, Autumn rushed to Wendy's side, touching the woman's arm before the paramedics carted her indoors.

One touch was enough.

Autumn trembled, frozen in place as the poor young woman was whisked away.

Winter was at her side in mere seconds. "What did you feel?" Her voice was low but intense.

"I'm going inside to find out what her status is," Noah called out, already jogging away.

Autumn made herself snap out of her daze, turning to her friend and wanting to break down entirely. "*So many* emotions, Winter. That woman just went through...she went through *everything*."

Winter threw an arm around Autumn and pulled her close. "So, she's still alive?"

Autumn allowed herself only a moment of comfort with her friend before pulling away and forcing herself back to neutral. "No. Not really. Or at least, she won't be for long. She's dying. They won't be able to save her. She's too close."

Autumn stared at the glass doors of the ER, and Winter stepped into her view, forcing her to look into her concerned blue eyes. "What is it?"

Shaking her head, Autumn tried to make it all make sense. "There's something different this time."

"What do you mean? Because they left her in the car instead of the swamp?"

Autumn shuddered, remembering the hand. That single piece of evidence that a human being once lived had been found. None of them would ever forget that.

"Yes, that, but also...not that. Before Wendy lost consciousness for the last time, she believed her baby was safe. It was the single hopeful thought in her mind." Autumn pondered the possibilities of what that could mean.

"What about the rest of her mind?" Winter stared at her as if she felt bad for even asking the question.

But the inquiry was legitimate.

"Nothing clear. Just a lot of pain and...despair. She had a rough life." Autumn's eyes welled with tears, but the sadness wasn't only for Wendy's plight.

That could be Sarah. If I don't help her—that could be my baby sister.

"How could she have possibly felt that her baby was safe? From what I've gathered, the scene was pretty brutal. She didn't get left there by the Care Bears and Rainbow Brite." Winter tugged at a loose strand of her dark hair, clearly trying to piece together a puzzle that was becoming more complicated by the minute.

"I don't know. I'm gonna call Sun." Autumn pulled out her phone, and Winter began walking toward the entrance.

"I'll be inside." She waved over her shoulder, and the two friends parted.

Autumn paced a few seconds, waiting for Sun to answer her call.

"Yeah?" Caller I.D. ensured that Sun never accidentally answered the phone with a polite greeting for Autumn. Or Winter. Probably no one.

"Have you run into any leads regarding couples suddenly having new babies in their homes? Couples that weren't known or detected to be pregnant by neighbors, co-workers, anyone?"

Sun sighed, and Autumn understood that she was just as exhausted as the rest of them. "I haven't come across anything like that. But Agent Logan has been checking adoptions that happened under questionable circumstances here in Florida. I'll give her a call."

This was good. Mia Logan was a superb agent who wouldn't overlook anything even remotely strange.

"Thanks, Sun. You were informed that they found Wendy?"

"Just a minute ago. I'll make sure the sheriff lets all the deputies and detectives know that they need to be on the lookout for a newborn. Detective Cohen is out helping with the search right now. I can also pass on any information she finds to the rest of you when she returns." This was possibly the most pleasant conversation Autumn had ever experienced with Agent Ming.

And all it took was four missing women and six stolen babies.

"Should we put out an Amber Alert?" Autumn knew doing so was the common procedure, but this wasn't the common case.

Sun sighed again. "I thought about that, but what exactly

would we be alerting people to? All newborns everywhere? The public would go crazy with that description. The phone lines would get completely jammed with useless information, and anyone who actually knew something important wouldn't be able to get through at all."

Autumn nodded, imagining the chaos. "Missing newborn. Sex unknown. Coloring unknown. Every damn thing that would make a search possible unknown." The public *would* go crazy. The description simply wasn't enough.

"Yep. I'll call you soon." Sun ended the call, and Autumn stood on the hospital sidewalk alone.

The Florida sun was high in the sky, and Autumn decided that she hated the state and everything about it. Screw Disney World and Orlando. Nothing good happened in this state, and wishing upon a damn star wasn't going to change a thing.

They *had* to find that baby. Whoever had the baby was the key. And for some reason, she deeply believed that they had a chance of doing just that. She even thought that they had the best chance of finding Wendy's baby *first*. Maybe it was part of the information she'd received from touching Wendy. But the majority of what she'd been privy to had been blurry and impossible to translate.

A chill raced up Autumn's spine. Apparently, that was what happened when you touched dead people.

Noah and Winter returned from the emergency room with somber faces.

"She's dead." Noah's voice was dull, and Autumn understood it wasn't only the loss of a life that burdened his thoughts. Finding Wendy could have broken the case wide open for them.

Could have.

Autumn gave him a wan smile. "I know."

"Baby gone. Wendy gone. Lead gone." Winter scuffed her shoe against the ground. "Hope gone."

Autumn didn't need any special powers to detect the despair amongst them.

What could Wendy have been if she'd lived? They could have helped her. Autumn *would* have helped her. Wendy could have led a completely different life than the one that brought her here. She could have been happy. She could have been an amazing mother.

Autumn put a hand to her stomach. Could have. "This case is awful."

Winter and Noah appeared to feel the helplessness in their cores as well. Missing baby after missing baby. Murdered mothers. Distraught partners.

A single hand in a swamp.

Noah's phone rang, and he put it to his ear without even glancing at the screen.

If another baby had gone missing already, Autumn thought she might lose her mind.

"What? Are you sure?" Autumn and Winter both whipped their heads toward Noah. "We're at the hospital right now." He listened a little longer and then jammed his phone into his pocket.

The women were waiting as patiently as possible. Winter's leg had started twitching in suspense. "Tell us!"

Autumn was positive that Winter hadn't meant to actually shout the words.

"They found Lindsay Welsh." Noah put a hand to his forehead in utter disbelief. "She's *alive*."

18

Aiden slammed the brake pedal to the floor beneath his lead foot. Lavender Lake Medical Center was barely ten minutes away from the sheriff's office, but Aiden managed to arrive in six.

Lindsay Welsh was alive. A group of hikers had found her unconscious on the side of a seldom used backroad and immediately called for an ambulance.

His rapid footsteps echoed off the stout brick walls of the hospital as Aiden charged toward the building. The electronic slide of the automatic entryway doors revealed Autumn, Winter, and Noah huddled together in the waiting area.

"Updates?"

A mixture of hope and sorrow cloaked Autumn's face. "Wendy Arnold is dead."

"And Lindsay?" Disappointment could be dealt with later. Aiden needed to know what they were working with.

"She had a pulse when they found her. Only caught a glimpse when they wheeled her in. Caked in mud," Winter grimaced, "a hell of a lot of blood."

Noah kicked at a metal chair leg. "We're waiting to find out."

An abrupt crash of falling office supplies interrupted their brief exchange. Aiden's head swung toward the commotion as a stapler flew through the air, and the team approached the distraught man shouting at the nurses and causing the chaos.

"Let me back there! Let me see my wife! You can't keep me away from my own wife!" Josh Welsh managed to secure one knee on the receptionist's counter before Aiden's strong hands seized his leg and pulled him back down.

"Easy! Easy now!" Noah gripped Josh's right arm while Aiden secured the left. They pressed him firmly against the waiting room wall.

"My wife is back there!" Josh screamed. His eyes were bloodshot and wild. Legs flailing, his thick fingers dug into Aiden's thigh. "Let me see my wife, you assholes!"

"Mr. Welsh, I need you to calm down. You will *absolutely* be allowed to see your wife as soon as the doctors say it's okay. But *only* if you pull yourself together." Aiden sympathized with Josh's plight, but hysteria was of no help in the current situation.

Spasmodic breaths heaved from Josh's lungs. Panic and affliction had melded into a madness that Aiden sensed was completely foreign to the grieving man.

Bright red flashed past Aiden's peripheral as Autumn came near.

"Josh. You have every reason to be freaking out, but you have to trust that the doctors are doing everything they possibly can to give Lindsay the proper attention she needs right now. You'll be able to see her shortly. Deep breaths. In. Out. In. Out."

Josh began to calm as he focused on Autumn. The two

were complete strangers, but Autumn's soft voice seemed to mesmerize the outraged man.

Aiden loosened his grip ever so slightly, testing Josh's composure. A quick nod of his head gave Noah the go-ahead to release his hold.

"Is she going to be okay?" The question was followed by a choked sob, and Josh collapsed on the cold tile floor.

Autumn glanced at Aiden and knelt beside him. "She's alive. They're doing their best to stabilize her."

Aiden noted that the actual inquiry had been smoothly side-stepped. "Let's get you seated, Mr. Welsh. Would you like some water?"

Allowing himself to be led to a chair, Josh vehemently shook his head. "I don't want anything. I just want to see my wife and babies."

Aiden exchanged looks with Noah. Josh was calm for now, but vigilance remained necessary.

Autumn sat beside Josh. "Do you think you could tell me a little bit about Lindsay? Any details about her at all could be helpful to the case."

Frowning, Josh put a hand to his forehead. He said nothing, and Aiden was convinced that Autumn's question would receive no answer. The man appeared to be too torn up to hold a conversation.

"She's so strong." He swiped at his wet face with his sleeve. "She's the strongest person I know. She didn't deserve this."

"Of course she didn't, Josh. And her strength may very well be the reason she's here right now. She's obviously a fighter." The tranquil nature of Autumn's voice appeared to soothe the man considerably.

"Why would anyone do this to her? She's a good person. She spent so much time trying to help other people. *So much time.*"

"I'm sure she's absolutely wonderful, Josh. Was there any particular way that Lindsay liked to help others?" The chat was seamlessly being maneuvered toward Lindsay's blog.

Good work, Dr. Trent.

"She had one of those...blogs. She called it *My Baby Miracle.* She wanted to help other women who struggled with fertility like we did. She was obsessed with it."

"That's a noble obsession to have, Mr. Welsh. I'm sure Lindsay's efforts were greatly appreciated by her readers." Autumn shifted in her seat.

"That whole damn blog was Lindsay trying to do something good in this world. And this is what happens to her. It's wrong!" His fist hit the vinyl-coated padding of the empty chair to his right.

Muscles instinctively tensed all throughout Aiden's body, but he maintained his distance.

Anger was expected and entirely acceptable as long as an escalation was avoided.

"Do you know if she became friends with any of her readers? Maybe she met with some of the women who commented on her posts?"

Josh shook his head. His eyes focused on Autumn for the first time since he'd sat.

"No. She would have told me. We didn't have secrets from each other. We were partners. If Lindsay made a new friend, I would have known." A sad little smile played on his lips. "Lindsay would have been too excited to not share the news."

Aiden fully believed him.

"How about the sperm bank you and Lindsay used? Could you tell me the name?" Warmth emanated from Autumn's bright green eyes.

"I don't remember. Not specifically. But our fertility doctor would know. Dr. Amanda Jenkins. She's a nice lady."

Noah's fingers tapped at his iPad, and he leaned in slightly, allowing Aiden to view the screen.

Results were already popping up for Amanda Jenkins.

"Try to pull up a list of sperm banks…local and nationwide," Aiden directed in a discreet tone.

Noah nodded and continued to type.

Josh's momentary loss of self-control appeared to be over. Aiden met Winter's gaze and gave a small nudge of his head in Josh's direction. She promptly advanced toward Autumn and the grieving man.

The two women ought to be able to keep the distraught husband occupied until an update on Lindsay's condition was available. Aiden had great faith in their conversational skills.

With Josh pacified for the moment, Aiden could assist with the internet search.

Nearly half an hour passed before a moderately harried doctor entered the ER waiting area, his eyes scanning the room for the federal agents.

Josh wasted no time introducing himself as Lindsay Welsh's husband, but this time, one glance at Aiden and Noah ensured his controlled demeanor.

"Lindsay is in critical but stable condition. We plan to transfer her to the ICU within the hour."

"And the babies?" Clenched fists trembled at Josh's sides.

The inquiry was expected, but the doctor flashed a nervous glance Aiden's way before meeting Josh's gaze again. "There is evidence that your wife vaginally delivered both infants and placentas, but no post-partum repairs were made. Your wife is our only patient."

The confirmation that his wife was still alive compounded upon the fact that his two daughters were simply *gone* brought Josh to his knees with an amalgamation of emotion. Autumn was at his side immediately, closely followed by Winter.

Consolation would do little to find his children, but Aiden understood the overpowering mercilessness of grief and the resulting necessity for commiseration. The intense sentiment would run its course regardless of its futility.

He also was cognizant of the implications the doctor's words had provided.

Post-partum repairs were only needed if tearing occurred during the birthing process. Mentioning it at all indicated that Lindsay had most likely torn badly yet received no medical care following the delivery.

She'd been found near a swamp, and the paramedic reports stated that she was covered with mud—especially her hands, knees, and feet. Aiden's theory thus far worked in direct conjunction with the findings.

Lindsay had been tossed into a swamp, believed to be dead or close to it, yet had managed to crawl out of the water before the gators made a quick meal of her weak and traumatized body.

She really *was* a fighter.

Sobs released from Josh Welsh's lungs at varying decibels. Positioned before him was Autumn, her soft voice once again working its magic. Winter was at his side, a hand gently placed on his back.

A few feet away, Noah Dalton stood tall, occasionally swiping a hand across his eyes. The lump in Aiden's own throat kept him from passing even the slightest judgment on anyone in the room.

Tragedy. Tragedy had come to Lavender Lake, and the emotional fallout was something they could all understand.

Loss was the ultimate equalizer of humanity.

"We will do all that we can to find your daughters, Josh. But what *you must do* is be with your wife. *Be with her.* When her eyes open, she will need every ounce of love and support you can give. Strong or not, she needs you to be her rock right now." Thick emotion blanketed Autumn's words.

Winter swallowed hard and added, "*We* will focus on bringing your babies home. That's *our* job. *You* focus on Lindsay. Okay?"

Josh's head dropped onto his knees as he nodded his compliance.

Moving swiftly, Aiden spotted and approached another attending doctor. "I would like my team alerted as soon as Lindsay gains consciousness, Doctor."

Resigned brown eyes met his stare. "Of course." The doctor glanced at Josh and lowered his voice. "But you should know...we aren't certain that Mrs. Welsh will regain consciousness anytime soon. She could quite possibly never wake up at all."

Aiden wanted to punch a wall but maintained his composure. "Understood."

She's a fighter. She's going to wake up.

Lindsay Welsh had been found with a pulse after enduring unimaginable trauma. The resilience she'd shown encouraged Aiden to hold out hope that she *would* wake up. They desperately needed her to.

She could be the ultimate key to solving this case.

A vibration against his thigh alerted Aiden to an incoming message. He immediately pulled the phone from his pocket and swiped.

The Lavender Lake crime lab had contacted him with the findings concerning the oxytocin vial. They had been able to pull a fingerprint from the container belonging to none other than Alexandra "Sasha" Romansky.

After making sure that Josh Welsh had been escorted away to be near his wife in the ICU, Aiden wasted no time gathering his team. "Agent Black, Agent Dalton, Dr. Trent...

come please."

The three rushed toward him, sensing the hint of excitement in the SSA's voice.

"The vial you recovered, Autumn, gave us a fingerprint that's been identified as Sasha Romansky's." Three sets of eyes grew wide, and Aiden didn't fight the smile that spread across his face.

"This is…" Winter blew out a breath.

"*Huge.*" Noah finished for her.

"And they can smell it." Autumn pointed to the large glass windows facing the hospital's parking lot. Multiple news reporters stood ready, microphones in hand and camera crews in place.

News traveled just as fast in Lavender Lake as anywhere else. A press conference was becoming unavoidable.

"They have to be told something." The sensation of being circled by vultures flashed through Aiden's mind.

"We don't have much to share." Autumn's frustration matched his own.

"I've held conferences with less." No one challenged this, and Aiden turned toward his team. "We have Wendy Arnold's disappearance and suspected homicide as well as her missing infant. We've identified Alexandra Romansky as a definite person of interest. If the media is going to get involved, we might as well use them for good."

"Spread the truth instead of conjecture," Autumn agreed quietly.

"Lindsay Welsh was found alive. They'll go crazy over that." Winter stared at the amassing crowd.

Noah nodded. "Crazy gets attention. Attention gets results."

"Sometimes. We should all keep our expectations realistic. Blind hope is often exactly that and nothing more." No one enjoyed the sentiment, which was precisely why Aiden found the warning necessary.

"Complete and total despair is worse." Autumn turned back toward Aiden, her green stare daring him to disagree.

He couldn't.

SSA Aiden Parrish exchanged confirmatory glances with each of them, straightened his tie, and walked straight toward the sliding exit doors.

Time to enter the lion's den.

MASSIVE, wrathful jaws crashed together, sending a fresh spray of crimson across Lindsay's face. A limp, hoof-footed leg hung from the scaly beast's treacherous jowls.

Retreat was impossible. Thick, oozing mud encased her body. Struggle only caused her to sink farther into the relentless mire.

Reptilian eyes locked onto her gaze. The deer was gone. The monster was still ravenous. No amount of flesh would satisfy the gargantuan fiend now approaching her.

This feast would carry on for all eternity. Blood would swallow the swamplands until nothing was left of them at all.

A dark red sea of terror and suffering filled with brutish, insatiable demons would spread across the earth until the entire planet had been purified with violence and horror.

The scream of infants surrounded her. Hundreds—*thousands*—of babies shrieking in fear. Lost—they were all lost—wailing for their mothers.

But their mothers would never come. Just the savage beasts and a never-ending wave of scarlet gore.

The ghoulish, anguished howls intensified with every passing second.

A cold-blooded, murderous creature hovered over her.

Golden amber eyes turned red, then slowly transformed into a frigid icy blue, and finally went black as night.

"Thank you for your service." But the words were hellish, slithering growls. Scaly, rough lips kissed her forehead and she struggled...knowing all effort was futile.

"My babies." Vermillion liquid filled her mouth, spreading through her body until each and every vein was infused with poison.

Voices broke through the wails—human voices. Her body was swiftly lifted from the carnage.

Ambulance lights swiveled in the sky as horrendous panic permeated her bones.

Don't take me. Leave me. Find my babies. Please find my babies. They're so close. Can't you hear their screams?

The human saviors didn't pay any attention. Sirens drowned out every other form of sound.

Fading into a foggy haze, the red sea grew distant.

Lindsay Welsh's eyes fluttered open only to find the handsome face of her husband looking back. Josh peered down at her with haunted apprehension, clutching her hand in his own. Tears crept down his cheeks in shimmering, glasslike tendrils.

The strength to rise was gone. Throat burning, Lindsay fought to plea with her husband.

"The babies."

Save our babies. You have to save...

The brief bit of light winked out, pulling Lindsay back into the darkness and the beasts waiting for their next meal.

19

Tangled thoughts always methodically straightened when I stepped into my personal laboratory. The polished white room instantly reminded me of the bigger picture—The Dream.

With no time to waste, I walked straight to my computer. A few swift clicks and three passwords later, and the internal database I'd paid a considerable sum of money to have created spread across my screen.

Sasha's disastrous decision was undeniably still plaguing my mind. Anger—*righteous* anger—over the morning's mishaps threatened to throw me entirely off track.

I would not allow that to happen.

Perhaps the time had come to more seriously consider Sasha's elimination, but that matter would have to be addressed later. I had orders to fulfill.

More importantly, I had selections to make. No one else could choose the vessels worthy of my seed. The spread of Eden's purity depended solely upon my painstaking attention to detail.

With the database open, I scanned through the latest

reports. Sixty-four couples seeking to purchase semen as the solution to their fertility issues.

What a blessing! Demand was high, and business was good.

With a tap of a few buttons, the medical chart of the first couple was revealed. The computer programmer I'd paid to create this system deserved every single cent he'd received.

Researching a couple prior to the system's installation could take hours, which was unfavorable in my mission to bring The Dream to life. Now, the information I sought was at my fingertips.

Tracy Hastings. Thirty-nine years of age.

Negative. Too old.

The next woman was too short and the following too fat.

The fourth image was pleasing—pretty enough with a pleasant fair complexion. But according to her chart, she'd been born with a congenital heart defect.

Eliminated.

Two dozen more candidates, but each unworthy for individual reasons. Poor facial symmetry, large ears, a history of severe depressive episodes...

So few in this world were meant to be my vessels. But I would not grow disheartened.

The next chart introduced Crystal Weiland. Blonde, blue-eyed, straight teeth, flawless skin...I began to grow excited. She was five-seven with a lovely figure and worked as a computer graphics engineer.

Brains *and* beauty.

After a careful scan through her medical history, I grew even more heartened to find only a few minor childhood illnesses, an ankle broken while skiing at fifteen years of age —nothing of consequence.

Crystal had spent three years trying to conceive with her

husband of only four. The perfect woman had married a male who produced poor swimmers. Such a waste.

She resided in North Carolina, which filled me with joy. Choosing couples from the same area had been unwise, and I would not make that mistake again.

Not that the last one was my mistake. I never could have predicted Lindsay Welsh's move to Lavender Lake, after all. She'd lived in Georgia when I selected her, and the chances of the couple choosing to come here were of microscopic proportions.

Yet Lindsay had come, bringing the total number of Lavender Lake vessels to three. My misstep had been in ever allowing that count to reach two.

The unexpected should always be expected. And unfortunately, *three* missing women had set off a decidedly louder alarm than *two* in the lovely city of Lavender Lake.

And Sasha nearly made it four.

Rage simmered low in my gut. That had been taken care of.

Sasha would be taken care of as well.

Close scrutinization of the Weiland file informed me that the couple had chosen Donor 3123057. With a few keystrokes and contentment in my heart, I changed the number to 9016710.

This was my personal donor number, and I had thoughtfully picked each digit, creating a numeral combination that was deeply spiritually associated.

Nine, for example, was connected to an individual's higher purpose and ultimate life mission. Zero was representative of the primordial void…the womb, while one reflected new beginnings and purity.

Six symbolized harmony, balance, sincerity, love, and truth. The epitome of Eden. Seven denoted completeness and perfection, while ten stood for the attainment of wholeness.

Any decisions made in my mission to fulfill The Dream required meaningful precision. Purifying humanity was an endeavor that could never be taken lightly.

A contented sigh escaped me as I saved the Crystal Weiland file changes.

Before the day was done, I would assign this particular case to an employee. He or she would simply pull the assigned sperm sample and combine it with the eggs that had been harvested from the vessel.

Soon after, an appointment would be scheduled, and Crystal and her husband would put into motion the fulfillment of a dream.

My dream. *The Dream*.

Embryos didn't always attach properly, which was greatly disappointing. As careful as I was, I still couldn't anticipate every contingency.

My faith that the right vessels would successfully bear my fruit kept me going. The beauty of Eden and my children was proof of a divine triumph.

I continued through the search results without finding even one more appropriate vessel, but tomorrow was a new day. The next time I opened this database, I would be opening a new list of possibilities.

Hope was never lost.

After closing down my computer and making sure all security measures were in place, I exited my office. The business with Sasha had left me restless and a walkthrough of my sprawling cryobank laboratory would assist me in regaining the peace I longed for.

A happy hum of activity met me as I entered the impressive, large room. Numerous employees, all clad in pure white, worked to fulfill the dreams of countless childless couples.

My mission was also being carried out by these dutiful worker bees. Of course, they didn't know this. Their fallible human nature would prevent them from ever grasping the concept of my spotless bloodline that was so vital to The Dream.

The secret stayed with me.

One day soon, I would begin instructing my children and mold their minds with The Dream's beauty. They would learn how to think, how to act and handle themselves in a world that desperately needed their purity.

I would raise them up in my image, and in time, they would march bravely into the world in perfect glory. The power of this—the sheer beauty of the thought—brought joyous tears to my eyes.

Friendships, couplings, groupings would all be arranged based on each child's specific strengths and weaknesses. These characteristics would be revealed over time, and my sole judgment would place them on their unique paths.

When they were old enough to mate, their superior genetics would combine to create offspring that carried on the purest, holiest DNA two parents could provide.

The process would be repeated with the next generation, and I would choose the brightest light from among them as my successor. This child would be groomed to perfection and entrusted with the gift of continuing my work.

My family would continuously expand, ascending to the greatest heights of every human industry. They would eventually control all forms of science, politics—*every aspect of mankind.*

My children would dictate the future.

A buzzing in my pocket interrupted my visions of sanctified grandeur, causing me a mild annoyance. I glanced at the screen to find a message from my assistant in Eden.

Watch the news!

The ripple of annoyance shot through me once again. I didn't tolerate receiving orders, then again, my faithful servant would have never given one if it hadn't been urgent. With mild apprehension, I found myself returning to my office to do as I was bid in privacy. Pressing the touchscreen on my desk, the door locked and the blinds closed automatically while light turned to illuminate the area to a degree I found most pleasing.

Another quick tap brought my flatscreen television alive, and I scrolled through the channels. I needed a news channel that repeated the latest developments ad nauseum throughout the day.

After making my selection, barely two seconds passed before a tall man with light brown hair and steady blue eyes stepped in front of a veritable sea of microphones. He introduced himself as Supervisory Special Agent Aiden Parrish of the FBI's Behavioral Analysis Unit.

An FBI press conference in Lavender Lake.

A ferocious wave of unease flooded my mind, and I turned up the volume so as not to miss a word.

"We have an update on the two cases we are currently investigating in Lavender Lake. The first update is that pregnant missing person, Lindsay Welsh, who was abducted two nights ago from The Greengrocer parking lot, has been found alive."

"No." The word was barely a breath.

"Mrs. Welsh is in critical but stable condition and appears to have given birth while in captivity. Her newborn twin daughters remain missing."

"No." The word was much louder this time. They were lying. Lindsay Welsh died. I replayed the scene in my mind.

Sasha killed her. She smothered her. I witnessed the act with my very own eyes.

But...

I mentally scrolled through all my options. Tamara. Tamara was on staff at Lavender Lake Medical Center. One quick call, and she would either confirm or deny this bit of news. Then, if it turned out to be true, she would ensure this problem was taken care of in an efficient and timely manner.

How thankful I was for Tamara's faithful service.

As I reached for my phone, the agent began speaking again.

"A second pregnant victim, Wendy Arnold, also went missing just this morning. She was found not long ago, alive, but expired shortly after her arrival at the hospital."

The agent's eyes were cool. Confident.

I disliked him immediately. The men of this world were entirely too pleased with themselves. Their incompetence was the exact reason my mission must be successful.

Think. You need to think.

I sank into my desk chair and blew out a long, calming breath.

Tamara would take care of Lindsay. And Wendy would have been found with her baby. The baby's presence severed the connection between the two women's abductions.

"Wendy Arnold also gave birth while abducted, and the whereabouts of her infant remain unknown."

Thumping, pulsating beats flashed through my brain.

The agent was lying. He had to be. The FBI was simply trying to flush out any information they possibly could by sharing falsehoods with the general public.

My eyes stayed locked on the television screen as I picked up my phone once again.

I could call my assistant, but he was on the island and of no help to me in this moment.

Roger.

Yes. My brother was nearby and always a faithful servant to The Dream. He would help in any way he possibly could.

The phone rang a single time before an automated message answered my call. *"I'm sorry. The number you've reached has been disconnected or is no longer in service."*

I stared at the screen, certain there must have been some mistake. Had I misdialed? Had the number been erroneously changed in my contacts? The phone dropped from my hand when the godforsaken agent held up a picture of a woman.

"We are currently searching for Alexandra 'Sasha' Romansky. She is a person of interest in both kidnappings."

Frozen, I could only gape at the screen.

Sasha's too-dark blonde curls, flawed, freckled skin, and abnormally large blue eyes stared back at me. I had allowed an unclean woman to play a huge role in the execution of my plans, and now an agent was showing her most recent mugshot to the crowd.

To the world.

"What in the hell is happening?"

So much time had passed since I'd experienced this sensation. I often witnessed it on the faces of others, but my pure heart ensured that I was spared from such a base, human emotion.

Yet here it was.

Fear.

I was trembling with fear.

20

Perfectly spaced palm trees lined both sides of the road as Winter drove them toward the office of fertility specialist Dr. Amanda Jenkins. Brightly colored business buildings appeared, one after the other, tidy and cheerful against the sunny Florida sky.

Brochure worthy scenes surrounding them, Autumn couldn't help but think of the thick backwoods and brutal swampland where women were being deposited directly after giving birth.

Those images wouldn't exactly bring the tourists in droves.

Neither would a few shots of the trailer park Sarah had ended up in.

A side-glance toward Winter assured Autumn that her friend's hands were clenched on the steering wheel. The time had come to share some details from her impromptu visit to Sarah's "house."

Winter couldn't drive and strangle Autumn at the same time.

"Last night...I tried to find Sarah."

Winter's head whipped toward her. "I *knew* it."

Autumn pointed back to the road, and Winter's head whipped back in the correct position for someone in control of a moving vehicle.

"Did you?" Autumn raised an eyebrow.

"Okay." Winter's thumbs beat an unknown rhythm on the wheel. "I suspected it. What happened?"

"The address the National Name Check Program gave me led me straight to a trailer park that was so run-down and old that..." Autumn wasn't sure how to finish. She had nothing against trailer parks or those who lived in them. Just this one. She stared out the window, opting to avoid Winter's gaze.

"And...?"

Autumn sighed heavily. "It was truly one of the most terrible areas I'd ever seen. Run-down. Trashy. Desperate. Not a pretty sight."

Winter remained silent, her eyes focused on the road. Autumn knew her friend was attempting to let her speak freely. Opinions would be shared later.

"There was a group of mailboxes right at the entry to the park...and I thought it'd be simple enough to check Sarah's." Autumn's stomach tensed. The string of events that followed flashed through her mind.

"Please tell me you didn't go through your sister's mail." Winter's tone gave a clear indication that she expected the story to get worse.

"Of course not. I found the mailbox with her address numbers and...I peeked. I *only* peeked. Her name was definitely on the envelopes." Autumn tapped her fingers absently on the arm rest. "So I decided to do a walkthrough and see if I could find her specific trailer."

"Late at night?" Winter shot her an incredulous glare. "In the dark? *Alone?*"

Don't worry. The next part is worse.

"I'm a big girl, Winter."

Winter's knuckles were slowly turning white on the steering wheel. "Yep. Keep going."

"I couldn't find it. The numbers on the trailers were mostly missing or impossible to read. I was going to leave but I ran into a..." Autumn bit her lip, trying to make her sister's situation sound not quite so awful, "friend...of Sarah's. He was nice enough to show me where she lived."

The hope that this sugarcoated version would pass Winter's intuition check had been a longshot. The possibility always existed, however, that Winter would go easy on her no matter what she sensed.

"Friend? He?" Winter's nostrils flared. "What little details are you leaving out?"

Okay. Possibility gone.

Autumn closed her eyes and decided the best route was to just spew the whole debacle out at once. They'd be at Dr. Jenkins's office soon and feeding Winter a tidbit at a time was exhausting.

"He mistook me for Sarah. We always resembled each other so closely. I suppose that never changed." Autumn wound a strand of her bright red hair around her finger.

"You *did* tell him you *weren't* Sarah, right?" Winter's tone had grown severe, and Autumn was surprised that heat wasn't rising from the top of her head. "Autumn? *Right?*"

"I knew he'd be a lot more likely to help me if he thought he knew me. He wanted to sleep with me...Sarah. So, I asked him to take me back to 'my place.'" Autumn finger quoted the words with an inward cringe. This story was even more terrible in the telling.

"And...?"

"And he did."

"Autumn Trent! You let a *complete stranger* who fully

intended on getting in your panties lead you around in the dark? Was he even *sober*?" Shouting. Winter was straight shouting now.

"He *wasn't* sober, and if he *had* been, he might have figured out I wasn't Sarah. He took me straight to her trailer, but before he had a chance to get inside, I pretended to get sick. I ran inside and locked him out." Autumn was aware of the risk she had taken.

She was also aware that the need to find Sarah had grown unbearable.

"I could spank you. Someone should. He could have turned violent in a split-second. What if—"

Autumn held up a hand. She wanted Winter to focus on what was most important. "Sarah wasn't there, but that trailer was definitely hers. She had a picture of us, as kids, on her fridge and more mail all over her table. The place was a mess...trashed. Depressing."

Autumn knew all the "what if" scenarios that were playing through Winter's mind because they'd already gone through her own. Winter's head was shaking back and forth, and her lips pressed firmly together.

"The guy broke in. The lock was shit. He assumed I was playing around. He asked me if his money wasn't good enough anymore." Autumn pressed her fingers to her temples. As horrible as this was, she was also glad to be sharing it with her friend.

"His money? He was planning on paying you...Sarah...for *sex*?" Disbelief and horror blazed in Winter's blue eyes.

"She's a prostitute, Winter. Sarah is a stripper and a prostitute. She works at some strip club called The Booby Trap."

"Tell me you did not go there next!" The words were closer to a savage growl.

"I didn't." *The only smart decision I made that night.*

"So how did you get *out* of there?" Winter demanded. Her

knuckles were ghost white against the wheel. Autumn wondered if her friend would have ripped it off entirely were they parked instead of driving.

"I kicked the douchebag in the balls and ran." Autumn chanced a side-glance at her fuming friend and quickly returned her gaze to the window. Autumn couldn't think of a single sentiment that would comfort or reassure Winter. The string of decisions *had* been reckless. She had fully expected this reaction from Winter, if not worse.

Winter was slowly inhaling and exhaling. Guilt spread through Autumn's veins when she thought of how easily the entire situation could have been handled differently. *Handled better.*

After a few minutes of tension-filled silence, Winter cleared her throat. "I understand better than anyone how badly you want to find your sister. You *know* I do. But you *have to stop* making these *ridiculously dangerous decisions.*"

Autumn turned in her seat to better face her friend. "Really? I seem to remember offering similar advice to this black-haired FBI agent I know who, in the dead of night, ran into a crumbling church searching for her sibling." Autumn's voice rose a few octaves. "A church, mind you, that screamed pure evil from its every brick and then tried to kill us by collapsing around our heads."

The last few words seemed to echo around the quiet interior of the Escalade as Winter's expression flashed through a series of emotions. Finally, she sighed. "You're right. I wasn't a very good role model, was I?"

Autumn snorted. "That depends on how you define good. If good means that you've modeled bravery and love and determination, then I'd say you're an excellent role model."

Winter peered over at her through narrowed eyes. "Are you shrinking me?"

Autumn laughed. "Depends on if it's working or not."

A growl rumbled low in Winter's throat, but she had relaxed, and her knuckles had returned to their normal color. "Maybe." She reached over and placed a hand on Autumn's arm. "I really am sorry. I forget sometimes that just because you're not Quantico trained yet that you can't take care of yourself."

Autumn covered Winter's hand with her own, absorbing the swirling emotions of her friend. "And I sometimes forget that I can't save the seven billion people of this world all by myself. I promise to start asking for help."

Winter sniffed, and Autumn's eyes burned from the love and respect the two of them shared for one another. She didn't need special powers to feel it either.

"Promise me." Winter squeezed her hand. "Promise me that, if you go searching for Sarah again, let me know. At the very least, I'll ride along with you."

"I promise. Totally. One hundred percent."

"Okay." Winter placed both hands on the wheel again, appearing to be finished with her lecture. She wasn't. "Aiden would absolutely *kill you* if you told him what you just told me."

A spark of rebellion flashed in Autumn's chest. "Aiden doesn't need to know. What I did wasn't work related. He's my boss, not my dad."

Or my lover.

Now, where in the hell had that thought come from?

A few minutes later, Winter pulled the Escalade to a stop in front of Dr. Jenkins's office building and turned to Autumn. She exuded support. "I'm not mad. I worry about you. Friends do that."

Heat rushed to Autumn's cheeks. "It's possible that I give you too many reasons to worry. I'll work on it, I promise."

Winter bear-hugged her, sending all her concern and love rushing through Autumn's mind.

Autumn nearly cried. Causing her friend this anxiety had never been her intention. She'd gone to find Sarah alone in part to *avoid* placing her troubles on anyone else's shoulders.

All the time she spent in foster care longing for a loving family and good home had taught her one very clear rule— do not make yourself a bother to anyone. Ever.

Autumn supposed the notion was still embedded in her psyche. Just one more spillover from her youth.

She'd work on it, she promised herself as they exited the vehicle and began approaching the large, brick building.

"Do you think Noah wishes he were here instead of back at the station?" Autumn carefully scanned their surroundings.

"I think Aiden needed his help researching sperm banks and fertility doctors. I *know* he needed his help handling the tip line. Can you imagine how nuts those calls have gotta be at this point?"

"Ya know, for not liking each other, they make a pretty good team." Autumn grinned mischievously. "A modern-day *Dukes of Hazzard* duo. Only crankier and in crisp suits."

Winter emitted one unchecked giggle before steeling herself back into professional mode. "Let's do this."

The glass front door opened into a reception area. The usual rows of padded chairs, a few coffee tables, and stacks of magazines gave the room a cozy, familiar atmosphere.

Nothing weird about this place. Yet.

A perky, small-boned receptionist greeted them right away. "Can I help you?" Focusing her gaze on the agents, she promptly became aware that the two women were not patients. The following gulp was audible.

"I'm Special Agent Winter Black with the FBI, and this is Dr. Autumn Trent. We'd like to speak with Dr. Jenkins if she's in." Winter's voice was calm but firm as she flashed her badge.

"Excuse me for one second. I'll check." The receptionist scurried away, and Autumn glanced around her work area.

Seems normal. Feels normal.

The tiny woman reappeared, her cheeks flushed. "Dr. Jenkins is on lunch break, but she said she'd see you in her office. So, if you'll just follow me please."

She led them down a main hallway and took a left, then opened and held the door to Dr. Jenkins's office. Winter stepped past her with Autumn close behind.

A pretty woman with a warm, friendly smile—Autumn guessed her at forty, perhaps a little older—was sitting behind a large and mildly disarrayed desk. Dr. Amanda Jenkins clicked a few keys with one hand and placed a half-eaten sandwich down with the other. She wiped her hands on a paper napkin as she stood.

Autumn studied the doctor's face for any signs of discomfort or panic. There were none as she examined the badge Winter held out.

"I'm Special Agent Winter Black, and this is Dr. Autumn Trent. We're here on behalf of the FBI, and we'd like to discuss a very important matter with you."

"Of course. Sit, sit." She indicated the two leather chairs facing her desk. "How exactly can I be of service to you ladies today?"

Winter took the lead. "We're investigating a case involving Lindsay Welsh. Perhaps you read of her disappearance or caught the news conference today?"

"Yes. Both. I had read about her going missing, and I've been praying for her ever since. As I understood the information, she's been found alive, yes? Her husband must be so relieved." Dr. Jenkins put a hand to her ebony forehead and her expression went somber. "This world."

"Lindsay was a patient of yours, correct?" As Winter

maintained the conversation, Autumn concentrated on the woman's mannerisms and body language.

"She was," Amanda confirmed. "I was honored that they traveled all this way for fertility treatments."

Winter frowned. "Do you know why?"

Dr. Jenkins's nodded. "Lindsay's family lives in the area, and from what I understand, they were impressed with the success rates our clinic has enjoyed."

"So, they drove from Georgia to Florida for treatments?"

"Yes." Her teeth were white against her dark skin. "It was a great compliment with wonderful results." The smile faltered. "Up to now, that is." She sighed. "That poor woman. Poor family."

"Would you be willing to answer a few questions regarding Mrs. Welsh?" Winter crossed her legs and leaned forward. "You may be able to help us immensely with this investigation."

"I promise to help as much and far as I possibly can, with respect to patient confidentiality, of course."

Autumn noted the genuine, caring energy emanating from Dr. Jenkins and smiled before asking her first question. "When Lindsay and Josh Welsh came to you seeking help for their infertility problems, what types of treatments did you recommend for them? And are those options different from what you would recommend to other patients?"

"These days, there are many roads to parenthood for the fertility challenged, and I always ask if adoption has been considered before the process begins. There are so many children in foster care just waiting for a place to call home."

Autumn endured the immediate gut punch and managed to keep her expression pleasant. "That is true. Do the couples you see often choose adoption?"

Dr. Jenkins shook her head. "Honestly, the couples that come to me usually haven't given up all hope of carrying their own genetically related child. Occasionally, surrogacy is considered, but the majority of couples want to carry a baby themselves."

"Aside from adoption and surrogacy, what are their remaining options?" Gentle prodding was important for these types of interviews, so no one could be accused of leading the witness, but a part of Autumn wanted to just jump past all the bullshit.

Dr. Jenkins waved a hand in the air. "There are many. We have medications specifically designed to enhance fertility, but they don't work for everyone. Then you've got assisted hatching, intrauterine insemination, and in vitro fertilization, just to name a few."

"In vitro fertilization as in IVF?" Winter tilted her head. "Josh and Lindsay Welsh used IVF to become pregnant, didn't they?"

Dr. Jenkins gazed from Winter to Autumn. "In vitro fertilization involves combining egg cells and sperm in a laboratory and then transferring the developed embryo into the woman's uterus for implantation. There are sperm banks across the country that allow couples to view and choose their own donor, if needed."

"Would you happen to know the specific sperm bank the Welsh couple used?" Innocent as the question came out, Autumn knew it crossed doctor-patient confidentiality lines.

But just that one tiny piece of information could break the case wide open.

Dr. Jenkins said nothing. She turned to her computer and tapped a few keys, then returned her attention to the agents. "If you'll excuse me, I really should wash these messy hands. Sandwich crumbs everywhere."

The doctor gave a very obvious and overly long gaze toward her computer and left the room. Winter flew around the desk faster than Autumn could even stand, grabbing a nearby notepad and pen.

Autumn glanced at the door while Winter jotted down the information, and both of them were seated in their chairs when the doctor returned.

"Anything else you need from me today, Agent Black? Dr. Trent?"

"I think we're good. Thank you so much for your time, Dr. Jenkins." Winter extended her hand, and the doctor gave it a hearty shake.

Autumn followed suit. The rush of warmth and genuine goodness flowing from the doctor's handshake set Autumn's mind at ease. Amanda Jenkins was a kind, honest woman.

No question.

Gazing at the numerous baby pictures tacked to the hallway wall, Autumn smiled. Dr. Jenkins had helped each of those little ones come to be. The world needed more people just like her.

As she followed Winter out the door and toward the Escalade, Autumn's smile faded.

All the good in the world didn't change the fact that someone—a very *bad* someone—was still out there, free as a bird, and capable of unimaginable cruelty.

21

"Tacos or burgers?" Food currently took priority over all else. Winter had fought herself not to eat the rest of Dr. Jenkins's sandwich when she left the room.

"Burgers. Too hot for tacos." Autumn was always hungry.

Winter snorted. "Wow. Limits on spicy food intake? I'm shocked."

Autumn turned the air vent until it hit her face. "I blame Florida."

"Dr. Jenkins is a saint, huh? She just saved us a load of time. We would have needed warrants to get that information by force. But voila...there it was." Winter pulled into a burger place and headed straight for the drive thru.

"Dr. Jenkins is an amazing person," Autumn agreed quietly.

"To say the least. I could have *kissed* that woman on the way out." Winter studied the menu. "Whacha want?"

Autumn raised her eyebrows. "Honestly? A super-sized one of everything."

"Roger that." Winter proceeded to place an order that

would have put the men to shame had they been there. "We gotta eat while we drive. We're not too far away."

Once the food arrived, Autumn doled out the burgers and fries from two large brown sacks while Winter drove. Autumn seemed off. Too quiet. Withdrawn. Granted, they were eating, but Winter knew something was up.

"Okay. Spill it. What's wrong?" Sneak attack or not, Winter was done dragging information out of her friend. They'd already played that game today.

Autumn didn't even attempt to put up a fight. "All those pictures. So many babies. Just got me thinking about the whole endometriosis thing."

"Do you want a baby?" Winter couldn't hide the surprise in her voice. It was something they'd never talked about in any depth.

"No. Yes. Maybe. I don't know." Autumn took a big bite of her burger and chewed thoughtfully for a while. Winter waited patiently until she swallowed. "It's so awful that so many people struggle to have a baby and are forced to go through IVF and whatnot to make that wish come true. And then some psychopath just *steals* that joy from them in such a horrible, brutal way." Autumn shuddered.

Winter observed her friend's slumped posture. "The abductions are terrible. Agreed. That's why we're trying so hard to find this asshole."

"Yeah." Autumn continued to stare at the passing scenery.

"You sure you're okay?" For the millionth time, she wished she could just reach out, grab Autumn's arm, and instantly know.

"I just...I don't like having my options taken off the table before...before I've even sat down." Autumn's green eyes were full of turmoil.

Winter understood. Becoming a parent wasn't something

she'd heavily considered yet herself. Work consumed her life. But being told that you *couldn't...*

That was different.

"Keep in mind, Autumn, that all of those baby pictures you're referring to belong to people who thought they couldn't have kids either." Winter was relieved to see Autumn's face brighten at the thought.

The GPS informed them that they were nearing their destination, and Winter brought the SUV to a slow crawl toward the main gate of XY Cryolabs.

"Jesus." Autumn craned her neck to take in the picture before them.

The building was quite impressive, towering up a full five stories of striking, gleaming white.

"How in the world do they keep anything, let alone the outer walls of a giant building, that incredibly clean?" Winter struggled to accept the sight.

Autumn poked her on the shoulder and pointed to three men pressure washing the building's east-facing wall. "There. That's how."

A guard approached their vehicle as they came to a stop. Winter whipped out her badge to show her credentials.

He didn't appear impressed in the slightest. "Wait here." He walked into the guard post to make a phone call.

A familiar ringtone filled the vehicle, and Winter lifted her phone. Noah.

"Make it fast, Dalton." Winter kept a careful eye on the guard.

"I miss you too, Agent Black. Update for you. I got ahold of Alex Gorski-Wilson, and she was more than happy to share Patricia's fertility doctor's name, Penelope Harris, *and* the sperm bank they used. XY Cryolabs." Noah was clearly pleased with himself and the information he'd gathered.

Winter shot Autumn a superior smile. "Well, Agent

Dalton, I guess it's a good thing that Dr. Trent and I are currently waiting at the gates of XY Cryolabs."

"Seriously?"

Winter would have laughed, but the guard was on his way back. "Hold on a sec, Noah."

"Dr. Russell Brandt is onsite and would be pleased to meet with you both. Pull in straight and park in the lot to the left. Just follow the sidewalk to the main entrance after that." Pleasant enough words but delivered with a cold demeanor.

"Thanks." Winter pulled ahead as the automatic gate slid open. The knowledge that it would immediately close and lock behind them was unsettling. "Still there?"

"Yes, and I have *more* news." Excitement edged Noah's voice.

"Shoot." Winter pulled the Escalade into a designated parking spot.

"I tracked down Wendy Arnold's ex-boyfriend. Complete and total douche, but he was more than willing to claim responsibility for their baby. He wanted to make the fact crystal clear that he 'didn't need no damn sperm donor 'cause he wasn't firin' no blanks.' I think I got that right."

Winter rolled her eyes. "How romantic."

Noah chuckled. "Exactly. Still trying to get Brad Conlon on the phone. I'll let you know if and when that happens."

"How's the tip line going? Anything?" Winter mentally crossed her fingers that something helpful had been phoned in.

Noah snarled. "We've got the usual influx of crackpots jamming the line. Detective Cohen is pulling in some more people to help handle the tips. All that basically means is sifting through the ocean of bullshit we're drowning in. But at least I'll be back out in the field."

Winter glanced at Autumn, who'd been privy to the entire

conversation. She was shaking her head in frustration. They'd known there'd be an insane rush of useless calls but dealing with people's stupidity in real time was always maddening.

"One last thing. We've been narrowing down the list of missing pregnant women across the country to *only* the ones with blonde hair and blue eyes."

"How many, Noah?" Winter wasn't sure she wanted to know.

"Fourteen. But we've only gone back three years so far. There'll be more."

By the time they ended the call, the mood was solemn as she and Autumn entered the XY Cryolabs building.

And holy hell, why was the interior so freaking white too? The glare was giving her a headache, and Winter had experienced enough of those to last a lifetime.

Two lifetimes. Maybe three.

The afternoon sun bounced off the spotless marble. Winter glimpsed Autumn squinting in protest as well. The extent to which the whiteness was maintained was utterly absurd.

"Hello. I'm Olive, Dr. Brandt's secretary. Follow me, and I'll take you to him." Neat and efficient, Olive's blue pencil skirt was the first splash of color XY Cryolabs had provided. The secretary was of average build, brunette, with friendly brown eyes.

She led them to a clear glass elevator centered in the first-floor foyer. Olive's face retained a decidedly professional smile as they soared to the fifth floor.

Fastest. Elevator. Ever.

Winter and Autumn exchanged a glance, and she almost smiled when Autumn touched her stomach. This ride was making her regret her large meal too.

The automatic glass door slid open, and Olive's heels

click-clacked down another gleaming white hallway as they exited the elevator. "Right this way."

They passed four identical spotless white doors before Olive opened one and ushered them inside. An attractive, smiling blond man stood as they entered but stayed behind his oversized desk. His impressive broad shoulders framed a fit physique. Light blue eyes sparkled, contrasting with his handsome tanned face.

Unsurprisingly, Dr. Russell Brandt was dressed in a white three-piece suit that appeared to be perfectly tailored to his tall, lean figure. He wore no tie, just a snowy linen button-down shirt left open at the neck.

"Dr. Brandt, here are your visitors. Would anyone like some refreshments? Espresso? Water? Croissant?" Olive's bright smile shot from the doctor to Winter to Autumn.

"No, thank you," Winter responded, and Autumn echoed the sentiment.

"Thank you, Olive." Dr. Brandt dismissed his secretary and sat, pleasantly waving a hand at two chairs that had clearly been placed for the agents' comfort.

The unrepenting white continued all throughout the doctor's office, and Winter began to wonder if perhaps the man was a germaphobe. The pristine cleanliness surpassed any protocol that Winter had ever witnessed. XY Cryolabs was *intensely* clean.

Winter also noted that, though his mannerisms were friendly, Dr. Brandt hadn't offered to shake their hands. He hadn't come near them.

He stared serenely at them across the giant desktop. Winter detected no trace of nervousness or unease in the man's demeanor. On the contrary, Dr. Brandt's eyes exuded blatant curiosity.

Odd. The man before them was very unmistakably odd,

and Winter wondered if Autumn had made the same deduction.

"Thank you, Dr. Brandt, for agreeing to see us so unexpectedly. I'm Special Agent Black and this is my colleague, Dr. Trent. We're here on behalf of the FBI."

Tread lightly.

Winter's vision blurred, and her head throbbed at the temples. A headache now—*here*—could completely ruin the opportunity they'd been granted.

One drop of blood on that Colonel Sanders costume and I bet his pretty head would explode right off his shoulders.

No vision came, however, and her eyesight cleared. Maybe the bright glow of her surroundings was to blame.

Refocusing on the doctor in his brilliant white suit, Winter was left with a definite impression that caution was necessary when dealing with this man. The straightforward truth of their investigation needed to stay with them. She needed a cover story. Fast.

The placid smile never faltered on Dr. Brandt's face. "How might I help you?"

Winter returned the smile. "The FBI is currently researching ways to curb the growing problem of siblings dating and even marrying each other, due to the fact that they had no knowledge of being born from the same sperm donor."

Autumn shifted in her seat but managed to keep a steady countenance despite Winter's bold-faced lie. This hadn't been the plan.

"We're hoping that you might be able to shed some light on the process and share how XY Cryolabs, in particular, works to prevent and avoid this problem." As she spoke, Winter steadily met the doctor's unwavering gaze.

Dr. Brandt steepled his hands together in a prayer-like

manner as he considered them. His unnerving, icy blue stare heightened Winter's sense of danger.

"XY Cryolabs is *the most highly trusted* sperm bank in the country. Our donors must pass a rigorous screening process. All potential donors are evaluated for medical, behavioral, and personality abnormalities."

Massive pride was evident in Dr. Brandt's tone, and Winter guessed that they were in for quite the speech.

That's just fine. Keep talking, Doc. The longer the lecture, the bigger the slip.

"We have an extensive medical and family history questionnaire along with an in-depth genetic testing procedure that rules out any potential donors who may have inherited genetic conditions."

A clock ticked tediously on the wall to her right and the mechanical beat only added to the uncomfortable order of the room.

Dr. Brandt thrummed his fingers together. "Donors who pass all the screening procedures continue to be tested while in the program. We require it. Regular physical exams, blood work, urinalysis...the monitoring of our donors is ongoing. Consistent. Thorough."

Perfect. He's obsessed with perfection.

"I personally created the XY Sibling Registry solely for this laboratory's use. Not every bank provides such an in-depth service, and as the registry is optional, not every client we see at XY Cryolabs chooses to utilize the program."

Autumn leaned forward slightly, seeming fascinated. "Does this disappoint you?"

"The lack of interest is a shame but not an unexpected one. Imperfect world, imperfect people, imperfect decisions." He shook his head sadly, but the smile remained.

Winter suspected that Dr. Brandt did not consider

himself included in that mass of "imperfect people." Pity was the word that came to her. He *pitied* the rest of the world.

"As investigators, I'm sure you're familiar with the Donor Sibling Registry that was created eighteen years ago?" Dr. Brandt raised an eyebrow.

Winter gave an authoritative nod. "Of course."

"A woman named Wendy Kramer and her son, Ryan, founded the DSR, which has become the largest online site for donor-conceived individuals. In simplest terms, the Donor Sibling Registry is a matching site."

Winter found the conversation tedious. "A truly innovative creation."

Dr. Brandt's eyes briefly narrowed, but he continued on.

"While not as refined as *my* personal program, the registry has made donor matching possible for many. A person can simply type in their donor number...an anonymous code assigned by the fertility clinic...and connect with others born from the sperm or eggs of the same donor."

"Remarkable concept," Autumn affirmed in a sweet voice.

"But again, only on an entirely voluntary basis. Contact is achieved through mutual consent. The semantics of such an undertaking are more complicated than the average human mind could possibly comprehend." The arrogance of the doctor was nauseating.

"We're specifically researching ways to integrate various registries." Winter was unsure as to whether such an integration had already been done and prayed that she hadn't just betrayed her complete lack of knowledge on the subject.

Were they truly investigating such an issue, the agents both, without question, would have entered this meeting with solid knowledge gained from hours of previous research.

Winter was positive that Dr. Brandt was intelligent

enough to know this, but the only option they had was to continue pushing for information.

"I see." His expression relayed no hint of suspicion.

Flipping through one of the many polished brochures Dr. Brandt proudly pushed toward them, Autumn tilted her pretty red head innocently. "Do you find that any particular donor gets chosen more than the others? Are there any limits in place as to the number of children one donor's sperm can produce?"

Winter had trouble pulling her eyes away from Dr. Brandt's face for even a moment. His smooth voice and crystal blue eyes were nearly hypnotic.

Something was wrong—off—with this man. She was certain.

But high intelligence often carried the weight of being different. Albert Einstein was a perfect example of that.

Puffing out a condescending sigh, Dr. Brandt addressed Autumn's question. "That particular subject is highly controversial. Many countries across the world have imposed limits on the number of offspring a single donor can sire, but not the United States. Here it is left to the individual sperm bank's discretion."

"What makes the topic so highly controversial?" Autumn persisted.

"There are many who believe that the proposal of imposing such limits infringes upon an individual's right to privacy and procreation. Should the government have control over who has children with whom?" Heat laced the words.

"What's XY Cryolab's policy?" Winter knew they had hit a nerve.

"The American Society of Reproductive Medicine sperm donor guideline recommends, but does not dictate, that there should be no more than ten same-donor births per population of 800,000. At XY Cryolabs, we strive to maintain those limits and even lower, if possible."

"How do you track something so *complicated*, Dr. Brandt?" The fascination in Autumn's voice was impressive.

He clearly enjoyed her attention. "Through highly sophisticated proprietary software. And rest assured that every single precaution we've discussed also applies to donated eggs. Eggs are also available for purchase at XY Cryolabs, though that extraction process is, of course, much more complicated than sperm donations."

Dr. Brandt had grown visibly bored, and Winter racked her brain for any other possible questions she could ask. Autumn appeared equally stumped.

Their time was running out.

"Would we possibly be able to take a tour through the facility?" Winter was aware that she was grasping at straws now, but what else could she ask? Did you happen to murder a couple of new mothers and steal their babies? The man's lawyer would laugh all the way through the shiny white halls.

"I'm afraid that would be impossible due to the highly sensitive nature of the labs. My apologies." Not a hint of regret shadowed Dr. Brandt's face.

"Okay. Well, I believe that's all." A quick peek at Autumn confirmed her statement. "Thank you so much for your time, Dr. Brandt."

He smiled graciously and hit a button on his desk phone. Within seconds, Olive was opening the door and ushering them out.

Dr. Brandt stood, but still didn't venture to step around his massive desk.

No Autumn Trent handshake in sight for us. Dammit.

Defeat weighed on her shoulders as Winter followed Olive and Autumn to the glass elevator. They had failed to unearth even a miniscule bit of evidence regarding the case.

The elevator began its streamlined journey down. As they passed level three, blood began to trickle from Winter's nose. Barely having processed its warmth, a vision slammed into her psyche.

A sea of blonde children, from newborns to what she discerned to be ten or possibly eleven-year-olds sprawled across a sandy beach. Numerous nannies, dressed only in white, tended to the children.

Babies gathered and played under sun shelters while the older children laughed and built sandcastles. The stretch of towheaded little ones was never-ending, covering mile after mile of beach.

"Dear…" Olive's eyes went wide, "are you okay?"

Autumn's arm shot around Winter, and she pressed a tissue into her hand. Once the doors opened, Olive quickly led them to the nearest restroom.

"I'll wait here while you freshen up." Olive showed a mild but genuine concern.

When the door closed, Winter grabbed a wad of paper towels and pressed them to her nose. "Please tell me I didn't just bleed all over the Angel Soft Palace."

Autumn snorted. "No sacrificial blood was spilled upon the holy shrine of Brandt. You're in the clear." She lowered her voice. "What did you see?"

Winter shook her head and turned on the water. "Let's talk about it in the car."

A few minutes later, Olive was indeed waiting for them. "Everything okay?"

Winter forced herself to look embarrassed, which wasn't a stretch. "Fast elevator."

Olive's smile faltered a bit. "Yes. State of the art, as is everything in this building."

Before exiting XY Cryolabs, Autumn extended her hand to the friendly secretary. "Thank you for your troubles."

Olive shook Autumn's hand without hesitation, and Winter closely studied her friend's expression.

As soon as the main door closed behind them, Autumn filled her in. "Olive is most definitely in love with her boss, but I didn't get the sense that she knew of anything bad going on in the building."

Winter sighed. Still nothing.

Autumn insisted she drive back to the station to reconvene with the team, and Winter gave her the details of her vision as she drove. Emitting a low growl, she pulled the Escalade back onto the highway. "So, we're supposed to go tell the team that the only thing we learned today was that sperm banks are moderately creepy places?"

Winter snorted. "No joke. We have zero evidence, aside from my disturbing intuition. No evidence, no warrant. And dammit, *we need a warrant.*"

"How many babies did you see in that vision?" The physical contact between the women had already informed Autumn of Winter's insight.

Winter shook her head, struggling to recall the details more vividly. "I don't think there was a number. Just a line of little blonde-haired babies and kids that stretched out to infinity."

"Infinity?"

Winter slumped in her seat, defeat heavy on her shoulders. "And beyond."

22

R ivulets of sweat slunk down Roger Brandt's body.
Missing newborn. Dead mother. Amber Alert.

The RV's radio relentlessly kept him informed of the current FBI investigation. Roger couldn't bring himself to turn it off.

A description of the baby wasn't yet available. He gained peace from that fact.

The baby in question could be a boy *or* a girl. White, black, Hispanic—no one knew.

There was absolutely no reason for him to believe a target had been placed on his back. Yet he had exited the interstate and taken to the north, heading for backroads almost immediately.

Better safe than sorry.

He'd said this phrase to Amanda when she asked about the route change. Bumping and bouncing along on ill-maintained roads in a giant vehicle wasn't ideal, but neither was prison.

The public had no real information because the FBI

couldn't provide any. They had nothing—just a dead woman's body.

Roger and his little family were going to be just fine.

He'd managed to clear out his bank account, purchase the RV, and pack only what they needed to travel and survive. The exit from the compound had gone smoothly enough, but Roger wished they had left sooner.

The Brandts had been on the road for less than an hour. They weren't far enough away. Roger didn't even have a clear recollection of what the time had been when he snuck Amanda and the baby off the ranch.

The plan was to just *go* and figure things out on the way. He knew there were ample campgrounds and RV lots where they could hook up to water and electricity. Granted, without a GPS, Roger wasn't quite sure where these havens were.

He wasn't lost, per se. He just wasn't completely sure of where they were.

But he planned to stop soon and buy a burner phone. That would provide a GPS and also give them a way to communicate if needed.

For now, just continuing to head north and staying off the grid would be enough.

He hoped.

Eventually, they would find a place to settle down. With new identities, they would have a real life far away from his psychotic brother and Eden and The Dream and the vessels and the murders.

The goal for today was simply to cross the border into Tennessee before stopping to rest. Even with the Amber Alert blaring out across the state, their plan seemed achievable.

The FBI issued alerts such as this when they were desperate.

And despite the constant spew of information from the radio, Roger's deep source of concern was presently not the FBI.

The baby would not stop crying.

Frequent checks in the rearview mirror assured him that Amanda had been and continued to do all she could think of to comfort the poor little guy.

They were fully stocked on formula, diapers, clothes—any possible item a baby could need. Roger had made sure to grab it all.

Yet the screaming continued. The baby wailed and screamed incessantly until he would finally fall asleep for a few minutes. But as soon as his eyes opened, the chaos resumed at full volume.

"Something's wrong with him, Roger." Amanda must have repeated this exact same sentence at least fifty times in the last half hour. She paced the narrow floor, holding the baby to her. She'd bounced, fed, patted, burped, sung, and checked his diaper repeatedly.

Absolutely nothing worked.

When the crying first started, neither of them had been keen on the idea of removing the baby from his car seat while the RV was moving. Doing so would be illegal and dangerous.

They were already fully stocked in both of those categories.

After the crying turned to flat-out shrieking, the car seat issue became the least of their problems. *Any* action that helped comfort the distressed infant was worth the risk, law be damned.

The predicament, of course, was that nothing had actually calmed the babe. He was screaming louder than ever, and Amanda was now sobbing along with him.

Hell. Maybe I'm not sweating. Maybe I'm crying too.

"He's turning blue!" Amanda howled, collapsing in the passenger seat with the inconsolable baby boy.

Roger took a quick side-glance. Amanda was right. The baby was a definite shade of blue. Was that normal? Did babies turn blue when they cried?

Roger didn't know. He was beginning to realize that he barely knew *anything* about babies at all.

"Amanda." He said her name but forced himself to stop. Surely he wasn't about to say the words that had almost left his mouth. Fear and doubt were simply messing with his mind.

This baby was their chance at having the family they'd always dreamed of. Amanda deserved that much, and dammit, so did he.

The stars had aligned to give them a precious baby boy. Fate had found Roger Brandt that morning.

Hadn't he promised the dying woman he'd save her son? And after placing the baby in Amanda's arms, he'd promised his wife that her days of endless tears were over.

Over.

The string of events had fit together like a jigsaw puzzle, and the resulting image was lovely—perfect.

But that image wasn't materializing. A bawling infant, a distraught wife, foreign winding backroads, and no actual destination at all.

Nothing was going right. Roger *had* to say the words. "I think it's time we abandon this entire thing."

Amanda didn't immediately understand. Her puffy, glazed-over eyes stared directly at him, showing no signs of comprehension whatsoever.

"We shouldn't have taken this baby. I shouldn't have. And we certainly shouldn't have left the family. This is repayment for our wrongs, Amanda. God is judging us. We abandoned The Dream and took what wasn't ours for the taking."

Amanda didn't move. She only held the baby tight and continued to stare at Roger.

"We can put the baby somewhere safe, someplace where he'll be found, and go home. We can pretend none of this ever happened."

And they truly could. Roger could have their phones reactivated and simply say the disconnect had been some type of fluke. No big deal. Stupid shit like that happened all the time with cellular companies.

He and Amanda only had to go home. Slide right back into their normal life. He'd tell Russell how they'd taken a shine to this sweet little RV. Just went on a fun little drive—a test run. That's all.

Russell would believe him, because Russell wouldn't want to believe the alternative. That his brother had attempted to leave the family. Roger had abandoned The Dream.

Intelligent as he was, Russell would refuse to consider any other possibility. Russell loved him, in his own way. His brother would simply be relieved to have his family intact.

Roger knew it would work.

Or at least, it *could* work. There was always the other possibility—Russell could be so far gone that he truly considered Roger equal to all of Eden's *other* "family members." Anyone who attempted to abandon Eden was dealt with in the same manner.

Elimination.

Roger shook his head in frustration. No. They would go back, and his brother would be nothing other than thrilled to see him. Roger was his *actual family*. That still meant something.

They had to turn around.

Another glance at Amanda informed him that she would never—not in a million years—go for it. And if Roger forced her to, she'd never forgive him. He'd lose her forever, even if she slept right beside him for the next forty years.

And he highly doubted that Amanda would allow herself to exist for another forty years.

Roger Brandt could not lose his Amanda. He'd loved her since he was twelve and she only ten. They'd been best friends, and the friendship had grown into something much more during their teenage years.

Roger had married Amanda the very day after she turned eighteen. The only issue that he'd never been able to fix for them was putting a baby in his wife's arms. That one missing piece had torn his wife apart for years, and now there was so little left of the girl he'd fallen in love with...

Amanda had reached a point of deep depression that absolutely terrified him.

But today, he'd put that baby boy in her arms, and she had smiled. For the first time in years, she'd *genuinely smiled*. Whatever was broken inside of her had patched in an instant.

Amanda had immediately loved the infant, and the baby had seemed equally enamored with his new mother.

But now. The screaming. The endless, hopeless wails.

"No." Amanda spoke finally. "*No*, Roger. You can't put shit back in the donkey. No."

The baby's screams were now tiny little gasps. Amanda gazed down at the little boy, and Roger became aware of one very certain truth.

Were the baby to die now, his wife would lose any last connection to reality. The thread would simply break, and alive or dead, Amanda would be *gone*.

He passed by a road sign that informed him they were exactly eight miles away from the town of Lovely Day, population fifteen thousand. The town was big enough to have a hospital.

Not giving himself time to reconsider, he shared his new

plan with Amanda. "We'll drive to this next town and take the baby to the ER. They'll be able to fix whatever is wrong with him. We'll just say we were on vacation. You went into labor a few weeks early."

Amanda's eyes lit bright with hope.

"We're just on our way home, and the baby started screaming. We didn't want to take a chance, so we stopped in. We're far enough away from Lavender Lake that no one will suspect he's the baby from the Amber Alert. They wouldn't even know what sex to check for."

"Yes! Yes. We'll do that. Thank you, Roger." She continued to rock the baby back and forth while he sped frantically toward the town.

The boy's cries were nearly *all* gasps now. Roger didn't think that Amanda had any awareness of this change. She only continued to rock and stare at the passing highway.

Her lips were moving, and he leaned toward her, attempting to understand what she was saying.

But Amanda wasn't speaking, she was singing.

In a soft, whimsical soprano, she sang, "Just one look at youuu...and I know it's going to beeee...a lovely daaaay...a lovely daaaay."

A sick dread sank into the depths of Roger's stomach.

Once they reached the town, signs led them straight to the hospital. As he pulled into the lot, Amanda let out an animalistic shriek. "He isn't breathing!"

Roger slammed on the brakes and reached for his wife. He knew what she was going to do, and if that baby really was dead, he had to stop her.

But he was too slow. Amanda had leapt from the RV with the infant clutched to her body. She was already running toward the emergency room entrance, screaming for help.

23

Sasha forced her lungs to take in a deep breath. Closing her eyes and concentrating very hard, she tried to recall any of the kind words the Father had spoken to her in the past.

She pictured his patient smile and warm blue eyes. She imagined the wonderful sensation of belonging that washed over her every time he kissed her forehead.

The Father loved her. He was the only person throughout her entire life who had loved her. All these mishaps and mess ups couldn't take away that love. The depth of his tenderness was too strong. He would forgive her, and she would do better.

She almost wished she hadn't spied on Tamara's phone conversation with the Father a few minutes ago. While the exact words and meaning had been difficult to surmise, Sasha had heard her name come out of Tamara's mouth more than once.

There had never been affection or kindness in Tamara's voice when she spoke to or about Sasha. Sasha didn't care— but she had certainly taken note.

And just now, she had been equally aware of an even colder edge in the dumpy nurse's tone. Tamara was speaking in the same flat, dead voice that she used when handling and disposing of the vessels.

But I'm not a vessel.

Was the Father angry? Of course. Sasha knew that. But she was a loyal, faithful, helpful servant. He would not remain angry forever.

Anger wasn't a part of the plan, and there was certainly no place for such a dark emotion in Eden.

When Tamara ended the phone call, Sasha had instinctively—silently—stepped into the hall bathroom. She didn't know what the punishment was for eavesdropping on the Father, but another wrongdoing could not bode well for her.

Sasha was certain of that.

She was also certain that Tamara would love nothing more than to go running straight to the Father with any news of another mistake on Sasha's part.

Hiding had occurred to her as a very attractive option. The last interaction she wished to have in this moment was with Tamara's bitchy face. She could stay in this bathroom until the nurse busied herself elsewhere, then sneak out.

Sneaking was what she did best.

But Tamara had all the information because she had spoken to the Father directly. Sasha would be able to read the Father's mood through Tamara's mannerisms. She needed to know just how bad her situation was.

This curiosity had been ingrained in her as a small child. Sasha had grown up in a home where she'd learned from a very young age that taking stock of each person's mood, schedule, wants, and needs could very well be the difference between life and death.

She'd trained herself to always stay one step ahead. That one step meant survival.

She didn't foresee herself ever breaking that particular habit, nor did she want to.

Once, when she was only five, she'd become aware of the fact that her father was on his last beer. He hadn't had this epiphany yet, but he would—soon. Worse than that, he was on his last beer and *still fully conscious*. When her father was drunk and awake, anything that angered him in the slightest turned into a beating for Sasha.

Sasha had endured many beatings.

She'd immediately stolen a twenty from her mother's purse and sprinted down the street to the corner store where her father bought his liquor and beer. The old man who owned and ran the store knew Sasha and her father—he knew the life she led.

When she begged him for a six pack "to keep daddy happy," the owner gave it to her. His eyes had been sad as her five-year-old body trudged out of the store, lugging the sack that was almost too heavy for her to carry at all.

Sasha hadn't interpreted the old man's act as one of compassion, and she wouldn't have cared regardless. Her vigilance had saved her from a beating. Nothing else mattered.

When Sasha's mother passed away, she hadn't known exactly what to expect. Her father had never been kind to her nor even pretended to love her. But he was all she had left.

He'd come to her room late one night, not long after the funeral, and sat at the foot of her bed. He was smiling, and Sasha had been filled with relief. Maybe her daddy was going to be different now.

Instead, he'd informed her that she had a new important job to do. Just like Mommy had, Sasha was going to get visits from many new friends. Man friends. And all she had to do was "make them happy."

She hadn't understood this entirely until her first new

friend put her tiny hand on the thing sticking out of his pants. As afraid as she'd been, she was more scared of what the man would do to her if she made him angry.

Men often got angry, in Sasha's experience, and the results were always terrifying.

She had done as the man instructed and kept the horror of what *he* was doing to *her* inside. The man didn't just want to play and touch. He wanted that big thing *inside of her*.

She bit her tongue until it bled while her new friend rammed her wide open. No experience in her fleeting ten years had prepared her for this level of invasion. The searing, burning anguish grew as her delicate flesh ripped to accommodate his thrusts.

Her visitor grunted and struggled to intrude her pre-pubescent body even deeper. Farther.

Sasha nearly screamed when a sharp, gashing sensation assailed her inner depths.

Her new friend seemed very pleased by this. His pounds became quicker and he emitted happy moans and groans that she was quite familiar with. She'd often heard these satisfied cries coming from Mommy's bedroom.

She was relieved by the memory. She knew this would be over soon. Mommy's visitors never stayed long.

That night she'd gone to her father, hoping for a single moment of pity from him. She was his *daughter*, after all.

She'd tearfully told him how bad the man had hurt her earlier that day, and then fell to her knees, begging her dad to never make her do that again.

He'd rolled his eyes. "It ain't gonna hurt after a few times. You ain't got no idea how much fuckin' money you made us today. You're used now, so the price is gonna have to drop, but I bet you make me more than your mama ever could."

When Sasha had continued to cry and beg, he'd simply backhanded her and gone to bed.

The visitors came every night. Sometimes two or three would come, one right after the other. Occasionally, two would come at the same time, and Sasha hated those visits most of all.

Her father let her stay home from school so that she could "rest up" during the daylight hours. Sasha asked him how she could know if she was making the visitors happy, knowing that her life could always get worse if she failed her only job.

"Jus' listen to your gut." The only advice her father had ever given her that remained helpful to this day.

And right now, her gut told her that assessing the position she was in was more important than staying hidden. She would have to face Tamara eventually anyway. Why not now?

Taking care to make just as much ruckus as she normally would, Sasha flushed the toilet, washed her hands, and splashed cold water on her face. She took a deep breath and stepped into the hallway.

Tamara was just walking her way, and shockingly enough, she didn't seem angry. Her expression was unpleasant, but that was just Tamara's normal, troll-like face.

"Sasha, have you seen Brother Roger or Sister Amanda today?"

Sasha shook her head, surprised at the question. "No. Neither."

"No matter. We need to make certain preparations. There's been a problem of sorts, and the Father wishes you to get rid of the surgical suite and any evidence of the women and infants who were ever there." Tamara gave the instructions as though they were everyday tasks.

"A situation? Is the Father okay?" She shouldn't have asked, but the questions slipped out regardless.

"All things work together for the good of those who love

the Father and are called according to his purpose." Tamara didn't so much *say* the words as bark them.

Sasha knew better than to press the matter.

"Can you be trusted to do what is necessary, Sasha?" Tamara put a hand to one ample, lumpy hip.

"Of course. Whatever the Father wants or needs." The relief that she was still safe under the blessing of the Father nearly made her giddy.

Tamara's mouth turned up at the corners as she placed a gentle, motherly hand on Sasha's head. "He needs you to not screw up."

Sasha nodded meekly, swallowing the urge to kick Tamara's teeth in. "What should be done with the birthing beds and nursery furniture?"

Tamara's face went severe again. "Anything that will fit in the industrial kiln should be deposited there. The beds are too large. Maintenance will be taking care of those."

"Okay."

"You need to use the special cleaner from the top shelf of the closet in the birthing room and scour every single inch of those rooms. *Every. Inch.* Do you understand?" Tamara raised an eyebrow.

A monkey could understand that, you godforsaken hag.

Sasha nodded obediently.

Tamara began to walk away, and Sasha wondered what the woman could possibly have to do that could be more important than her own task.

"Where are you going?"

Tamara's eyes were blank when she turned back around. "There's a problem I need to take care of at the hospital before we can leave."

As Tamara disappeared down the hallway, off to perform her "mystery task," Sasha considered her words.

Her stomach rolled with nervousness, but she decided to ignore the new wave of fear.

She had an important job to do as well.

An untold amount of DNA was waiting to be scrubbed out of the nooks and crannies of the surgical suite, and she would remove every drop.

The Father needed her, and she would obey.

24

How dare those women come into my office and lie straight to my face? The fact that they were with the FBI was of no importance to me. Agent, doctor, nun—those two females had no idea who they were dealing with. A line had been crossed.

The lack of respect was difficult to swallow.

The notion that the FBI was researching ways to avoid consanguinity was borderline hilarious. Agent Black—the dark-haired one—should have come up with something much more convincing.

But she was human, imperfect, and I was willing to guess, unclean.

The redhead had left me with *no* doubt as to her status. The filthy ways of the world had been written all over her. The woman's hair had even been *dyed*.

I knew a Jezebel when I saw one.

And "Doctor" Trent? I'd almost laughed when the agent introduced them.

I was the doctor.

She had been a dirty little girl with a title she did not deserve and would never live up to.

Filthy, unworthy, disgusting females. In time, my seed would purify the Earth in such a way that there would be no room left for such sinful beasts. They would be annihilated.

With love.

But none of that was of any importance. I needed to know what they *actually* wanted. What they suspected.

Were they just following procedure and putting out feelers to numerous sperm banks? Did XY Cryolabs just happen to be the closest to the heart of their investigation, the lovely Lavender Lake?

Their reasoning had to be one of those options. Surely, I was panicking for nothing.

What could the FBI possibly have as evidence?

A dead woman in a car with a missing baby? While that may have made for a dramatic press conference, the news had nothing to do with me. More importantly, that information would never lead them to me.

Tamara was on her way at this exact moment to take care of the Lindsay Welsh problem. While Sasha's ability to correctly perform any task was questionable at best, Tamara did not make mistakes.

Buzzing alerts vibrated on my desk. *Tamara.* Smiling, I placed my phone against my ear.

"Yes?"

"I have Sasha attending to the birthing rooms. She was *happy* to do so. A staff member is keeping an eye on her, just in case she decides to screw something up again. She is *very* aware of the fact that she disappointed you a great deal." Tamara's breathing was ragged.

The stress of her mission was substantial.

"Sasha's shame should inspire her to perform her task

very well." I knew the woman would do anything to please me. Especially now.

"Are you sure that we shouldn't just eliminate her right now? I could easily take care of her for you." The eagerness in Tamara's voice was apparent.

Not for the first time, I wished I'd gone ahead and order the kiln to be made big enough to accept a human being into its depths instead of utilizing the swamps as I'd decided. Ashes to ashes would have been less risky. I wouldn't make that mistake again.

"Ah, my child. You know we may need Sasha again. Although she most definitely deserves to be eliminated, she still has a purpose in my plans." I sighed, relieved that I had arranged the details so well. "Sasha will take the fall for all of this madness, if necessary."

"Yes, Father." I sensed Tamara's disappointment. She'd been wise to recognize Sasha as a risk from the very start.

That being said, I'd known what Sasha was capable of doing in service of The Dream. She had that quality of character which enabled her to perform tasks that many of my servants could not.

Sasha was valuable for the precise reasons that she was dangerous.

Soon, she would be nothing more than collateral damage.

"Did you succeed in procuring the strands of her hair to place in Lindsay Welsh's bed?"

Tamara emitted a rather unattractive snorting chuckle. "The woman sheds like a cat. I gathered the strands without incident. Sasha was unaware."

"Excellent, my child. Excellent. And you are confident that you can take care of the Welsh woman?" Such a horrible thorn in my side this vessel had turned out to be. Her ability to survive was uncanny.

"I will make sure she is properly attended to, Father."

Tamara was proud to bear such an important weight upon her shoulders.

She *should* be proud. My plans, Eden, The Dream—Lindsay Welsh threatened all of them. The honor of eliminating her and thus serving The Dream so dutifully was great.

"Any word on the location of my brother?" Roger's disappearance had become more troubling by the hour.

I had entirely too many irons in the fire.

"Roger and Amanda are still missing, Father. I am sorry."

Why? Why would Roger simply vanish? Had the Feds taken him?

Why would the Feds ever want Amanda? She was utterly useless.

Amanda couldn't even bear one single fruit for my brother.

I couldn't fathom any possible reason that Roger would leave. My brother was a true believer—he'd dedicated his life to The Dream.

Roger would never abandon the family. Perhaps he had his occasional bout of frustration, but that was understandable. Amanda was a disappointment, and she always had been.

I often wondered if my brother wouldn't be much more joyful were Amanda to quietly be eliminated. But there wasn't time to think of that now. Later, perhaps. The task would be simple enough.

"Keep me apprised, should you gain any news of them."

"Of course, Father."

I ended the call and allowed myself to relax. Worry had no place in Eden.

Still, I went through all my fail-safes.

My private computer was heavily firewalled. God himself couldn't hack into it. Even if the Feds attempted to infiltrate my virtual vault of work, they would activate the kill switch set in place to render the system wholly useless.

Sasha was tending to the removal of all possible evidence left behind in the birthing rooms. When she had taken care of this task—and I had great faith that she would do her best work yet, considering her recent grievances—all that was left to do was simply wait for the right time to take care of Sasha.

The ranch could never be traced back to my name. I wasn't a foolish man.

Even the island of Eden was in no way legally connected to me.

My yacht was hidden beneath a layer of shell corporations.

I had allowed my helicopter, penthouse, and cabin cruiser to be placed in my name because I was a *wealthy* man. How very strange would it appear to have *no* assets in my name, considering my financial success was public knowledge?

After today, what exactly would the FBI even have in the name of evidence?

A number of couples who had used XY Cryolabs as their sperm donor source?

Any decent attorney could squash that bug in their sleep. And I could afford far better than a *decent* attorney.

My bank provided sperm to thousands of recipients each year. *Thousands*. The odds of interconnected couples enlisting the help of XY Cryolabs were not so improbable as the Feds might wish.

On top of every other precaution, I had been very diligent in assuring that my seed was never used more than ten times maximum under the same donor number. After ten uses, I always went straight into the system and altered the donor profile number myself.

The FBI was grasping for straws. None of those straws could be connected to me. And once Tamara had finished her task for the day, Sasha would be served to them on a beautifully solid, DNA-supported plate.

I'd thought of everything—planned for every contingency.

I sank down into my office chair, solace flooding me once again.

My vision was unstoppable. The Dream itself was unbreakable.

I was born to carry out this cleansing. My seed was meant to spread across the planet.

The FBI couldn't stop that from happening. Those conniving agents were sullied by their own humanity.

The divine power and purpose that had been bestowed upon me was superior to any obstacle. The Dream would work out beautifully.

No one could stop me.

25

Coffee sloshed in the Styrofoam cup Winter placed before Autumn. "How you holdin' up?"

Autumn glanced at the mood ring Aiden had placed on her finger. Black.

Well, according to this little beauty, I am tense and/or nervous.

"I'm fine." Autumn flashed an unconvincing smile.

No doubt, Winter knew she was anything but fine. Neither of them was "fine."

Just as predicted, the hunch they'd both been afflicted with at XY Cryolabs was about as helpful as rubber lips on a woodpecker. Even if Winter's visions were able to be presented as evidence in a court of law—and that was never, ever going to be the case—they'd gained no clear direction whatsoever from her "headache."

A sea of blonde children.

Your honor, I would like to present to you this airtight piece of proof that...something is strange about the dude we met at the sperm bank. You see, my friend saw a bunch of blonde babies in her head. This infallibly points to the guilt of one Dr. Russell Brandt, and possibly Alexandra Romansky...somehow. Case closed!

Autumn shook her head. They had nothing. Facts, figures, actual confirmation of any data whatsoever—the team desperately needed these.

"I've got something!" Noah's shout blasted across the sheriff's office.

Autumn whipped around to find Agent Dalton standing stark still with a phone pressed to his ear. He held up his finger to quiet the room, and the agents and officers alike fell into a deathly silence.

The seconds stretched painfully while Noah finished the call. When the conversation was over, he slapped his hand on the desk. "Hot damn! Finally, *something*. We might have found the baby."

Autumn stood so fast her chair nearly toppled over.

"A couple going by the names of Roger and Amanda Brandt rushed into an ER just north of here in a town called Lovely Day. They had a *newborn baby* experiencing respiratory distress. The ER doc grew suspicious when the supposed parents couldn't answer basic questions like the baby's birth date or gestational age when born."

Pulses of adrenaline pumped through Autumn's veins.

Yes.

"The couple also couldn't name an obstetrician or a pediatrician. And apparently, Amanda Brandt did not resemble a woman who had just given birth."

Brandt. Roger and Amanda Brandt. Dr. Russell Brandt was the owner of XY Cryolabs.

Autumn's eyes widened at the blatant connection, and Winter took her turn slapping down a palm on the desk beside her. "I knew it!" For a moment, Autumn thought Winter was going to do some type of victory dance.

All eyes were on Winter now, and Autumn offered the explanation while Agent Black regained composure. "XY Cryolabs is owned by Dr. Russell Brandt. He was the person we interviewed at the sperm bank. He was creepy and just *off* somehow."

"And we both sensed it. He's a part of this. That last name can*not* be a coincidence." Winter's declaration echoed off the walls.

Could the connection really be this glaring, just falling into their laps like a gift from the sky?

"Lovely Day is only about an hour north of here. Orange County may have a copter we can use." Detective Cohen was already dialing the number.

Aiden caught Autumn's eye, pointing at her, Winter, and then himself. The trio were immediately in action.

"I'm not going with?" Noah demanded, his green eyes full of protest.

Aiden spoke over his shoulder as he walked away. "I need you here. For now."

In only ten minutes, they were running to board the promised helicopter which had just landed at Lavender Lake's helipad. Twenty minutes after that found them arriving at North Star General Hospital.

A physician and a security guard were already waiting at the roof door.

"Every exit is covered?" Aiden demanded as soon as he'd finished ducking under the blades.

"Yes, sir." The guard's face was flushed. Autumn assumed he probably had never witnessed this much excitement at the hospital before—nor expected to.

"I'm Dr. Sheila Malone. We've managed to keep the Brandts in a private room, but there's a bit of a situation. The Brandts must have picked up on our suspicions that the baby wasn't theirs."

Dr. Malone stood tall and thin, wisps of her dishwater blonde hair sticking to the sweat on her forehead. Autumn noted the strain and severity in her murky gray eyes.

"We had stabilized the infant at that point. He was on oxygen while we awaited further test results. The Brandts attempted to take the baby and leave the hospital. Security barred them from even exiting the room, and Roger Brandt pulled a gun." Dr. Malone shook her head in frustration.

Winter appeared ready to charge. "They're holding the baby *hostage?*"

"Well, sort of. They refuse to let go of it." Dr. Malone led them down a series of stairs to the proper floor. "Amanda Brandt has him clutched to her chest, and the only person they've allowed into the room is a pediatrician. No one else."

"How did the couple arrive at the hospital?"

A stationed security guard fielded Aiden's question. "A motorhome, sir. Follow me. I'll show you." The guard led Aiden away from the group and toward the nearest exit.

"We've evacuated everyone from the hospital who was able to leave or be transported." Dr. Malone called out over her shoulder, not slowing her pace for a second. "Here." She abruptly stopped and pointed at a closed door.

"I'll go in." Autumn knew this was her territory.

Winter's face clouded with concern, but she said nothing. Instead, she removed her vest and put it on Autumn.

"The door doesn't lock from the inside. You'll have no trouble entering." Dr. Malone stood to the side, making way for Autumn. "But like I told you, Roger Brandt has a gun. He's threatened to shoot *anyone* else who opens that door."

Autumn knocked anyway. "Roger, my name is Dr. Autumn Trent, and I'm unarmed. I'd like to come in and talk to you and Amanda. Would that be okay? I think this might all be a big misunderstanding."

"I'm not giving you the baby." Roger's voice was gruff.

"I won't try to take the baby from you. I promise. Can I come in?"

The room door opened just a crack. "You better not be lying. I *will* shoot you."

Autumn fully believed him. Dr. Malone's expression was grim as Autumn put a hand to the doorknob. Wondering if a bullet would hit her before she even began talking, she cautiously entered the room.

The shiny barrel of Roger Brandt's handgun was Autumn's immediate greeting. He slammed the door shut behind her.

"Easy. I'm only here to help." Autumn held her hands up, scanning the room.

Roger, who appeared sicker with upset than violent with rage, kept the gun raised. Amanda Brandt stood in the far corner, holding the baby and sobbing. The pediatrician had a stethoscope to the infant's chest and was clearly focused on the little one's heart.

"Doctor?" Autumn chanced to speak.

The pediatrician turned toward her, his face grave. "The baby has a heart defect. I believe he may have transposition of the great vessels, and if he does, immediate surgery is his only chance at survival."

Amanda's sobs intensified.

"I've told this to the Brandts, and they've allowed me to give the child Prostaglandin E1 to keep the PDA open, but that'll only buy us a short amount of time. I need additional testing done quickly, but I can't do it if they don't give me the child." He shot a worn, angry glare at the distraught looking couple.

Autumn sat on an orange plastic chair, keeping her hands visible. She looked from Roger to Amanda and back. "Mr. Brandt, do you and your wife understand what this doctor is telling you?"

Amanda continued crying, but Roger nodded. He'd been crying as well.

"Roger, we know that this child was born to Wendy Arnold. You should know that she died believing you would take care of her son." The words had the desired effect Autumn had wanted, lifting the trance of despair and desperation that had fogged-over Roger Brandt's mind.

He seemed to be truly aware of Autumn's presence for the first time.

"That baby boy will die if you don't let the doctors perform surgery immediately, Roger. *He will die.* I know this situation you're in seems bad, but how much worse will it be when that precious life is sacrificed simply because you're afraid?"

Roger's shoulders slumped, and Autumn let out a low breath of relief. He was coming back to his senses. He was going to make the right decision.

He stepped slowly toward his wife, whose eyes were wide with the realization that she really had to let the baby go. "We have to," he whispered, embracing them both.

Amanda only nodded, and they both kissed the infant before handing him carefully to the doctor. Autumn gently pulled the gun from Roger's hand while the baby was rushed from the room.

The split-second touch informed Autumn of what she'd already guessed. Roger Brandt was not a bad man at his very core. He was a weak man, but he deeply loved his wife and had indeed intended to give Wendy's baby a good life. The Brandts weren't criminals at heart—they were just desperate.

Aiden and Winter dashed into the room at the precise moment that Roger Brandt broke down. Through his tears, he described how he had found the baby.

"The baby just screamed and screamed…and that girl was dying, just lying in the back of that car. So much blood on the seat…I only wanted to save him." His eyes pled with Autumn to understand.

Though her heart ached for Roger and Amanda, there was a bigger picture to focus on. "Roger," Autumn kept her voice calm and kind, "would you and your wife happen to be related to Dr. Russell Brandt?"

Roger's face immediately went hard, and he pressed his lips together. His silence was in vain because Amanda threw up her hand and began ranting madly.

"This is *all* Russell Brandt's fault! Him and his ridiculous, idiotic mission! He's ruined our lives! He's taken everything from us!"

Roger put a hand on her arm, his eyes wide, almost frantic. "Amanda, hush. Please, you must *hush*."

"I will not hush! No! No more! Your brother is an evil, horrible man, and now he's taken away the only thing I ever wanted!" She ripped her arm away from her husband. "I've hushed for far too long!"

Autumn gave Aiden and Winter a side-glance. The unspoken consensus amongst them was very clear—let Amanda Brandt rave on as long as she liked.

The distraught woman was giving them exactly what they so desperately needed to solve this case. She was single-handedly filling in every individual blank.

"He thinks because he had some stupid dream that he's above the rest of humanity! *Everyone* has dreams! He's just a psychopath trying to *purify* the world with his own insanity! All of those babies he stole, and he wouldn't even give us *one*!" Amanda was screaming now.

"Honey, please. You have to stop saying such—"

Amanda smacked Roger across the face. He froze in shock while she continued shrieking. "*I will not stop!* He's a murderer! He's a crazy, crackpot lunatic! I hate him! *I hate The Dream!*"

With the last words, she collapsed, folding into the fetal

position and wailing into the floor. Roger sat beside her and patted her back, saying things Autumn couldn't understand.

She's grieving. Mourning. She can't carry her own child. And he's...broken.

Autumn's stomach twisted with empathy. Amanda wanted to be a mother more than anything else in the world. The natural desire had driven her to a place where she mentally could no longer function.

And Roger had just been trying to give his wife the infant they both felt they deserved. Probably trying to save her sanity as well. Tragic.

Staving off her own rattled emotions, Autumn began to replay the highlights of Amanda's impassioned disclosure.

Roger and Russell are brothers.

Russell has a "mission."

She called it "the dream."

An evil, horrible man convinced that he is superior to the rest of the human race who believes he must purify the world.

Psychopath. Murderer. Lunatic.

All those babies he stole.

The vessels recycled in the swamps.

"He has a ranch. We all live on it. A giant ranch south of here. A compound. I'll give you the address. Go get the son of a bitch." Amanda spoke desolately from her position on the floor. Roger no longer attempted to shush her.

The information was phenomenally valuable, and Autumn committed to make sure the D.A. of the case knew how these two had been so helpful.

Autumn turned to Aiden and Winter. Aiden already had his phone to his ear, his jaw flexing.

"Noah's phone is going straight to voicemail. I'll try Bree." The frustrated SSA left the room.

Autumn and Winter locked eyes. Winter shook her head

sadly, but Autumn also noted the bright spark of determination in her friend's vivid blue gaze.

This case was coming down to the wire. The team had urgent work to do.

Within minutes, the stunned agents were back in the helicopter for the return flight to Lavender Lake.

Autumn closed her eyes and attempted to recenter.

The monster in the closet was no longer a mystery.

But would they be able to catch him before he killed again?

26

Dressed in freshly pressed scrubs, Tamara strode through the peaceful halls of Lavender Lake Medical Center. Killing Lindsay Welsh was the most crucial task the Father had ever given her.

Leaving Sasha's hairs beside Lindsay's cold, dead body was just a particularly delightful bonus. Letting the little whore be the fall guy was a perfect plan.

Just as everything the Father did was perfect.

Tamara was smiling as she headed with great purpose to the medical-surgical floor.

How pleased the Father would be when this was done. She'd hoped for a long time that he might change his mind about allowing her to be an Eden mother. Tamara knew she didn't fit the qualifications, but sometimes a person grew more attractive the deeper you got to know them.

The Father knew her well. A few more months of over-whelmingly faithful service, and she might begin to seem like a possible vessel after all. No one loved the Father more than Tamara.

Even if she was never selected to bear the holy fruit,

Tamara held tight to the fact that she was the Father's most vital servant. She would stand by his side until the day she died.

Reaching the proper floor, she made her way to the computers at an otherwise empty station. In a few swift taps, she entered the password she'd happened to glimpse just the other day while in conversation with an ER nurse downstairs.

The moron hadn't even had an inkling that Tamara spied it. Humans were forever letting their guards down at the wrong moment.

Not quitting her day job had been the Father's wise suggestion, and she was glad she'd followed it. Her hospital access had proven to be very handy many times over, making her an essential member of the Father's family.

After today, her place in the Father's inner circle would be cemented forever.

And soon she'd be rid of Sasha as well. How long had she patiently put up with that mouthy, dirty woman's shenanigans?

Too long. But that was over. *Sasha* was over.

Life was beautiful.

"Hey, Tam. I didn't know you were working today?" Betsy, a nurse Tamara was friendly with, approached her with raised eyebrows.

Betsy annoyed the living hell out of Tamara, but you could never have too many people who believed they were your friends. People were tools, and Tamara used them at the Father's discretion.

"Nothing like being called in at the last minute." Tamara rolled her eyes and gave Betsy a grin.

She'd actually chosen this exact time to complete the Father's task because she knew all the supervisors were in a big meeting. The less prying eyes walking around the hospital, the better.

"Tell me about it. I got called in *three times* in *one week* last month. I mean, the paycheck is great, but do they not care that we have lives too? Honestly. So obnoxious." Betsy prattled away while Tamara nonchalantly pulled up Lindsay Welsh's chart.

Good. Lindsay had been moved to a step-down unit after stabilizing in ICU. Ideally, Lindsay would have been moved to her own private room, but the change was positive regardless.

Tamara would have fewer one-on-one staff lurking around which meant more opportunities to do what must be done.

Betsy's soliloquy continued. "My husband says nurses are one of the least respected professions in the country. *Everyone* needs us, but people barely notice you're there."

Tamara was banking on that.

The cameras still troubled her. They presented a problem that she would have rather avoided altogether.

But the Father had promised her that if she was caught or implicated in any way regarding Lindsay's death, he'd simply move her to Eden where she could continue to be a nurse.

In paradise.

The reward was so great that the tedious mission and its possible consequences were duly balanced out.

Ten minutes of mind-numbing small talk later, Tamara excused herself from the nurse's station. She walked down the hallway until she was comfortably far from Betsy. Slipping into the public restroom, she bolted the door and got to work.

Opening her tote bad, she donned a different change of scrubs, a mousy brown wig she'd cut into a bob, and a pair of glasses with thick, pink rims. The final touch was a heavy layer of pink lipstick and dark blush, and the most important of all—tiny clear circles of tape attached to the pads of her fingers to ensure no prints were found.

At precisely three o'clock, Tamara headed up to the step-down unit. The staff would be busy filling out reports during the shift change, and visitation wasn't allowed during shift changes either.

Perfect opportunity.

Fingering the syringe in her pocket, Tamara smiled at the guard standing outside of the room Lindsay was recovering in. He checked her badge and nodded.

"Thank you, Ms. Gardner."

She gave him a heartfelt smile and promptly pushed her way into the room.

Stillness greeted her, filling Tamara with glee. No obstacles at all.

Lindsay's blonde head rested peacefully on a bright white pillow as she slept on the standard hospital bed. Just another quiet day in Lavender Lake.

Time's up, Mrs. Welsh.

Tamara made an obvious show of charting her observations, and then went to the IV pump, making sure her back was to the main camera focused on Lindsay.

Under normal circumstances, she would take great care when administering drugs through the medication access port. The port would be sanitized for the recommended fifteen seconds, then she would flush the line, watching carefully for any problems at the injection sight.

But sterilization wasn't necessary today. Lindsay Welsh had much bigger problems, although she wouldn't live long enough to know it.

Tamara pulled on a pair of gloves, knowing one touch to her skin of the syringe's contents could kill her. "Easy peasy," she murmured happily.

She lifted the syringe from her pocket and was split-seconds away from screwing off the needle so that she could attach the barrel to the port when the machine's alarm began to sound.

Tamara glanced down at Lindsay, only to meet the woman's wide-open eyes. She stared at Tamara with absolute horror, but that didn't last for long. Almost immediately, Lindsay's gaze turned into an all-consuming rage.

The heat in the vessel's eyes nearly caused Tamara to run away.

She knows exactly who I am. How could she possibly recognize me?

There was no time to worry about that. Her hands shaking, Tamara fumbled with the syringe and grabbed for the port, but Lindsay moved her hand to cover it more swiftly than she should have been able in her current state. The movement infuriated Tamara, and with a curse she was glad the Father couldn't hear, she knocked Lindsay's much weaker hand away.

You are not getting out of it this time, you stubborn, bullheaded bitch.

Two nurses rushed into the room, the security guard on their heels. "What are you doing?" one of them yelled at her back.

Tamara met Lindsay's feral, triumphant gaze beaming out of her perfect vessel eyes. She had never hated a vessel before, but she hated Lindsay Welsh with every fiber of her being.

Why this perfect blonde bitch? Why not Tamara? Her brains made up for what she lacked in beauty, and no one was more deserving of carrying the Father's seed than her.

No one.

Lindsay tried to speak, but her voice came out in more of a gravelly hiss. "It's her. Took...babies."

Tamara swung around, her pulse hammering in her throat. How had this happened? The Dream was blessed, and each action taken to secure it should have been equally sanctioned. She'd been so sure of her success that she had given no thought of escape. Her eyes darted across the room, desperately seeking a way out of this predicament.

The guard pulled his gun. One of the nurses rushed to Lindsay, stepping on the locking mechanism and pulling the bed away. The other nurse slid the bedside tray between Tamara and the patient.

"Drop the weapon and put your hands up!" As she stared down the barrel of the gun, Tamara understood that this hadn't been just a guard. He was an off-duty police officer stationed outside of this room for the sole purpose of keeping Lindsay Welsh safe.

Why were they all so obsessed with this woman? She was nothing. She should have been processed through an alligator's bowels by now.

Lindsay Welsh was just a pretty idiot who'd been stupid enough to try and help a complete stranger. *At night. Alone.*

Tamara fought the urge to scream.

Other officers were already gathering behind him. Windows were to her back, and even the bathroom door was blocked. She was trapped. There truly was no way out.

"Drop the weapon. Now!"

Time was short. Time was *gone.*

Tamara gazed down at her only "weapon." The plan had been so perfect. A lethal dose of "gray death," as the kids called it, and Lindsay would have instantly ceased to be a problem for the Father.

She'd chosen this particular drug because there was no chance for anyone to come back from the gray death. Nearby doctors and nurses would have been useless.

This little syringe would have ensured that the cursed vessel did not resurrect. Again.

The guard stepped closer, the gun pointed at the center of her chest. The nurses stared at her with shock and disgust as they hovered over Lindsay, who was, even now, trying to claw her way to Tamara.

Just can't leave well enough alone, that one.

How had it come to this?

It was a silly question, really. For her whole life, Tamara had fallen just shy of her dreams.

She'd been second chair clarinet as well as only half a point away from being valedictorian. While she'd dreamed of becoming a doctor, she'd settled on being a nurse.

Why would this be any different?

Swallowing hard, Tamara closed her eyes, picturing the blond man she adored with all her being. She would meet him again, she knew, but she'd miss him until that day arrived.

"Tell the Father I love him."

In her final act of service to Eden, Tamara jammed the needle into her leg. With an anguished cry for all that she'd miss, she pushed the plunger all the way in.

27

Noah tapped his phone against his forehead. He'd spent a lot of time taking and making calls to the tech team in Virginia, trying to learn any detail possible about Dr. Russell Brandt.

The team had already managed to find some shell corporations that could possibly be traced to the doctor. They were working on finding the links but had made clear to Noah that such research took time.

If Russell Brandt was the asshole taking all these babies, what was he doing with them? He certainly didn't need the money. The man's portfolio rivaled some of the richest men in the world.

Was he keeping them? All of them? If so, why? Where? Somewhere private, of course. Much more private than the penthouse apartment he kept near his XY Cryolabs office.

So, where? According to the records the tech team had pulled up so far, Brandt had made sure his name was on nothing unusual.

Intelligent son of a bitch, but that doesn't mean we won't catch you.

Chris and Sun were helping with the computer tech searching in Lavender Lake. Parker sure hadn't loved the fact that his profile was wrong, but he'd come around.

Agent Parker wasn't a bad guy, once you waded past all of the obnoxious bravado.

Regardless, Russell Brandt had become their number one suspect—the ultimate target. Chris had jumped right on board to help once he'd licked his wounds for a few minutes.

And the added help was needed. They were also still attempting to locate Sasha Romansky. The woman wasn't the kingpin of this sick operation, but she was heavily involved.

"Shit." Noah scrolled through his recents and spotted the missed call from Aiden. Too much chaos, not enough brain cells.

He was about to call Aiden back when Bree rushed into the room. She had Aiden on speakerphone.

"Roger and Amanda Brandt have confirmed their relation to Russell. Roger is Russell's brother. Seems that Russell has a type of god-complex influencing all his decisions. He believes himself to be chosen to purify the world."

Noah hadn't realized he could hate that Brandt douchebag more than he already did. "Amanda Brandt broke?"

"Like glass." Noah could hear the victory in Parrish's voice. "She gave us all that information and more. We have the address for his ranch in Central Florida. Dalton, I want you to gather a team and head to the ranch while we get the search warrant approved. I'll—"

A sudden commotion in the sheriff's office cut Aiden off. An officer had charged in and was frantically relaying that, although the current details were sketchy, something bad was going down inside Lindsay Welsh's hospital room.

Aiden overheard every word, and Noah was immediately

receiving new orders. "I want Agent Dalton and Agent Stafford to head to the hospital before you go anywhere else. Agent Black and Dr. Trent are going with me to XY Cryolabs. By air, we'll be there in fifteen minutes flat."

Noah grabbed his keys and gave Bree an eager nod. He'd been ready to go for eons.

"And Noah," Aiden's voice boomed, "make sure Lindsay Welsh is taken care of. She is a vital witness. Top priority."

Noah and Bree were speeding down the highway in less than two minutes. Noah couldn't imagine what would happen to the case if Lindsay had been further hurt or killed. In addition to Brandt's sister-in-law, she was the key to stopping all this psychotic madness.

But by the time they made it to Lindsay's room, the chaos was over.

Relief flooded Noah as he caught sight of Lindsay Welsh. She was alive and resting on her bed, but the nurses surrounding her looked to be preparing her for a move.

He understood why when he spotted an anonymous dead woman on the floor. A wig lay twisted on her head, and her lips and protruding tongue were a deep purple.

"Is it possible that we've just found Sasha?" He stared at Bree, who stared at the woman's face.

"She doesn't resemble the sketch or the mugshot at all, Noah. I think this is another individual that's somehow been involved in this mess." Bree knelt to make a closer examination. She nodded up at him.

This wasn't Sasha.

Noah strode across the room, standing near Lindsay's bed. He hadn't expected the woman to be awake, but she was, and her eyes were wild from the recent altercation.

She yanked Noah down by his tie, not stopping until he was at her eye-level. Lindsay Welsh still appeared very unwell, and Noah guessed that she was operating on a pure adrenaline high in this moment.

"That woman..." Her eyes flicked to the unknown suspect on the floor. "She was the nurse who helped a man deliver my babies. Another girl helped as well. Her name was Sasha. They held me down and stole my children straight from my womb."

Noah's heart ached for Lindsay and her husband, and there was a part of him that simply wanted to take this brave woman into his arms and protect her from the brutality of the world. But he also needed the vitally important information she was giving him.

"Sasha was the one who kidnapped me." Her voice was growing hoarser by the second. "She held a pillow over my face after the babies were out. She was *honored* to kill me!"

A nearby nurse cast a concerned glance Noah's way, and he held up a finger. He was almost done here.

"They were sure I was dead. They left me in a swamp. I don't know how we got there, but I crawled out." She frowned and lifted a hand to press to her forehead. "Yes. I remember. I crawled out because the gators got the deer instead of me." Lindsay's eyes glazed over with a reel of horror movie worthy scenes that Noah couldn't even imagine.

He whipped up his cell and tapped on a picture of Dr. Brandt. "Is this the doctor who delivered your babies, Lindsay?"

Lindsay stared at the screen and took the phone from Noah's hand. Her eyes poured tears, but she nodded vigorously. "That's him."

Noah was unsure if the poor woman would be able to share anymore. She appeared dangerously close to passing out.

"I don't know where they took me. I couldn't see...until

the room. The room I gave birth in was sterile...and white. *So white.*" Lindsay's eyes began to flutter closed. "And I woke up in a swamp...I don't know how far we drove..."

After giving him every detail that was important, Lindsay Welsh fell asleep.

She certainly hadn't given them a roadmap, but she *had* identified Brandt. There was no longer any question that this was the bastard they were hunting for. The proof was finally there.

Gritting his teeth, Noah called Detective Cohen to get going on the warrants. They'd need them for XY Cryolabs and any other property they discovered belonging to Brandt.

"We're bringing this bastard down, Jackie," Noah declared.

"Roger that." She ended the call.

Noah immediately called Aiden next.

"Dalton?"

"Lindsay Welsh is still alive and...not necessarily well, but she was able to confirm that Dr. Russell Brandt was the man who delivered her babies. She also confirmed that Sasha was there assisting."

Noah met Bree's eyes, and she nodded toward the body on the floor.

"Apparently a third woman, a nurse, was also present for the delivery. She caused the ruckus here, trying to take Lindsay out for good. She's dead."

Aiden didn't miss a beat. "We're only a few minutes out via air from the laboratory. While we go there, I want you and Bree to gather a team to raid the ranch."

"Done."

"And lastly, Amanda Brandt told us that in addition to the ninety-two acres of ranch in Central Florida, Russell also owns an island somewhere off the coast. That's where he keeps the babies. She didn't know anything else about it. No specifics including a location other than it's an hour or so away by helicopter. Roger claimed he didn't know anything about the island, either, although I don't buy that."

Noah tried to process all the new details Aiden had just shot his way. How intricate was this whole operation? Was Russell Brandt just a murdering psychopath or had he lost touch with reality altogether?

The two weren't mutually exclusive.

Before he and Bree exited the room, Noah pulled on gloves and searched the dead woman's pockets. Retrieving a cell phone, he dropped it in an evidence bag. But as they prepared to leave, Noah decided to take the phone with them.

This breach of protocol would make the phone useless for the prosecution, were it to contain anything of importance to begin with. But they needed information now, or there might never be a case or a court or a prosecution.

With Bree behind the wheel taking them to the lab, Noah called Sun. He gave her the ranch address.

"Think you could track down the ranch owner?" Noah knew that if anyone could, Sun was their girl.

"I can try," Sun shot back as a tapping commenced, her fingers already typing away at lightning speed. "I'll get our folks in Virginia on it as well. All hands on deck."

Noah nodded his approval. "If we can get a name for the ranch, we might be able to link it to whoever legally owns the island. The island is top priority because apparently Brandt keeps the babies there. We need to get to those babies before Brandt does. No telling what he'll do with them now."

"You think he'd just get rid of them? *All of them?*" Sun's normally cold voice filled with disbelieving horror.

"I think he's smart enough to know that if the babies are gone, there's no way to prove his complicity. A good attorney will rip Lindsay Welsh apart on the stand. We need those babies." Noah ended the call and turned to Bree.

"I know the rest of us are blown away, but you've seen a lot. This doesn't shock you, does it?" Noah studied her face as she considered the question.

Bree sighed and ran a hand through the tight curls of her hair. "There's a lot of sick people in this world, Noah. People who are capable of doing hideous, unthinkable things to others. We catch one and celebrate, but there'll *always* be another shortly after. I learned that a long time ago."

Noah pinched the bridge of his nose. "Yeah. I'm beginning to learn that for myself."

Bree gave him an encouraging smile. "But *today*, we're going to catch *this* bastard. Let tomorrow be tomorrow."

28

I had nothing to worry about.

But I paced back and forth through my office regardless.

Divinity cloaked my being. I'd been called. *Chosen.*

My mission was pure. Righteousness could not be felled by the sword of sinners.

Still, fighting off this humanistic emotion—this *fear*—was growing wearisome. My frustration mounted at the relentless struggle.

Worry was such a pathetic display of humanism.

While I could admit that I was currently trapped inside a human body, my actual essence was pure, beaming white light.

"Thou shalt have no fear," I murmured, straightening my posture.

No fear. None.

The Dream was my purpose and *only* focus on this sin-ridden planet.

My smile returned, sure my brief moments of uncertainty would soon be in vain.

Tamara would call soon and cheer me further with the confirmation of Lindsay Welsh's demise. She'd assured me that "the gray death" left no chance for revival.

That plucky little vessel would be eliminated *for good* this time.

I chuckled. Lindsay's nature was most pleasing. My daughters would be brilliant warriors of light.

I considered calling Tamara. The immediate relief the call would provide was tempting.

Love is patient.

I trusted Tamara to properly carry out her task. Her call would come at the right moment. No intrusion from me was necessary.

Possibly, she was in the final stages of her work right this instant. A ringing phone at an inopportune moment could be a detriment to her success.

I glimpsed a flash of crimson and turned to the flatscreen. A red "breaking news" banner met my gaze.

I stepped closer, focused on the footage.

Two humans were being escorted by officers from a building...a hospital.

My legs wobbled with sudden weakness, and I nearly fell to the floor.

Roger and Amanda were the two individuals. My brother. My sister-in-law.

Shaking, I grabbed the remote and tapped up the volume.

"...the Brandts entered North Star General Hospital with a sick newborn, seeking immediate assistance. Hospital staff became suspicious when the couple couldn't answer the most basic of health-related questions about the infant."

I placed a hand over my mouth. "Oh no, Roger. No."

"...refused to turn the infant over to the doctors. Roger Brandt then drew a gun, and the baby was held hostage by the couple until federal agents were able to negotiate the infant's release."

Roger had always been too soft. Even as a child.

"...received word from a source who claims that the baby involved was the same infant stolen only this morning after its mother was found nearly dead in her car."

Roger. He must have been nearby when Wendy Arnold gave birth. My orders to abandon the mother and child had given him opportunity to...take a baby for himself.

Cameras zoomed in on my brother's face as he was guided into the back of a police car. He appeared incredibly mournful.

As he should be.

Roger had begged for a child for himself and Amanda for years. I'd told him no on enough occasions to have lost count of the pleas.

The right time would come for them—possibly. But The Dream required much toil from the faithful. Roger's service was needed to help Eden thrive.

Amanda's seeming inability to carry Roger's seed was not a coincidence. I knew that her failure was just another beautiful piece of the plan.

Roger and Amanda weren't meant to have a child. Not right now.

Why hadn't they trusted my wisdom? I knew what was best for *all* the children of Eden, including my brother and his wife.

When had Roger stopped believing?

He'd taken the unclean child and fled with Amanda. That plan had almost immediately derailed.

"You should have trusted me, brother." Heavy sadness filled my heart.

How long until the Feds connect him to you? They will *connect him to you.*

Would Roger turn on me? He'd already betrayed me *and* his family. Roger had walked away from Eden. The Dream.

Was Roger capable of stabbing me in the back so grievously? Surely he couldn't simply hand his own brother to the Feds on a silver platter.

But Amanda would. Amanda had hated me for quite a long time. On more than one occasion, I'd accidentally been privy to her complaining about me to Roger.

She'd all but perfected the ruthless, nagging wife routine.

Amanda resented living in a small cabin on the ranch while I lived in the luxurious main house. She couldn't comprehend—even as a loyal follower—the superiority I'd been blessed with.

I lived lavishly because *I was the chosen one.*

The cabin had been a temporary dwelling for Roger and Amanda. After a few more years of learning their place, I intended to upgrade them.

A *moderate* upgrade, of course. Favoritism was not a part of Eden, and I took great care to be mindful of that fact when I made decisions regarding Roger and Amanda.

I gritted my teeth at the mere thought of the woman's name. What had my brother seen in the woman? She was weak in every way possible.

Amanda most certainly would sell me out. She probably already had.

So exactly how long did I have before…

Chuf chuf chuf chuf. Chuf chuf chuf chuf.

…visitors.

Rushing to the window, I spotted a helicopter circling the XY Cryolab parking lot. The pilot was obviously searching for a place to land.

A sudden flash of bright red hair followed by a glance of ebony locks from within the chopper wasn't surprising. It was *them*! The fact was abundantly clear that these particular go-getters were here for me.

My new federal agent friends were back. How wonderful.

I hit the kill switch for my computer system with one swift slap. Any information contained on this computer was currently eating itself alive, and soon there wouldn't be a byte left.

The hysterical giggle that escaped my lips was concerning, and I clamped my mouth closed.

Every last little file would be erased in a manner so thorough that nothing and no one would ever be able to restore it.

No problem. I had hidden backups the Feds would never find.

Forcing myself to walk calmly to my wall safe, I turned the dial, choosing each digit of the combination with great care. Another fail-safe locked the vault tight if the wrong password was entered even once.

No time for mistakes now.

I'd placed a go-bag behind the steel door of the safe the first day I moved to this office. My past wasn't free of blunders, but I'd gained valuable insight from previous error.

The escape plan I'd created for this precise moment was flawless. Foolproof.

I strode with confidence into the hallway and headed for the main floor back exit stairs.

"Dr. Brandt! Dr. Brandt, is anything wrong?" Olive's chirpy, girlish voice called from behind me. The rapid click-clacking of her heels echoed off the walls as my faithful secretary ran to catch up.

"Stay where you are, Olive! I have an emergency I must tend to. I'll be taking the helicopter." I delivered the order in a severe tone, and Olive's clack-tastic symphony abruptly halted. I could almost imagine the sorrow on her face when she discovered I was gone forever.

A holy adrenaline kicked in. I covered the five flights of

stairs in seconds and busted through the exit, then ran the remaining distance to the helipad.

Once I was securely in the pilot's seat, I started the engine, going through the pre-flight checklist at lightning speed.

Time was of the essence. My helicopter was traceable, so I'd have to choose an alternate way back to the island.

My stomach lurched. The ranch was most likely compromised as well.

Two swipes dialed Brother Brian Dunkin, my most trusted staff member at the ranch. He answered after one ring. My throat wanted to close, but I forced the words out. "Evacuate Plan E now."

"Yes, Father." Calm and collected, just as I had expected from my faithful servant.

I ended the call and finished the systems-check. When the chopper was ready, I grabbed my go-bag and pulled a shiny metal device out. I forced myself to take a deep breath, letting any lingering anxiety fade away. I was still in control. I just needed to follow my own carefully laid out plan.

Taking the device from its protective case, after flipping the power switch on, I entered the orders through the tiny screen.

Set timer one for twenty-five minutes. Check.

Set timer two for thirty minutes. Check.

Set timer three for thirty-five minutes. Check.

Set timer four for forty minutes.

"Check."

Triumphant, I pressed the start button on the device, allowing the countdown to begin. How beautifully smooth my escape had begun.

Satisfied, I pointed the nose of my helicopter toward the marina.

The Dream was unstoppable.

The filthy agents would learn that soon enough.

GLEAMING. The birthing suite was positively gleaming.

Sasha's mouth stretched into a wide smile, surveying the fruit of her labor. The walls, the floors—she'd scrubbed until the entire room sparkled.

There couldn't possibly be any speck of blood or strand of hair left.

Her scorched eyes burned terribly, as though they might bleed themselves. The mixture inside of the "special cleaner" bottle had seared her lungs until coughing fits overtook her.

The ingredients were very likely not meant for human inhalation. A mask would have been wise. But Tamara hadn't even suggested one.

She's probably crossing her fingers right now, just hoping I breathed in enough of this shit to knock me out dead.

Sasha smiled. Maybe she'd let Tamara have a drink of the same mixture before she killed her.

Just fill the bitch up with poison and smile as she drops.

What a beautiful day that would be.

However, right now, she had to focus on the specific tasks of *this* day.

The birthing suite, aside from the bed and larger pieces of furniture she'd been instructed to leave, was spotless. Sasha hadn't simply *cleansed* the space—she'd made the room *Eden white*.

The Father would forgive her. One peek into this room and he would understand how special she really was. He would want her by his side *always*.

Sasha had been gleefully surprised by the pleasure she found in observing the room's smaller items slide into the industrial kiln. The idea that the fire instantly made unwanted burdens disappear was fascinating.

Maybe she'd cut off Tamara's arms and legs and toss *her* into the kiln. So many delightful choices. Too bad the oven wasn't bigger.

Focus.

Sasha centered herself. This work was done, but the Father's plan required many more acts of service. She would call Tamara and ask what—

Voices came from all different directions of the compound.

Loud, panicked voices.

The compound was nearly always peaceful and hushed, exactly as the Father preferred.

Something's wrong, and you better get one step ahead of it.

Sasha rushed to the main hall, where all the compound's wings converged. Men and women alike were running across the marble floor, many carrying suitcases, others simply appearing terrified and confused.

She spotted Brother Brian in the midst of the pandemonium and hurried toward him.

"Brother Brian!" She shouted to ensure he would understand her over the racket. "Where is everyone going?"

He turned to her, eyes cold and hard. "None of your concern, Sasha. You were tasked with cleaning the birthing suite. You should return and finish your job."

"I *did* finish." Sasha hated Brother Brian. He always eyed her with disgust, as though just the sight of her might actually make him puke.

The Father never treated her like trash. He had instantly known who she really was deep inside.

"Then perhaps you should go over it one more time. Make sure you didn't mess it up somehow." Brother Brian raised an eyebrow at her and smirked.

Sasha didn't know how much he knew about her recent screwups, but he quite obviously knew enough. Brother Brian was useless to her right now.

She pretended to walk back in the direction she had come from, but ducked behind a large potted plant as soon as she knew Brother Brian wasn't keeping an eye out for her. That asshole wasn't going to tell her anything, so she would simply spy.

Spying was always her go-to when she wasn't sure of how to act.

"…must leave."

"…alerted to immediately…"

"…if we evacuate quickly enough…"

"…pack only what you need…"

Sasha wasn't a genius, but she knew a mass exodus was happening at the compound. The children of Eden were fleeing. The matter was urgent.

Except that she had been told *nothing*. Neither the Father nor Tamara had mentioned anything before, and they certainly weren't contacting her now.

Brother Brian had lied straight to her face, and he was the Father's most trusted employee at the ranch.

Surely the Father hadn't instructed him to *leave* her. Despite her mishaps as of late, Sasha knew she was still of high importance to the Father. He *needed* her. He had said so himself many times.

He'll deal harshly with Brother Brian for this. When the Father finds out, Brother Brian is toast.

Her current concern far outweighed the hope of retribution.

Sasha stood and ran full speed. She'd left her bag, which contained the only few items she absolutely needed, in the hall near the birthing suite. When she reached the satchel, she glanced over the contents, was satisfied, and ran again.

Outside, numerous vehicles were being loaded with harried followers. Sasha knew that she had to be in one of those vans. She crept along the massive drive, hiding behind the decorative bushes and shrubbery.

A few vans were already leaving. Sasha nearly screamed at the injustice.

The Father loves me! He needs me! He would never leave me here!

She honed in on the last two vans and scanned the faces of the people piling into them. No one familiar. No one important.

Figuring that everyone who might stop her had already fled, Sasha sprinted toward her targeted van and swung inside. The door closed behind her as the vehicle began to move.

She'd been right. No particularly familiar faces. No one who knew much about her, who she was, what she did, how badly she'd messed up this morning…

For now, she was safe.

The general chatter amongst her fellow passengers didn't inform her of much more than she'd already picked up on in the hallway hiding behind that plant.

There was an evacuation alert. Residents of the ranch were to travel to the Marina at South Vero Beach and board the Father's yacht. They were going to Eden.

Sasha no longer cared why the ranch was being deserted.

They were going to Eden.

The ecstasy that flooded her more than made up for the sting of Brother Brian's words.

Brother Brian would get his.

All the same, she made sure to stay amongst her fellow passengers when the time came to board the yacht. She used the group as camouflage, keeping a hood over her curls and her face downward, knowing Brother Brian would never let her board.

He might not even be the *only* one who wouldn't let her board.

Once she was on the boat's deck, Sasha immediately sought a hiding place. She ran to the lower deck and down the hall, choosing the unlikely to be used maintenance closet.

The engines were starting, their roar vibrating through the large boat. Sasha wobbled slightly as Eden's Paradise pulled away from the dock.

Whatever had happened to cause this, she knew her circumstances would be okay now. She'd managed to sneak onto the mammoth boat, and the Father would right all the wrong that had come her way when he arrived in Eden.

Eden. I'm on my way to paradise.

Sasha smiled. She was finally going home.

29

Autumn leapt from the helicopter and ran after Aiden and Winter. Adrenaline pumping—she was ready.

Time to catch this son of a bitch.

Instantly, security guards sprinted toward them.

"We've got company!" Autumn called ahead.

Aiden threw open the main entryway door to XY Cryolabs. He and Winter held their badges high. "FBI! Don't move!"

The main floor receptionist was the only person in the entry foyer, and she appeared close to fainting. Five XY Cryolabs security guards rushed in seconds after the agents, surrounding them with hostile glares.

And guns. They definitely have guns.

Autumn shuddered.

"We're here for Dr. Russell Brandt," Aiden boomed with an authority that made people stand to attention. "He's currently the main suspect in an active case. Tell us where he is."

The receptionist turned her wide eyes to the guards surrounding the agents, as if seeking permission to respond.

A taller than above average guard stepped boldly toward Aiden, his rebellious dark eyes surveying the three intruders with distrust.

"Now, hold on there. I don't care if you were sent by the damn president. You can't be here without a warrant, cowboy." The guard glared down at Aiden, who was at least half a foot shorter.

Autumn raised her eyebrows. *Cowboy?* Aiden's expression betrayed his raging-inferno level of pissed.

"I am Supervisory Special Agent Aiden Parrish with the Federal Bureau of Investigation." His phone pinged, and after a quick glance down, Aiden raised the device triumphantly. "Here's your warrant."

Autumn glanced at Winter, who met her gaze and gave a slight nod toward a large door to their right labeled "stairs." Autumn slowly stepped to the side, eyeing the armed security guards one by one.

The men were all intently focused on Aiden, as though female agents were nothing more than afterthoughts.

Typical.

"Show me an actual, authentic, *printed* warrant, and I might take you seriously. You can shove your cyber Google bullshit back up your ass." The guard refused to be intimidated, and Autumn noted that Aiden's free hand was clenched into a fist.

"Here's the situation, genius. You *will* take me seriously *right now* because you're dealing with *the FBI*. This can go one of two ways..." Aiden's voice faded as Autumn padded away, focused on the doorway.

Winter mouthed, "Now." She stepped quietly toward the stairwell exit and pushed the door open.

Autumn followed her friend, briefly wondering if they both were about to be shot in the back. But they closed the stairwell door without incident, and Winter began mounting the stairs with gazelle-like ease.

Autumn cursed herself for the lack of physical training she'd pulled off recently. Her huffs and puffs grew more severe as she trailed Agent Black on the five-story climb.

Thank god there aren't fifty floors. Winter would have to let me piggyback her.

The duo burst through the stairwell entrance of the fifth floor, the door slamming forcefully against the wall of the executive office's reception area. A startled, familiar figure whirled around.

Olive appeared frazzled, a sharp change from her tidy, professional visage earlier that day. She raised her chin and managed to regain a bit of secretarial authority and composure.

"Wonderful to run into you again. How can I help you, ladies?"

Autumn noted the hostile tone. It was yet another three sixty turn from the previous sweetness Olive had shown only hours ago.

"We're here for Dr. Brandt." Winter's voice carried an authority similar to Aiden's. "We have a warrant, and we *will* be searching the premises. Where's the doctor?"

"I want to see the warrant." Olive's voice waivered slightly.

"Well then, you're free to go down to the main floor. Agent Parrish will gladly show the document to you. Super friendly guy. Loves questions." Winter took off down the hallway, no longer finding Olive of any use whatsoever.

Autumn swallowed a giggle and followed. Within seconds they were entering Dr. Brandt's creepy, immaculately clean office. The formidable atmosphere remained, but Russell Brandt was not present.

The two searched every room of the fifth floor. A bathroom, a conference area, and what appeared to be an expansive, glistening laboratory.

White was everywhere. Brandt was not.

Autumn's frustration mounted with each passing minute, until a large, moving white object caught her eye through one of the many crystal-clear windows.

"Helicopter," Autumn shouted, running for the stairwell door. "He has his own helipad. He's leaving!"

Winter reached the doorknob first, her expression filling with rage when the door wouldn't budge. She turned to the elevator, slamming her palm across the down button.

Nothing.

Autumn frantically sought Olive's form. As expected, the secretary was standing near her desk, arms crossed, a smug smile spread across her young face.

Olive had placed the floor on lockdown.

Winter emitted an audible growl and charged toward her. Autumn quickly stepped between the two women, holding a hand up to stall her friend's impending takedown of the woman.

"Olive. You seem like a very intelligent, caring person. Are you aware of the horrible atrocities that your boss has been committing?" Autumn calmly and deliberately pronounced each syllable.

Olive's once friendly brown eyes filled with disdain. "Dr. Brandt is a good man."

"Well, that 'good man' has been abducting pregnant women, stealing their babies, and murdering the mothers after they give birth." Autumn studied the small woman's face before reaching out to touch her hand.

Olive wasn't involved in any of this. Her only crime had been believing that Russell Brandt was a saint. Falling in love with him probably hadn't been wise either.

But could she process this new information despite her personal sentiments?

"I don't believe you. I won't." Olive shook her head, her neat brunette bun beginning to loosen.

"He's groomed you, Olive. You don't *want* to believe me. He's brainwashed you into believing that he's a noble, kind person. I promise you, he isn't."

Autumn's soothing voice and gentle mannerisms had brought many people to their senses quite effectively.

Olive was not one of those people.

She was too immersed in a fantasy world where Dr. Brandt was her lover. That world was supposed to become reality one day. Being with Russell Brandt was her dream.

"Baby stealing mommy murderer" didn't digest too easily.

Winter stepped around Autumn and grabbed Olive's bun, yanking it backward until Olive yelped. The agent got nose to nose with the woman, her voice low and filled with threat. "Maybe you're an accomplice. I think that's *exactly* what you are. Maybe we should take you into custody as well. Aiding and abetting."

"No! I haven't done *anything*! I don't know *anything*!" Olive grasped at Winter's hand, but the agent's grip held firm.

"Then unlock these damn doors right now." Winter released the woman's hair, and Olive stumbled to the button near her desk that reversed the lockdown.

Autumn was sure the secretary was near tears as she obeyed Winter's orders.

But there wasn't time to care about Olive's ruffled feathers. When this was all over, Olive would be forced to accept the fact that her dreamboat boss was, in fact, a monster. Autumn knew they couldn't help her in the present moment.

Descending the stairs was much easier than climbing them. Less huffing on her part at least.

"You know," Autumn attempted to laugh, but her rapid breathing allowed only a raspy chuckle, "I think I'll have to disagree with your earlier assessment. You've convinced me that the hammer method can be *much* more effective than a cotton ball approach."

Winter used the rail to swing onto the landing and hit the next flight of steps at a run. "Ha. Occasionally, Dr. Trent. Only occasionally."

Reaching the main level, they burst into the reception area, where Aiden was *still* having a verbal standoff with the unyielding security guard. Autumn guessed he'd purposely kept the conversation going—as well as the pissing contest— to divert the guards.

The distraction had worked.

Their undertaking had failed.

Autumn tapped Aiden's shoulder while Winter jogged toward the front entrance. "He's not here. Private helicopter."

Aiden cursed under his breath and turned on his heel. Without a word, they headed toward the door, leaving the security guards to process what had just taken place.

The trio boarded the borrowed police copter again. Winter and Aiden sat in the two rear, forward facing seats, while Autumn sat directly behind the pilot, facing her co-workers. This arrangement allowed them all to have a window view but placed Winter and Aiden closer to the back cage where the guns were kept.

Once they were secured and their headphones in place, the pilot spoke into their ears. "I saw Brandt take off, and I've been working with the ground crew to track his path. But keep in mind, he's got a pretty good head start on us."

Aiden's phone buzzed, and he hit a button to Bluetooth the call into the headsets. "Give me some good news, Dalton."

Noah sounded out of breath. "The Brandt main compound is almost completely cleared out. Officers are checking every building, but whoever was here seems to have fled already."

Aiden tapped at his screen, and when Autumn leaned forward to get a better look, she realized he was looking at a map. "That's a ninety-two-acre ranch, Dalton. I don't want buildings 'checked.' I want every last inch of that compound *scoured!*"

While Aiden barked order after order, Winter's phone buzzed. Autumn glimpsed that Sun was the caller. Winter ripped the headphones off and pressed the phone to her ear.

While she burned with curiosity, Autumn could do nothing but attempt to read her lips. Eavesdropping had become impossible between the roar of the chopper and Aiden's urgent order shouting.

Winter ended the call after a couple minutes, and Aiden halted his conversation with Noah to get her update. "Sun's found Brandt's yacht. Same dummy corporation that owns the ranch. Currently moored in a Cocoa Beach marina."

Aiden repeated the news to Noah. "You're an hour away, and we need immediate help. Call in the local SWAT and HRT and get them moving in the marina's direction. Rally the Coast Guard as well in case the teams can't get there fast enough."

Aiden disconnected the call, and Autumn asked a question she wasn't sure she wanted the answer to.

"Hostage Rescue Team. Why do you need them?"

Aiden stared at her, his cool blue eyes grave. "They have the two newborn Welsh girls, and those are just the infants we know about. There's a good chance those babies are on that boat."

Autumn dug her nails into the leather of her seat.

Even saving just two babies would be a wonderful feat. And if they were able to stop the boat, they could probably force someone to cough up the details of the island's location. Assuming anyone aside from Brandt even knew that information.

Their helicopter had an ETA of fifteen minutes.

Autumn wondered helplessly if that would be fast enough.

30

Fifteen minutes wasn't exactly a never-ending period of time, but Winter was convinced this flight was the longest she'd ever experienced in her career. Maybe her life.

The only action that Winter, Autumn, or Aiden could take was to hope. Hope that Noah and the ground teams could get the state of affairs organized and operating at the Cocoa Beach Marina.

The wait was excruciating.

But the destination was near. Winter was aware that the great expanse of the sparkling blue ocean water was getting larger—closer.

The pilot's voice crackled through her headset just as her phone began buzzing again.

Sun.

Before she could take the call, the pilot said, "The craft we're in pursuit of has deviated." He sounded grim. "I repeat, *deviated* from the expected flight path."

Trying to understand why Brandt would do such a thing, Winter took the call. "Sun, what's happening?"

"The Cocoa Beach Marina is a decoy." Winter felt the

anger and frustration drip from the words. "Brandt's actual destination is Vero Beach. I've already let Noah know, and he's on his way. He's closer to Vero Beach than your copter at this point."

Dammit dammit dammit.

"Brandt's chopper just changed course, so that aligns with what we're seeing from the air."

After Sun assured her she'd keep digging to see if Brandt might have any more surprises for them, Winter disconnected the call.

"We've been duped," she told the group. "Agent Ming just informed me that Cocoa Beach was a decoy. The real target is *Vero Beach*." Winter shouted a list of expletives in her head.

Why was this case such a godforsaken circus?

Because the man was both brilliant and wealthy. That combination let a number of really bad guys go free, she knew. She didn't like it, but that was the way it was.

"Changing course. Heading south. Let's hope we have enough fuel to actually get there." The pilot muttered the last part. Clearly, he was just as irritated as they were.

Winter exchanged glances with Autumn and Aiden.

How fun. Another wish to blindly hope for while we sit here doing absolutely nothing.

The three of them would all need immediate transport to the psych ward by the time this ride was over.

No more than five minutes passed before Winter's phone buzzed once more. She glimpsed Noah's name and pressed the phone to her ear.

"You all right, Dalton?"

"Sure, I'm *great* considering all the time I wasted getting the SWAT teams and Coast Guard alerted to the situation at the *wrong fucking beach*!"

Winter unbuckled and moved forward to tap the pilot's shoulder. "Can you put this call through to everyone's headset?" He nodded, and Noah was immediately yelling into Autumn and Aiden's ears as well.

"I've alerted all teams to the new destination, but Vero Beach has a problem. An accident involving two civilian boats, and all available vessels in that area are busy working to save the seven people involved in the crash. Three children are being rescued. One is missing."

Winter sighed deeply while Autumn's eyes widened with disbelief. Aiden smacked a frustrated hand to his forehead.

"Cutters are being sent to assist as well as a copter out of Miami. But their ETA is at least five minutes behind your arrival. I do have the local SWAT on ground and ready to go. We'll have the boat pinned down from at least four points. Not six, but better than nothing."

Noah was running. His ragged breathing was broken only by the echo of his shoes slamming against the wood of the dock.

"Shit." Noah added a few more expletives before shouting, "Hey! You! FBI! Lookin' for a yacht called Eden's Paradise!"

Winter strained to make out what had to be a dockhand responding but couldn't. Noah's panting resumed.

Winter turned to the pilot. "Is Brandt's helicopter still in flight?"

"Affirmative, but we still don't have a visual."

Dammit.

"Noah, tell me what you're seeing."

"This place is huge, and no one seems to know anything. I'm searching but—"

Boom!

What sounded like a clap of thunder exploded into their ears, making them all jump and scramble to pull the radios from their heads. Everyone except Winter. She knew that sound. It wasn't thunder...

"Noah?" Winter's entire body flooded with ice-cold panic. "*Noah*! Are you okay? Noah! Say something!"

No response.

"Noah! *Noah*!" Winter was screaming now, her heart beating so hard she thought the savage pulse may strangle her.

Nothing.

She looked at the phone. The call had disconnected.

Autumn's arm slipped around her, pulling her close. A gesture of comfort.

People only needed comforting when something terrible happened.

Fighting back tears, Winter ached at the onslaught of memories that assailed her. Noah's wide grin and quick wit that he used often, especially when he wanted to bust any amount of tension in a room.

He was so smart, and he used that big grin and easy-going manner as camouflage so that people would underestimate him. She couldn't even begin to name the number of times she'd seen others do a double take when he transformed from a Texas hick to a steel-trap mind in a blink of an eye.

Noah was good at his job for so many reasons, but more than anything, he was good at it because he cared about people so much. He wanted to right the wrongs, avenge those who'd been hurt. Make a difference in as many lives as he could.

He was insanely beautiful and had a body that could win awards. But he didn't seem to notice or care. He enjoyed dressing up and dressing down. He ate anything from the finest cuisine in elegant restaurants to pizza on the living room couch.

More than anything...he loved her, even with all her flaws. He didn't try to change her or fix her or judge her. He simply accepted her, warts and all. He wanted to make her happy just as much as she wanted his happiness in return.

She'd even been thinking more and more about their future. About marriage and babies and a home to raise them in. They'd even spoken about tying the knot, but she'd put the idea off as though being his wife was an obnoxious errand she could take care of later.

The boom of the explosion vibrated through her mind.

Would there even be a later now?

Please be okay.

She needed him to be okay.

"Noah…" she said one more time, the word barely escaping her dry lips.

There was no answer.

He was gone.

31

Noah sputtered and spewed brackish water as he surfaced. Gasping for air, he attempted to process what in the hell had just happened.

Whatever that explosion was, the force of the blowup had sent him flying ten feet through the air. He was damn lucky to have landed in the water instead of slamming into a much more solid surface. His face and neck stung from the small pieces of shrapnel that hit him from the blast, but other than that, he was damned lucky. He was certain of that.

For a frantic second, Noah thought that Brandt might have blown up his yacht, babies and all. He spun in the water, treading fervently and seeking the source of the blast.

It didn't take him long. Black smoke billowed from the raging fire that seemed to take up a great deal of the coast.

The damn marina is on fire!

As that information sank in, he spotted his gathered SWAT team and other law enforcement rushing toward the blazing building where the fiery eruption would leave an empty shell.

Shit!

They *had* to respond. Their jobs required instant action to the most immediate need.

As a screaming man ran toward the water, his clothes a fiery halo surrounding him, Noah knew exactly where that most immediate need was.

While Noah understood, he also came face-to-face with the fact that he was almost entirely on his own now. Bree was back at the ranch overseeing the search of the gargantuan compound. Sun was in Lavender Lake, dutifully working her magic on her computer.

Winter, Autumn, and Aiden were still in the air.

Winter.

The blast had knocked his phone straight out of his hand, and the cell was likely somewhere at the bottom of the Indian Lake Lagoon by now.

He couldn't reach Winter, couldn't assure her that he was still alive. Knowing she must be terrified made him sick, but nothing could be done to rectify the situation right then.

Ears ringing like relentless church bells, Noah swam toward land, searching for a place where he'd be able to climb back up to the docks.

Seconds before the explosion, a dockhand had shown him the general direction to follow in order to find Brandt's yacht. The mega-craft of Eden's Paradise was well-known throughout the marina.

Heaving his body back onto the dock, he ripped off his sodden suit jacket. The water-weight of the clinging fabric would only slow him down.

His shoes squished with every step as he ran down the pier, and he considered taking them off to increase his speed. He didn't. He was afraid he was already too late and didn't want to waste the precious time to kick them off.

Deal with it. Nothin' you can do about it now.

He spotted a giant white ship at the end of the longest pier in the marina. Of course.

Why's it always gotta be at the very damn end of wherever I'm trying to go?

Nearing the monstrous craft, Noah realized the ship was pulling away from its slip. And sure enough, Eden's Paradise was boldly imprinted on the back.

This was Brandt's yacht, and the beast was leaving at full speed.

Noah made his stride longer, faster, but the powerful engines of the boat were running to their full capacity. If yacht clubs had a wake zone rule, the captain of Eden's Paradise sure didn't give a shit about the stipulation.

Frantically scanning the remaining dock, Noah sought a point where he could possibly intercept the fleeing vessel. At the very end of the pier, another slip jutted out to fit what must have been an even *larger* yacht than Brandt's.

The slip had to be close to two hundred feet long. The concept of anyone actually needing a boat that size was asinine. Not that he'd turn something like that down.

Damn. How can I get an introduction with that *guy?*

Gauging his angle, Noah eyed several men and women scurrying around on the deck of Eden's Paradise. There was far too much movement to even attempt a count, and he was certain that he didn't spot any babies.

But surely the infants had been secured within the safety of a cabin below decks.

He was damn well sure about to find out.

Noah's soaked shoes slid while he made a sharp turn onto the last slip, nearly causing him a hard fall. Pinwheeling his arms, he planted a hand on the pier and pushed himself back up. Hating that he lost that precious second, he charged toward his target, cursing as he calculated how close this was going to be.

The ship was moving fast, but so was he.

Zeroing in on the craft, he noted that the crew hadn't yet raised all the mooring rope they'd used to secure the yacht to the dock. The thick braids dangling down the side were his last hope of getting on that ship.

He only needed to get ahold of one. Just one.

With only a few feet left to run, Eden's Paradise pulled past the pier, the huge engines churning the water and causing the dock to rise and fall with their force. Noah leapt into the air, reaching for the dangling ropes. His fingers touched the scratchy surface, but he was millimeters away from grasping hold.

Cursing with every inch he fell, Noah plunged into the murky saltwater once again. The moment he surfaced, he began swimming for the dock, furious over his failed attempt.

Boom!

A second explosion erupted, causing the water around him to ripple with the force. He turned, intent on locating the source. The blast was farther down the coast this time, but the resulting fire and smoke were easily visible.

What the hell is going on?

But as he pulled himself up and out of the water for the second time that day, he thought he already knew. Collateral damage.

Noah didn't believe in coincidences and had no doubt the Brandt cult was responsible for the explosions. It was a distraction, he knew. A good one. Rescue personnel would have no choice but to focus on saving those they could.

How many bombs had these crazy brainwashed mother-fuckers set? Brandt and his followers were obviously one hundred percent okay with killing innocent civilians in the name of escape. In the name of their mission.

Bastards.

Noah stared as the yacht cruised away, rage burning through his veins.

Fueled by a renewed flood of adrenaline and disgust for Russell Brandt's very existence, Noah reached the dock and pulled himself out of the water.

No phone, no radio. Noah had to find a way to warn the local police of possible impending explosions. They needed to get all the coastline buildings evacuated immediately.

Running back up the slip he'd just sprinted down, Noah thought of the stolen babies on board that boat.

So close.

But right now, there was nothing more he could do to save them.

The frustration was maddening.

Chuf chuf chuf chuf!

A familiar timbre vibrated the air, moving closer and louder with each second that passed. Shielding his eyes from the relentless Florida sun, he spotted a shiny white helicopter flying his way.

He scanned the craft. The XY Cryolabs logo was proudly displayed on the side. The copter was moving fast but also...low.

Through the cacophony of smoke and sirens, Noah's training kicked in, and his breathing returned to normal as every last ounce of his attention focused on the chopper heading his way.

He had no means of communication, but he had this... Noah pulled his Glock from its holster, grateful for the gun's water resistance, and gave the steel a quick kiss.

The beauty had taken two dips in the sea within the past ten minutes, but a Glock was a Glock. If the gun couldn't hold its own against a little water, then the damn chunk of metal didn't deserve its name to begin with.

As the aircraft approached, Noah calculated the approximate angle and speed of the chopper as well as the breeze coming from the sea. He worked to slow his breathing, and a sudden wave of déjà vu thrust him back in time.

Dust swirled as the hostile's chopper flew closer, nearly blinding him with a curtain of sand. He would either make this shot or witness his fellow marines get blown apart without mercy. They were his friends—his brothers. Hell or high water, he had to take this sputtering copter down.

"Shake it off, Dalton." Noah refocused on the present moment. The current war.

Right now, it wasn't his buddies' lives at stake. Right now, he was fighting for the lives of innocent babies...how many, he didn't know.

He knew only one thing. He'd only have seconds to take the shot.

Beastly main rotors of steel and brass graced the sleek XY Cryolabs helicopter. One bullet, especially from his angle, couldn't possibly take them out.

A lucky shot could disable the engine or strike a critical hydraulic line of the chopper's body. But the odds of pulling off such a hit were highly unlikely. That left two choices, and even though he'd probably get his ass suspended for firing a single shot, he didn't care.

The pilot or the tail rotor. Shoot one of them. Shoot both of them.

Flexing his grip, Noah blinked the last of the water from his eyes as the chopper flew within range. He might not be able to stop the cult leader, but he had a chance of slowing him down.

Muscle memory was a beautiful thing, and Noah fell into the zone he'd learned during sniper training. His breathing slowed and his jaw went slack as he transitioned into the almost tranquil state needed to take long shots.

He'd flushed out of the course because he simply had too

much energy to stay still for that long, but he'd picked up some skills. Tension was the enemy of a good sniper, and as Noah zeroed in on the bird closing in, his heart rate slowed, his body doing whatever was needed to support him when it was time to take the shot.

"Engaging." There was no one to hear the word, but it needed to be said. It was part of the process.

Calm and relaxed, he went to one knee for better stability, then aimed at the windshield and the pale circle of the doctor's face behind the glass. Maybe he could crack the glass enough to force Brandt to land.

"Yippee-ki-yay…"

Taking one last breath and letting it out, Noah pulled the trigger during the pause. One…two…three…

The bullets pinged off the windshield as though he were merely shooting a long-range Nerf gun. Reinforced. He wasn't surprised…and he was ready for his last option.

The copter barreled overhead, and Noah turned, gun still at the ready. He took aim, this time targeting the tail rotor.

Miss.

Miss.

Miss.

Hit.

Special Agent Noah Dalton let out a triumphant roar as the last bullet clipped a rotor blade, causing the aircraft to lurch to the left.

"Please spin, please spin, please spin!" Noah begged through gritted teeth. He'd done all he could do with what he had. Gravity, he hoped, would do the rest.

Just when it looked as if the helicopter would go nose first into the ocean, Brandt righted the aircraft, and Noah knew he was only able to do so because of the insane speed the damn white demon had been going. The maniacal asshole had been flying at top speed, around one hundred fifty or sixty miles an hour at Noah's best guess. That speed had allowed the vertical surfaces of the body to stabilize the copter and prevent a fatal spin.

Even though he hadn't immediately crashed, the controls would be working against the good doctor now, and if that damn blade he hit would just break off completely, the real trouble would begin. Although a marvel of mechanics, the tail rotor generally consisted of light materials—vulnerable materials—such as fiberglass and hollow aluminum.

The contraption most certainly wasn't bullet proof.

For now, Brandt could steer by manipulating the engine speed and the pitch of the main rotor blades. But that required expertise and extreme concentration, and Noah guessed Brandt didn't have much of the latter to spare right now.

He'd given that psychotic bastard a few unanticipated problems to deal with.

Currently, it was the best he could do.

32

Autumn pressed the binoculars to her eyes, searching the distance for any glimpse of what was happening at the marina. Behind her, Aiden was on the line with emergency personnel, and a frantic Winter called Noah's phone over and over.

The air reeked of chaos.

Autumn didn't want to brood about Noah right now—not that she could stop entirely. The multitude of unfortunate events that Agent Dalton could have run into were so innumerable, contemplating them would drive her insane.

"ETA in two minutes!" Their pilot's deep voice cut through the commotion.

Up ahead, Autumn spotted the marina with its long line of boats. Another helicopter invaded her vision, gleaming white and heading straight for—

A riveting flash of orange and red appeared in the far-right corner of the binocular's lens. "Shit!" Autumn yelled, nearly dropping the field glasses.

Winter and Aiden both swiveled their heads toward her.

"What happened?" Aiden barked while Winter, looking pale as death, tapped Noah's contact number again.

"Another explosion. This time a building farther south went up in a ball of flames." Autumn had trouble believing what she was witnessing. That was the second blast within only a few minutes.

How many more?

She lifted the binoculars back up, not wanting to lose sight of Brant's helicopter.

"There it is. Shiny white chopper. Going south over a bay or lagoon..."

Autumn gave the play by play, unsure if Winter or Aiden were even able to follow her words.

"Now, it's over a thin strip of land and—" Autumn gasped as the hind end of the craft lurched hard to the left.

Winter pressed next to her. "What? Another explosion?" Her voice was loud in Autumn's headset.

"No...it's..." Autumn peered harder. "I think shots were fired at Brandt's chopper." She focused the wheel, attempting to zoom in more closely.

A man was on the end of the dock, down on one knee, his hands raised toward Brandt's helicopter. Was that—

"I think that's Noah!" Autumn pointed as Winter ripped the binoculars out of her hands, taking a few moments to focus in on the correct location.

Winter's heavy sigh of relief nearly made Autumn cry. Pressed together as they were, she knew exactly what Winter had been tortured with. Her friend had believed Noah to be dead.

"I think so too," Winter agreed, her entire body relaxing heavily against Autumn.

One less horrifying possibility to worry about.

Autumn pulled the binoculars back and zeroed in on the XY Cryolabs gleaming white copter. It was flying crazy.

Please crash. Please crash. Please crash.

Now that she was able to focus on something besides fear for Noah, Winter had regained some color to her cheeks and was back in action. She located a second pair of binoculars and joined Autumn in scanning the horizon.

"The yacht is up ahead! My ten o'clock."

Autumn oriented herself and scanned farther south until she located the mammoth white vessel. She focused the wheel again until she could make out two letters. "I think you're right. I can spot a big E and P."

Eden's Paradise.

"Brandt must be either color-blind or color adverse," Winter muttered.

"Just a god complex." Autumn wrinkled her nose at Winter. She could think of about ten clinical reasons why the man preferred white, but she didn't want to dig into his psyche just yet. "Wants everything to be as lily white as his ass."

Winter snorted and shifted her binoculars again. "Brandt's chopper's in trouble."

The pilot agreed. "I think a tail rotor blade got hit. That's gonna make flying that duck a lot trickier."

Aiden slammed his phone on his thigh. Alarmed, Autumn turned toward him. "What?"

"Multiple emergencies happening on the ground. Law enforcement doesn't currently have the time nor the manpower to worry about a few escaping fugitives."

"If they knew the main fugitive was Satan himself..." Winter muttered beside her.

"They're evacuating all of the buildings along the coast and trying to save anyone they can from the explosions. The bombs *had* to be set for this exact purpose. Distraction. Chaos. We're on our own." Aiden pressed his lips together and shook his head.

Autumn knew the SSA was beginning to doubt a successful outcome was likely for their mission. Neither she nor Winter could say anything to the contrary.

She returned to the view of the XY helicopter and eyed it going even lower, its tail wildly swinging back and forth. And then she spotted the helipad on the back of the yacht.

Winter had discovered it as well. "He's going to land—"

"The idiot is *trying* for a controlled descent because of the tail rotor issue." The pilot didn't sound like he had much faith in the attempt. "'Trying' being the key word."

The babies. Autumn pictured their tiny helpless bodies lying peacefully in cribs. If the chopper crashed into the yacht, what happened to the babies? What chance did newborns stand against fiery wreckage and deep, dark waters?

The helicopter circled Eden's Paradise with movements that screamed *uncontrolled aircraft.* Their pilot was correct. In addition to being pure evil, Brandt was a complete idiot.

Dr. Russell Brandt would rather take his entire operation out in one catastrophic collision than sacrifice himself. Autumn held her breath as people on board the huge boat scurried in different directions as the chopper turned in erratic circles.

Stressed seconds passed before the copter became still. It had landed, but just barely. Only a portion of the craft was on the helipad circle, while the rest teetered over the top landing, its weight held only by the boat railing.

Autumn's breath rushed out of her distraught body. She needed to start taking yoga again, or practice deep meditation so she didn't end up having a heart attack by the time she was thirty.

"Now what?" The question came out steadier than she thought it would, which was good.

Surely there was an action they could take to save the

yacht's precious occupants. This mission *could not* end with infant children sinking to the bottom of the ocean. All the psychotherapy in the world wouldn't be able to make that image fade away.

Aiden and Winter stared at her blankly. Autumn understood. Their options for stopping this madman were growing slimmer with each passing minute.

The pilot gave them a glance over his shoulder. "We're getting severely low on fuel. We won't be able to follow for long. But someone should be able to pursue the boat with the signal from the chopper so that—"

Autumn gasped. "Oh no! It's not going to hold."

She was right. As they watched, Brandt's helicopter began to slide from its perilous perch. A man clad in an all-white suit—geez, she wondered who that was, the bastard—jumped from the chopper seconds before the railing gave out, letting the giant aircraft fall into the ocean with an enormous, Hollywood-worthy splash.

"Shit. Guess we're gonna have to follow the signal to hell instead, folks," the pilot quipped in a deadpan tone.

To the right of them, another red explosion blasted into the sky even farther down the coast. Flames and smoke decorated the coastline like a raging garland of fire.

Autumn sank back against her seat, trying to order her thoughts. Across from her, a golden glow of reflection adorned the depths of Winter's sapphire eyes as she stared at the massive blaze in silent horror.

Autumn forced her attention back to the yacht. They didn't even *need* a signal. "I think we've already *arrived* in hell."

33

F ive million dollars falling into the sea.

Just. Like. That.

I loved my heli, but the copter's demise wasn't my main frustration right then.

Money was just money. I'd have a replica built. Or maybe I would just upgrade altogether.

Right now, I was angry because the elaborate plan that should have worked to perfection had been effectively ruined. Destroyed.

I hadn't intended to land just yet, and not just because the merry little ride along the coastline had proven more enjoyable than I ever expected.

What a treat!

As a boy, I wasn't allowed to play sports or do anything that might be even remotely dangerous because my parents didn't want me to put myself at risk. My schedule was rigorously dictated, and I was allowed to watch only one hour of television per day, which almost always consisted of shows that involved a great deal of chase scenes. Chase scenes just like the one I was personally involved in today.

Of course, my nannies never let me watch all that I wanted before I was thrust in front of my tutors again. My parents had even built a personal study just for me, where my tutors worked with "one of the greatest minds of our time."

That was me.

I'd graduated from high school at twelve and had my bachelor's degree by fourteen. I was Dr. Russell Brandt by the age of twenty, though my father had been greatly disappointed that I hadn't followed in his surgeon's steps.

Creation.

That was what fascinated me most. Watching two miniscule cells combining and then dividing to create a human being. It was the biggest miracle of all. I'd loved being part of the process for those unable to conceive themselves. I'd been happy, or so I'd thought at the time. I hadn't known true happiness until The Dream.

And now, The Dream was at risk.

Because of a single bullet.

Not only had that bullet cost me the most adrenaline-fueled ride of my life, being forced to land put my loyal family members at risk. They hadn't yet traveled far enough away to be safe from human law.

Which shouldn't have happened.

Hours of intricate detailing had been spent creating this extravagant exit strategy.

The performance of my life now marred by one single bullet from a common man.

I'd intended to give the Feds an even longer chase, leading them across the ocean while Eden's Paradise sailed away to the *actual* paradise of Eden.

I'd dutifully calculated the agents' flight time when they traveled north to confront my brother and sister-in-law.

Just the thought of Amanda made the icy rage I was

hiding from my faithful followers bubble up like lava. I rather wished she'd accidentally been eliminated during the whole kerfuffle, but that was apparently hoping for too much.

If you want a job done right…

But that was the thing…I had done the job just right. I'd even done the math and determined the FBI returning flight time to XY Cryolabs, over to Cocoa Beach, and down the coast. Based on how long I anticipated them being in the air, I was certain they'd run out of fuel incredibly soon.

While I still enjoyed a full tank.

I had to confess—to myself alone at least—that my journey south had been mostly driven by my desire to witness the explosives I'd so carefully set years ago do their work.

Finally.

And my oh my. The fireworks were fabulous. I hadn't been this alive in months.

Classic, cartoonish, TNT-like blasts—so satisfyingly magnificent. All that was missing were giant word bubbles in the sky reading KABOOM!

Delightful.

Of course, I sobered myself momentarily with each explosion, thanking the souls who fell victim to the flame for their humble sacrifice. They would never know that their deaths helped ensure my survival…and the new hope for this rotting planet.

The only hope.

They were martyrs, really. Unaware martyrs. But the ending was the same, and they'd still died for a noble cause.

All acts of service to The Dream were righteously pure. Virtuous.

Being shot at had certainly been unexpected. How had the FBI even known where to go? They should have stayed on course straight to Cocoa Beach, where absolutely nothing —aside from a group of very hyped up and worried law enforcement—would meet them.

But one of their demon federal techies had dug up the Vero Beach information.

And if they knew that, would they be able to find Eden's location as well?

No. Absolutely not.

The island was hidden under layers of corporate infrastructures that no other asset I owned could be connected to. But so was the ranch…

Disturbing.

Roger and Amanda knew *of* the island, of course. They'd even visited the paradise, but I'd never told either of them the GPS location. Divine wisdom had kept me from making that mistake.

Amanda could betray me all she wanted, but she didn't have the power to give away Eden. *I hadn't allowed her that might.*

Only *one* other person knew Eden's location, and that was the captain of Eden's Paradise. Not even the attorney who'd originally set up the legal infrastructures was a threat. Apparently *that* poor man had fallen on a bit of bad luck shortly after finishing his services for me. Overwhelmed, he'd ended his own life with a well-placed bullet to the brain.

That was the official story which the authorities believed, anyway.

To this day, I still chuckled when I thought of him. Such a nice guy. Always good for a joke. We'd even made plans to go golfing together.

He'd been just one tiny cog in the great machine that was The Dream.

Certainly, the compilation of all my cautious preparations wouldn't be destroyed simply because I'd been forced to land *on my own yacht.* But the turn of events *was* truly exasperating.

I wanted to scream to the heavens in frustration but held the urge in. My children were already scared. I must show them that all would be well.

If I could stop obsessing over that stupid bastard on the dock, I might be able to concentrate a bit better.

The fact that he was there in the first place was maddening. Then for him to have been able to damage the tail rotor *so easily*. The yoke had immediately grown sluggish, and high speed alone had kept me from finding myself in a tailspin that rendered all control unrecoverable.

The damaged rotor blade had forced me to set down on Eden's Paradise. Even then, I'd been aggravated but not too terribly worried. Every law enforcement official in the state of Florida was busy dealing with the explosions.

Such a clever idea, planting those distractions. I'd placed them three years ago, and even back then, I hadn't thought I'd ever need them. Not really.

But human life was full of hardship. I had long ago accepted that.

Expect the unexpected.

And today had proven that not every surprise was a bad surprise.

The explosive show had been nothing short of glorious.

And the bombs weren't the only important part of my elaborate escape plan.

Upon my move to Florida, I'd gone so far as purchasing and registering this very yacht I stood on in Ecuador. The country was famous for offering asylum. I'd also registered a plane in Ecuador, which sat in a hangar on the island of Eden.

The plane was a fail-safe, in case I needed to make a longer journey than the helicopter or yacht would allow.

I had taken every possible outcome into deep consideration.

My wealth had been used wisely, carefully diversified into many different accounts. My patents and copyrights were listed to various aliases just in case the government ever attempted to freeze my finances.

All of that genius effort, and yet...here I was.

"Father?"

I froze as the soft voice registered...

No.

It couldn't be her. Maybe I hit my head as I steered the helicopter back on course? Surely that must be it.

"Father?"

Absolutely not. It could not be her.

The very idea of that familiar voice turned my blood to ice. She shouldn't have been this near. But that was unmistakably her voice.

How? Where? Why? *No.*

I turned, gazing down into the dark blue eyes of Sasha. Eyes that were too large. Eyes that could be mistaken for no one else's. And those cursed too-dark curls framing her horribly freckled skin.

Maybe this was her ghost.

I had distinctly ordered that she be left at the ranch. Her presence there would give the authorities someone to tie the crimes to. She would have been the perfect scapegoat on which they could place the blame and drop the chase of my beautiful family.

"What are you—"

Before I could even finish the question, a police chopper appeared in my periphery. The craft circled my ship, probably trying to determine what weapons my people might have, if any.

The children of Eden *did* have weapons, but not many. A

few rifles and pistols were kept on the yacht, but not enough to ever be accused of running guns for profit.

I now regretted that call.

I had my own personal cache of weaponry and ammo onboard the helicopter, which by now was sitting at the bottom of the Atlantic.

My inner scream was building.

"Father!" A different voice this time—a man's voice.

I forced my attention away from Sasha's abhorrent face and turned to the captain of my ship. Brother Warren Tharp appeared cool, composed, and confident.

His eyes were telling me a much different story.

Stepping away from Sasha, I followed Brother Warren back to the bridge where he pointed to the radar. "Coast guard." His foreboding gaze locked with mine.

"How many?" Every muscle in my body tightened into a violent knot.

"Just one for now, Father. But—"

"There will be more," I finished for him.

The time had come to discuss a new plan of action. We couldn't simply lead the authorities straight to the island. The notion was ridiculous.

But we *were* on a gigantic glistening white yacht. Hide and seek wasn't exactly an option either.

My distractions had all worked...but they weren't enough. I'd underestimated the power of those intent on stopping The Dream.

Evil. Corrupt. Wicked.

As the last word came to mind, it was followed by an idea. Turning to face the wide windows of the bridge, I scanned the deck until I found the wicked one I sought.

Sasha.

She lifted a hand as our eyes met, a worried expression on

her face. I smiled, and like I'd waved a magic wand, the worry was replaced with pure happiness.

I beckoned her to me, and gazed down into her loathsome face.

"I need your assistance, my child."

Joy radiated from her every pore. "Yes, Father. Anything."

The plan in my mind was fully formed by the time I sent her back outside. Pleased, I turned back to Brother Warren.

I inhaled deeply. "I daresay it's time for Plan B, Brother."

34

"I'm in the wrong profession," Autumn muttered, getting her first close-up view of Dr. Brandt's yacht.

Enormous, gleaming white, and so sleek that the impression of a bullet in the water wasn't a stretch. Apparently, being a psychopathic, delusional murderer paid quite well.

"Coast Guard vessel is approaching at an intercept angle," the pilot updated.

Autumn's entire body sagged in relief.

She studied the boat and its passengers, pointing to a few specific individuals. "Those men have pistols."

"We're out of range. Pistols only shoot fifty yards, and I don't intend to get that close." Their pilot seemed confident in his flight skills, which eased a tad of Autumn's distress.

However, the majority of her torment would only be quelled when the babies were safe and far away from Russell Brandt's madness.

"Our low fuel situation is getting more serious. Another chopper should be coming to replace us. For now, we're just gonna tail the boat until we have no choice but turn back, or until we can board the damn behemoth without issue."

Autumn turned to the pilot, her brow furrowed. "How long will the replacement copter take?"

He shook his head. "Don't know. I'm guessin' with all of the explosions along the coast, they could take a while."

Autumn glanced at Aiden's burdened face. The waiting had darkened his features considerably.

"Can you give me control of the external speaker?" The SSA was ready to take action. The pilot hit a button and gave Aiden a thumbs-up.

"Go time," Winter murmured.

"This is Supervisory Special Agent Aiden Parrish with the FBI." His voice blasted over the water. "I'm ordering you to turn off the engines and stop this vessel. Drop your weapons and lay face-first on the deck with your hands on your heads. Now."

Not a single person followed his commands. Autumn knew Aiden hadn't expected them to, but protocol was protocol. She didn't need Quantico to understand the importance of following each and every step.

"What now?" Autumn asked.

Aiden opened the caged doors behind him and grabbed a pair of police issued rifles. He handed one to Winter, and they both carefully trained the borrowed firearms at the yacht.

Autumn blew out a breath. Though they'd said nothing, she got the picture clearly enough.

Minutes later, the Coast Guard cutter appeared and swiftly approached Brandt's ship. They announced themselves as well and were met with the same lack of response. Though their boat was much smaller, the craft was also much faster.

Autumn spotted the military personnel on board. They all had guns, and they certainly knew how to use them.

Receiving no acknowledgement at all, Aiden repeated his orders verbatim.

There was an immediate response this time, and not one they had foreseen or wanted.

Brandt himself approached the railing, and while Autumn watched, he grabbed the arm of the woman by his side. It was Sasha, the woman they'd been looking for.

Winter seemed to agree. "It's her. What is he do—"

Autumn gasped when he picked the small woman up… and threw her overboard without a hint of warning.

"Shit!"

Autumn couldn't agree with Winter more. Scrambling for a better view, she waited until Sasha's head bobbed above the water. She didn't even have time to be relieved that the young woman had survived the fall when Brandt pushed two more unsuspecting followers into the sea.

Autumn could barely believe what she was witnessing. Weren't these Brandt's faithful subjects? Pressing the binoculars to her eyes, she could make out the expressions of the others on board.

They appeared startled—horrified—backing away from their leader in rushed steps. Clearly, Brandt had surprised them all with this part of his plan. The passengers of Eden's Paradise were as mortified as Autumn felt.

That's when she understood. "Another distraction," she murmured.

Winter nodded as the Coast Guard immediately diverted to pull the thrashing bodies from the water. "Another damn good distraction."

A flash of pure white caught Autumn's attention again, and she focused back on the deck. She watched the doctor going down a set of steps, and within minutes, he returned holding a…

"No," Autumn breathed, her hand moving to her mouth. Surely...*no.*

Dr. Russell Brandt was holding a baby.

"What the hell?" the pilot yelled.

Autumn wildly scanned the water for help. There wasn't any. The Coast Guard was even farther away now, still rescuing Brandt's human diversions.

The maniacal doctor walked directly to the side of the monstrous boat and held the little bundle out over the rail.

Overwhelming panic surged through Autumn's veins. She gazed down at the water. Their helicopter was only fifty feet or so above the sea. "Get closer!" she screamed at the pilot. She shot a brief glance toward Aiden and Winter. "Cover me!"

Winter immediately gripped her arm, and Autumn swung around to reassure her friend. "I'm a *good* swimmer, Winter. A *strong* swimmer. We *cannot* let that baby die!"

Winter's fingers released, and Autumn peered from Winter to Aiden, who both nodded their approval. All three of them knew Autumn's plan was the best chance they had of saving the newborn.

"He won't do it." Aiden shook his head, but his tense posture told Autumn that he wasn't sure of that.

"If the babies are gone, we can't prove a genetic connection, and a huge majority of our case is down the drain. Gone." Autumn had ascertained a pinnacle point.

Aiden's jaw tensed, but he remained silent. He knew she was right.

Autumn leaned toward the pilot. "Can you swing around to the side closest to Brandt and go as far down as we can possibly hover?" The pilot nodded, proceeding to follow the instructions.

As she opened the helicopter door, a man on the deck lifted his pistol, and Winter instantly gave off a warning shot.

All the guns on the ship deck lowered, but Winter kept hers raised. "This waiting is driving me insane," Winter barked.

Autumn understood. Winter had been conditioned for action. She was trained to bring the hammer down, and right now, the three of them were as impotent as flies on a wall.

Aiden emitted a low growl and raised the megaphone again. "This is Supervisory Special Agent Aiden Parrish with the FBI. I am issuing your last—"

Russell Brandt beamed a freakishly wide smile up at them, then opened his hand and let the bundled infant drop.

He was laughing.

Laughing why?

Because he knew that nothing she did would save the child?

It was Autumn's fear. Not losing her own life. She feared living with the knowledge that she'd failed to save another.

Sarah.

She ignored the wild pounding of her heart. "Closer! Get closer and lower!" Autumn screamed the order and yanked off her headset, tossing the device along with her cell onto her seat. The pilot immediately heeded.

Autumn frantically pulled off her shoes and waited until the pilot said, "This is as low as I can go."

She jumped from the helicopter without another word.

In high school, she'd been on the swim team, and had taken an interest in diving, although her school was too small to have an actual diving team. The beautiful marvel of muscle memory brought the skill back, and her body tightened into a vertical line straight down to her pointed toes as she hit the water. She was quickly reminded of how hard the water hit back.

Autumn had expected the sting and wasn't worried for her own well-being. But the baby had fallen from a high height as well. Could those fragile little bones and tender head even survive such a drop?

As her body shot back up through the millions of bubbles her intrusion had created, Autumn angled toward the yacht. She began to swim the moment she resurfaced.

Even if the baby didn't survive, they would need its tiny body as proof of the evil doctor's horrendous plan. She would not let the infant perish in vain.

Autumn half-expected bullets to begin raining down as she raised her head to get an idea of her position. In the time she had taken to swim around forty yards, the yacht had gotten much farther away.

She surveyed the stretch of sea ahead, searching with desperation.

Then she saw it—a white blanket floating in the distance.

Autumn inhaled a deep breath and swam again. The bundle was closer, closer, closer—until she finally could reach out for the baby, be it dead or alive.

Grasping the blanket, she pulled the infant to her chest, turning the child so she could see its tiny face, praying the entire time for some miracle.

It was a bottle.

More accurately, it was a half-empty two-liter bottle of Sprite with a baby blanket taped around it. That unbelievable bastard had tossed out a decoy.

Autumn had fully believed she was swimming toward a helpless newborn. She'd also been nearly positive that the newborn was dead and had mentally prepared herself for the sight as well as the task of bringing the tiny corpse back. Tears of frustration and pure hatred burned her eyes as she continued to tread water.

Her thoughts were drowned out by roaring engines and swirling chopper blades that were becoming louder by the second. The sound brought her no joy.

Thanks to that Brandt son of a bitch, the Coast Guard would now waste precious time hauling her impulsive ass out of the sea.

From behind her, even louder engines and rotors drowned out all other activity. Autumn turned in the water, and her jaw dropped as she witnessed one of the biggest helicopters she'd ever seen barreling toward the mess that was their mission.

She blinked the salt water from her eyes, identifying the giant aircraft—a Blackhawk. Multiple soldiers stood at the door dressed in head to toe black, their automatic weapons at the ready.

A sharp voice filled with authority ordered the captain of the yacht to stand down, and the men on board were dropping their weapons even before they received the barked instructions. Guns were tossed away as every person Autumn could see moved to the rails, hands on their heads. Autumn would have shouted for joy were she able to get a deep enough breath.

A neon life preserver landed with a splash only a foot or so away, causing Autumn a heart-stopping moment of alarm. As caught up as she'd been by the action taking place in front of her, she hadn't forgotten that she was bobbing like a cork in a body of water that held predators who might decide she'd make a tasty lunch.

Grateful, she grabbed hold of the ring with one arm while clutching the fake baby with the other. Moments later, Coast Guardsmen pulled her over and up onto their boat.

Fascinated, Autumn stayed riveted to the scene unfolding before her. Navy SEALs rappelled from the Blackhawk and dropped onto the deck of the luxury boat with an ease that made her jealous.

Eden's Paradise had surrendered. And in the middle of all the activity, a blond man dressed in a pristine white, three-piece suit was on his knees, his hands on top of his head.

"Not so divine now, are you, asshole," she murmured to herself, still holding the baby decoy in her arms as a heavy blanket was draped over her shoulders.

"Where did the SEALs come from?" Autumn asked a nearby guardsman.

"They were doing training maneuvers not far from here and answered the distress call for help." He shrugged. "Good timing, huh?"

Good timing indeed. Their arrival was an absolute miracle.

The SEALs arrival could have been the difference between seizing Eden's Paradise or failing the mission entirely.

A few minutes later, the police chopper carrying Winter and Aiden landed on the yacht's helipad. Autumn had almost forgotten the low fuel situation altogether in the midst of her quest to save the castaway baby soda bottle.

Her heart warmed as she viewed her friends safe. Alive.

The moment they landed, Winter jumped from the helicopter and headed below decks. Autumn barely breathed while the minutes passed.

Would Winter find the Welsh twins? Would she find *more* infants? What if there were guards waiting for her who refused to give up the babies, or thinking they had no choice, opened fire at the sight of a federal agent below decks?

Just when Autumn was convinced she would grind her teeth to the nub, Winter finally emerged on deck. Her arms were empty. As Autumn watched, her best friend marched straight over to Brandt and hauled him to his feet by the front of his shirt. Autumn just wished she could hear the tongue-lashing the arrogant man was surely receiving.

Autumn smiled. "Let him have it," she murmured.

The cutter's radio squawked, and Autumn listened as each cabin and room on the yacht was cleared by the SEALs. She shivered in the hot sun when no infants had been found.

How could that be possible? *Where were they?* Already transported to an island that no one knew how to find and Brandt would most assuredly never give up?

The radio went off again and shared a piece of information that raised her soggy spirits.

The captain of Eden's Paradise had made a mistake—and a rather large one at that. The GPS coordinates of the island were still logged into the history of the navigation system.

They were going to Eden.

35

W inter studied the disgraced Dr. Russell Brandt being led into the courtroom. His bright orange jumpsuit was a far cry from his usual meticulous white attire.

She bet the color was driving him insane. Well. *More* insane.

The last three days had been hectic, to say the least. Winter's normally pale skin was slightly burned from all the time she'd spent on the island, helping the hoard of law enforcement officers and social workers process through the children.

So. Many. Children. One hundred and eight, to be exact.

But the three days they'd spent on Eden working to uncover Brandt's hidden secrets had been a mere drop in the bucket compared to hundreds of days that would be spent closing this case and getting these innocent children back into the arms of the people they belonged to.

The press had been brutal—not that anyone was shocked by that. Once the island's location was leaked, reporters and journalists had arrived by plane, helicopter, and boat. Circling the island like starving sharks, they waited hours upon hours just to get the scoop or maybe a one-up on the other news outlets.

Shortly after the press, parents of missing children from all across the country also arrived. The hope they hadn't allowed themselves to entertain for so long was clearly visible on their strained faces.

Winter's heart ached for them as they were told, one after the other, that they would not be leaving the island with a child in their arms. Their disappointment was crushing, but nothing could be done to change the situation...yet.

DNA tests would take a couple of days, even with the rush the labs were promising. The children then had to be transported to mainland hospital facilities and given thorough physicals.

But in a happy twist of fate, every single child appeared to be healthy and well.

The only positive remark that could ever be said about Brandt was that he had assured the stolen young ones received round-the-clock, first-rate, loving care.

Winter was still shocked by the elaborate nature of Brandt's operation. The degree of precise planning required to accomplish an undertaking the size of Russell Brandt's would take years to comprehend and dissect completely.

Luckily, the mad scientist had pissed off a multitude of his faithful followers. Roger and Amanda, as well as Sasha and a number of other loyal subjects were ready to squawk like parrots all day, every day, *any day* for a chance at reduced sentences.

The insight these jaded individuals provided was speeding up the process of understanding the scope of Brandt's "mission."

The "Eden mothers," as they'd been called, had all believed they'd been saved by the Father when he took them to the island. He'd promised them a long, happy life taking care of children in a peaceful "heaven on Earth" utopia.

None of them had any idea that the children had been stolen. They believed themselves to be running a type of orphanage. Having no contact with the outside world ensured that they would never know any different.

Villains or victims? That question was being argued constantly on the morning and evening news, as well as twenty-four-hour information outlets across the country.

Personally, Winter found the Eden mothers all a bit dim-witted. An orphanage that only housed blonde children? This hadn't seemed off to even *one* of the women?

Then again, they called him the Father. They'd walked way too far down Brainwash Avenue to operate with any critical thinking skills.

She gritted her teeth, knowing she had to keep that thought to herself. Autumn had already cautioned her to be careful with how she treated the cult members, stating that, in many ways, they were victims too.

Winter didn't want to buy that for a second, but she'd learned enough about human emotion that she could see how being promised a perfect paradise like Eden could be enticing for many. The need to be included and loved was seductive...addictive.

Other legal ramifications were also coming to light. Nearly a dozen partners of missing pregnant women across the country were currently in prison. From the beginning, these men had proclaimed their innocence but had been found guilty anyway. In the days and weeks to come, Winter wondered how many of them would indeed be found inno-cent of murdering their wives and unborn children.

Those men would be freed, but did freedom repay the living hell they'd suffered through? Winter wasn't the psychologist of the team, but she was seasoned enough to know that nothing could ever make their tribulation "better."

Then, of course, the partners had all learned that the child they planned on embracing had been sired by a madman with a god complex. Those realizations were the saddest part of the entire mess in Winter's eyes.

Several fathers had already refused to claim a child, even when the DNA came back proving the child belonged to their late wife. So many emotions were involved, making the situation overwhelmingly complicated.

And sad. Maddening.

Would the children of Eden ever be able to truly find happiness after such a traumatizing event? Would they miss Eden and wish they could go back? Would they even remember Eden at all?

The questions were endless, and the answers mysteries that only time would solve. Winter wanted to believe that all the children could go on to live normal, healthy lives.

But Winter knew as well as anyone possibly could...there wasn't always a happy ending.

Justin...

Forcing her brother from her mind, she focused back on the people in this room. The courtroom hosted several parents seeking justice for themselves and their families. Russell Brandt hadn't just stolen their children. He'd annihilated these people's dreams.

Brad Conlon appeared pale and dejected sitting next to Alex Gorski-Wilson and the Welsh couple. Lindsay still was visibly drawn and exhausted, but she exuded a strength and happiness that Winter hadn't observed in her before.

Since the Welsh baby girls had been the two tiniest of the discovered children, DNA tests had been done immediately and were over. The twins were back home where they belonged, in the lovely nursery Lindsay had designed for them long ago.

Lindsay had secretly mentioned to Winter earlier that Josh was still trying to come to terms with the fact that Brandt was the girls' father, but she was hopeful that he'd see the girls as the innocents they were. He'd told Lindsay that they were a family and they loved each other. To Winter, that was a solid beginning.

"All rise!"

The judge swooped in, calling the court to order. The multitude of charges against Brandt that they knew so far were read aloud.

Surprising no one, the mad doctor smiled the entire time.

"How do you plead?"

"Not guilty, Your Honor." The entire team had expected this, but witnessing the bastard actually say the words out loud was insufferable.

What no one had expected was the prolific speech the doctor launched into.

"I have devoted my life to building a better world...a world that would have improved the lives of all mankind. Every decision I've made has been in the good interest of all humanity. I do not believe that a passionate dedication to spreading peace and love to the suffering masses is worthy of this hateful bombardment."

Winter's jaw dropped. Russell Brandt's narcissism knew no limits.

Brandt looked around the room with an exaggeration that made Winter narrow her eyes. What was he up to now?

"Why isn't Roger here?" Brandt said when he returned his attention back on the judge. "My brother is responsible for gravely endangering a sick infant's life. I only ever took pristine care of my little ones." The mind-boggling aspect of

Brandt's speech was that he wholly believed the crap coming out of his own mouth.

A low rumble of protest arose from the crowd. The judge slammed his gavel.

"Order! Order in the court!"

Brandt closed his mouth and resumed his incessant smiling.

Winter glimpsed Brad Conlon rising from his seat. The poor man was probably—

Brad went from still to running in an instant. Before Winter or anyone else could react, the grief-stricken husband leapt the bar between the gallery and the defense table. With a roar of triumph, he stabbed something straight into the doctor's throat.

A macabre fountain of blood spurted from Brandt's neck. The doctor clutched at his throat, his blue eyes frozen with fear and disbelief as his lips moved without even a whisper of sound.

"You killed my wife! You stole my family! You took everything away from me! *Everything*!" Brad shoved the pen deeper as he screamed, and the crimson geyser sprayed with assiduous vehemence.

Chaos descended upon the courtroom. Shouts, cries, frenzied disarray. The quiet scene had escalated into a hellish nightmare in the span of only a few moments.

Brad had appeared so *controlled*. Miserable and defeated, yes, but Winter had discerned nothing in the man's countenance that could have warned them of his intentions.

As guards cleared the mess of people from the courtroom, Brad Conlon was taken into custody. As he was forced onto the floor, his screams morphed into rageful sobs.

Dr. Russell Brandt had gone limp at the defense table, his head dropped forward to rest on the scarred wood. Scarlet now decorated his bright orange jumpsuit with bold, mortal splatter as his eyes eternally locked in a portrait of holy horror.

The "chosen one" drew his last breath, exhaling the dream of Eden into the sullied air of a fallible planet.

Winter couldn't stop staring at the now dead mastermind.

At her side, Noah lifted his shoulders and sighed. "Case dismissed."

36

D r. Autumn Trent yawned in the passenger's seat of Noah's rented Escalade. After Brandt's courtroom fiasco died down, the team had stayed for the arraignment of each person in the Eden cult.

"Not guilty" pleas declared one after the other until Autumn had fought the urge to scream.

The stolen infants, murdered women, distraught part-ners...so many lives ruined. Not a single person who'd placed a foot on that stand was innocent.

They were *all* guilty to a degree, cult members or not.

Cults were such a complicated phenomenon. Entire groups of individuals obsessed with a vision or mission they wholly believed to be the one and only path to...what?

Forgiveness, purification, immortality, righteousness, heaven, *purpose*...goals attained only by strict adherence to a divine design dictated by a single "flawless" individual.

A chosen one.

These leaders were usually incredibly charismatic, persuasive, and narcissistic as hell. But most importantly, they offered answers to questions that humans had grappled with since the beginning of time.

Questions that, in reality, could never be answered. Not in this lifetime.

Occasionally in droves, but more often person by person, a following was amassed to bring to life the fantasy of a mentally and emotionally unstable megalomaniac. This person's delusions of grandeur and self-importance became an unbendable way of life for loyal "believers."

Critical thought faded away into the fog of cognitive dissonance and rendered intelligent human beings nothing more than zombies in a state of blind—and often seemingly insane—devotion.

Autumn knew in her heart that Brandt's followers, for the most part, had been brainwashed. There was a certain level of victimization to that.

There also was a very graphic magnitude of victimization in having nothing left to relay the horror you experienced except a single, floating hand in a dank, miry pit of predator-filled water.

Autumn fought the urge to vomit.

The mothers—the actual mothers—were the true victims of this case.

And aside from Lindsay Welsh, they were already dead.

How did you find justice for a ghost?

Exhausting. The Lavender Lake case had taken a physical toll on the entire team. None of them had slept much since arriving in the Sunshine State. There were still reams of paperwork to be dealt with.

And Autumn was certain that the majority of her co-workers needed a healthy round of quality psychotherapy. Herself included.

"You still awake up there, Trent?" Winter's sleepy voice

told Autumn that she wasn't the only one on the verge of crashing.

"You know it. Can you guys start talking though, so I don't straight pass out?" Autumn wasn't joking even a little.

"Oh, I can keep you awake. Let me think. Life story time. It all started back when—"

"Not you, Dalton," Winter cawed from the back seat.

"Just trying to help." Noah's shit-eating grin grew wider.

Winter took what sounded like the last sip of her drink because the slurping from the straw held more air than soda. "No one seemed to want to help much when Brad Conlon stabbed Brandt right in the damn neck. Was it just me, or did we all kind of just let that happen?"

"I'm pretty sure none of us could have helped him at that point." Autumn meant the words, but she also was repulsed by the idea of trying to save Russell Brandt's life in any situation *ever*. She still held an enormous grudge against the dead man for creating a situation in which she nearly killed herself.

"Darlin', you don't yell at the garbage man when he picks up your trash," Noah quipped.

Autumn wasn't able to stop the laugh from bubbling up. "You know we would have stopped Brad if we'd known. Occupational hazard."

"Sometimes you have to protect the psychopath," Winter agreed.

Noah let out a huff. "Conlon's sitting in a jail cell facing murder charges. I'd say he's getting his due punishment."

He was right. Autumn had learned just hours ago that Brad and Sheila's two-year-old son would be staying with Sheila's parents while Brad dealt with the consequences of his actions. The toddler's twin sister had apparently died during birth, the evil, all-knowing Brandt having not realized she was in distress in time.

"Roger and Amanda Brandt are in for a fun ride too. Child endangerment and kidnapping charges are the best those two can hope for, considering..." Winter let the sentence drop, and Autumn was grateful.

Wendy Arnold's baby had died on the operating table. The doctors involved insisted that the death may have been avoidable had the time-consuming hostage situation not occurred.

Autumn imagined Roger was devastated. Her touch had allowed her to know without a doubt that, at heart, Roger wasn't a criminal. But he and his wife had committed criminal actions, nonetheless.

Amanda's mental state appeared so fragile that Autumn made an educated guess the woman would likely end up in a mental ward instead of prison.

Sad. Overwhelmingly sad conclusions.

"Alex Gorski-Wilson is adopting Patricia's baby. That's a positive. She didn't care that Brandt was the sperm donor. She's set on raising the babies as siblings, just as Patricia wanted." Autumn attempted to cheer her friends—and herself—with a happier story.

The case hadn't left the team with many encouraging tales to share.

"And Lindsay...she's got to be one of the toughest women I've ever met," Winter declared. Like Autumn, she was still awed by Lindsay's resilience.

Autumn smiled. "Coming from one of the toughest women *I've* ever met, I'd say Lindsay just received a huge compliment."

Noah snorted. "Winter's tough and all, but she's not the one who dove out of a helicopter straight into the Atlantic."

"Thanks, Dalton," Winter retorted, laughing at the jab.

Autumn threw up her hands. "I was trying to save a baby.

A baby. Even Aiden understood that. *Come on.*" Autumn knew she would never be free from the teasing.

"You valiantly rescued a rather unhealthy floating beverage instead." Noah cracked up, and Autumn couldn't help joining him.

The decoy situation truly wasn't funny, but humor seemed to be the key to keeping your sanity in this line of work.

Winter chuckled. "I think you're a little unclear as to just how upset Aiden was about that jump. Thought his damn veins were going to pop out of his forehead while you were in the water."

"That's nothing compared to his expression when that guardsman was flirting with you hardcore. I feared for the dude's *life.*" Noah was still laughing.

Autumn blushed, attempting to ignore the comments. So much had happened in just a few days. She didn't have the energy to think about…that…right now.

She decided to change the subject. "I'm just glad that so few lives were taken in the explosions."

"Five explosions, twelve fatalities, and twenty-seven injuries," Winter recited.

"Could have been *so much worse.* Who knew Brandt placed the bombs for maximum impact and minimum casualties? You wouldn't think he'd care one way or the other." Autumn stared out the window, wondering when she would cease to think about Russell Brandt every other minute of the day.

"Yeah. You never can get a good read on those crazy bastards. *Super* annoying." Noah shook his head while Autumn marveled at his bulletproof satire.

"He didn't seem to care if *Sasha* died," Winter reminded them. "Man, there is *bad blood* between the two of them. I think she'd claw his heart out and make him watch while she ate it, if she could."

Noah's eyebrows raised to his hairline. "Geez, Black. That's dark."

Winter yawned. "Call it like I see it."

"Also medically impossible." Noah didn't let up.

"Shut up, Noah." Winter was laughing again, but she leaned forward and laid a gentle hand on his shoulder. Autumn knew she still wasn't completely over thinking that Noah had been killed.

Autumn appreciated the banter, but whenever Sasha's name came up, she immediately thought of Sarah.

That was, if she wasn't already thinking of Sarah to begin with.

Autumn's deeply engrained need to find her sister hadn't let up for a moment, and that desire was the sole reason for the scenic little drive they were on right now.

The team would be leaving Florida early the next morning, and Autumn knew she'd never forgive herself for not trying one more time.

True to her word, she'd informed Winter of her intentions. Winter had, of course, immediately agreed to ride along. Autumn hadn't argued. She knew she would need her friend's support.

Noah ended up on the trip by default. When he eavesdropped on what they were talking about and planning to do, he grabbed the keys and ran to the driver's seat. Autumn was too tired to protest. Winter simply rolled her eyes and hopped in the back.

Now, they were almost there.

Winter sighed. "You know, this is gonna sound weird, but this case really made me think about my biological father a lot. I know nothing about the man except his first name. But all these DNA sites and whatnot...maybe finding him is possible after all."

Autumn froze at Winter's idea. While Noah expressed his

encouragement, Autumn thought of the numerous ways Winter's quest could end badly.

What if Winter's father was a horrible person? What if he was a normal person but wanted absolutely nothing to do with her? What if he was in the last stages of a horrible disease?

Winter had been through so much already. Autumn couldn't bear the thought of her friend hurting even more.

Sometimes, not knowing was best.

Simultaneously, Autumn knew she'd support Winter no matter what.

And she was also very aware of that burning, incessant need to find long-lost family. Just as she was aware that there was a strong possibility she'd wake up tomorrow wishing she'd never attempted to track Sarah down.

Noah turned into the parking lot of The Booby Trap, and Autumn groaned. Even the building was awful. Cheesy, flashing pink neon signs advertising the amazing and not at all disturbing services offered by this establishment.

So I just walk into this bar and...what? Ask for my stripper sister? Or maybe I'll just be able to pick her out amongst the other pole dancers without any help.

Horrible. Coming here had been a horrible idea. She should have just gotten up early tomorrow morning and driven back to her sister's trailer by herself. Maybe catch her sister before "business hours" began.

It took a full minute for Autumn to feel brave enough to open the door after Noah had parked. Winter and Noah had lost their teasing attitude and simply waited for her to make the first move.

Open door.

Get out of SUV.

She could always come back another day. She wasn't on a deadline, after all.

Noah and Winter stared at her from the sidewalk, sensing her hesitation. Noah stuck out his elbows dramatically, ready to gallantly lead the women in.

"Try not to enjoy this too much, Agent Dalton," Winter muttered testily as she and Autumn each laced an arm through his.

Autumn gave Noah's shoulder a half-joking, half-serious punch. "If I catch you looking at my sister's boobs, *I will kill you*. You've been warned."

"I second that. I'll *help* her kill you." Winter smiled sweetly at Noah, who appeared to be attempting to force himself somber as quickly as any man could.

Autumn shook her head and took a deep breath as they walked across the gravel lot, their shoes crunching to the beat of "Sweet Dreams Are Made Of This." That wasn't so bad. Autumn had been a big Annie Lennox fan for years.

Just listening to the song brightened her mood as it grew louder and louder. The door to the place might be shaped like titties, but that was just advertisement. Good marketing.

This was fine. What Sarah did for a living didn't matter.

She was going to find her baby sister and love her no matter what.

With that promise to herself, she nodded at her dearest friends.

Together, they stepped inside.

The End
To be continued...

Thank you for reading.
All of the Autumn Trent Series books can be found on Amazon.

ACKNOWLEDGMENTS

How does one properly thank everyone involved in taking a dream and making it a reality? Let me try.

In addition to my family, whose unending support provided the foundation for me to find the time and energy to put these thoughts on paper, I want to thank the editors who polished my words and made them shine.

Many thanks to my publisher for risking taking on a newbie and giving me the confidence to become a bona fide author.

More than anyone, I want to thank you, my reader, for clicking on a nobody and sharing your most important asset, your time, with this book. I hope with all my heart I made it worthwhile.

Much love,
Mary

ABOUT THE AUTHOR

Mary Stone lives among the majestic Blue Ridge Mountains of East Tennessee with her two dogs, four cats, a couple of energetic boys, and a very patient husband.

As a young girl, she would go to bed every night, wondering what type of creature might be lurking underneath. It wasn't until she was older that she learned that the creatures she needed to most fear were human.

Today, she creates vivid stories with courageous, strong heroines and dastardly villains. She invites you to enter her world of serial killers, FBI agents but never damsels in distress. Her female characters can handle themselves, going toe-to-toe with any male character, protagonist or antagonist.

Discover more about Mary Stone on her website.
www.authormarystone.com

Connect with Mary Online

facebook.com/authormarystone
goodreads.com/AuthorMaryStone
bookbub.com/profile/3378576590
pinterest.com/MaryStoneAuthor
instagram.com/marystone_author

Made in United States
North Haven, CT
21 April 2022

18455984R00183